Xavier

FLIGHT TO AMBROSIA

EM COOPER

BOOK TWO

Snowfall on St Griswold

Xavier Jones stood alone on the quadrangle of St Griswold College and gazed at the billowing clouds. He marvelled at the magnificent indigo formation gathering and rolling in a restless churn overhead. Ice and electricity crackled in the air, feeding his anticipation. During the thirteen years he had lived in the northern town of Ravenwood, he had never seen clouds like these, but then again, he had never seen snow. Ethan said he was sure it would fall today. Although it was spring, he said snow often came late to the Southern Lands. Excited and unable to sleep, Xavier had risen at dawn hoping to glimpse the first flakes.

The cold, yet magic silence broke as a white vulture shifted in a nearby tree. Without looking, Xavier knew it was watching him. A few more of the creatures scratched in the undergrowth by the perimeter wall, the largest fixed a beady eye upon him while two roosting in an apple tree slowly turned in his direction. The Boundary Keeper, who lived on the southern edge of Mourn Forest, which surrounded the school, had called them Zullites.

Shuddering, Xavier recalled the First Strike, a deadly clash between angelic and demonic forces he, Gabe, Ethan and Beth had witnessed a few weeks earlier. He tried to block the memory of the vultures' curdling screeches as they descended on the field after the battle to scavenge the carcasses of demons, wraiths and other beasts—but the visions crept in. He sighed and watched his warm breath pass from his lips to chill and mist silver in the icy air.

Gabe emerged from the west wing of the school building and walked across the quad towards Xavier. 'Well, where is the snow?' Like the other boys at Griswold, his blond collar-length hair was now short and ragged. Ethan had cut Gabe's hair with nail scissors a few days earlier, which accentuated his strange blue eyes. After four months at Griswold, Gabe's frame was leaner although he was still the same relaxed boy who had revealed his guardian angel identity to him in the gardening shed.

'It's definitely cold enough.' Xavier pointed at the sky. 'Look at the clouds.'

'Nimbocumulus, I think. Ethan's prediction of snow might be valid.'

Xavier hoped he wouldn't launch into a long-winded scientific explanation.

'That is the name of the cloud formation. They hang low but reach high and often carry rain or snow. Might be an ice risk.'

Xavier frowned.

'You know—a risk for flying. Angels need to know clouds.'

In a lower tone, Xavier said, 'I wouldn't be talking about flying or angels. Not with the white birds about.' He tipped his head. 'And those things.'

'Gargoyles?'

'Their eyes are closed—like they're asleep.' Xavier wiggled his toes to ease their numbness in the growing cold. 'No, don't look now.'

'You have not noticed that before?' Gabe shook his head. 'Like demons, they always sleep by day. I am sure if gargoyles were not made of stone, they would hide away from the sun too.'

Xavier shivered in the drizzle.

'You need longer pants to keep you warm. Look at you—a scraggy, black-haired scarecrow.'

Xavier shrugged. 'Thanks, but I can't help that I've grown. Anyway, back to the gargoyles. Why do they hate light?'

'I do not know if all of them do. Demons hate light and ...' He gazed open-mouthed at the sky and then turned in a circle with his arms outstretched. 'I can see it now.'

Xavier hoped none of the boys were watching from the windows above. He raised his eyes to check but then understood why Gabe was acting so strangely. The sky had turned from indigo to grey to the colour of drizzle. But now the drizzle had changed too. Raindrops fell in slow motion until gradually they feathered and floated.

'Snow!' Gabe said.

Both boys stood and gazed in wonder until a soft, whirling whiteness filled the air as it fell slowly to earth.

'Stupendous, stunning, sublime,' Gabe said. 'I can see each one, each flake, perfect and unique. Surely they are not of this world.'

'It's all white to me.'

'You must look closer. You are one of us now.'

'I didn't get your super eyesight,' Xavier said but focused intently on the falling snow.

'Can you see each flake now? Each one is different; each with its own personality. It is incredible. We are so lucky.'

Xavier ignored Gabe's last comment and squinted to catch a glimpse of what he could see. The light seemed to intensify and everything became more distinct, yet he couldn't decide if it was due to the snowfall, his eyesight or just him wanting to believe. He wondered if his family were close enough to Griswold College to see the snow. He hoped they were safe.

'What are you two doing?'

Xavier jerked back to reality when he heard Ethan's voice through the snow flurry. 'Enjoying it,' he said with his face to the sky.

Ethan shook his head and laughed. 'You idiots, you'll get frostbite.'

A few more boys emerged from the west wing with arms crossed or hands in pockets. They gave them strange looks as they hurried across the quad towards the relative warmth of the dining hall.

'Come on,' Ethan said as though he were speaking to a pair of halfwits. Small and fine-boned, he felt the cold acutely, so his jumper was well padded underneath with a thick wad of newspaper. Despite the padding, he jiggled and jogged on the spot partly to keep warm but also because he could rarely stay still.

'We were going to breakfast,' Xavier said, 'but just stopped for a moment.'

'It is so beautiful, breathtaking ...,' Gabe said. 'I quite like rain too, but this is more exciting.'

A clod of dirt and ice hit the side of Xavier's head, and he heard laughter from another group of boys walking towards them.

'Come on,' Ethan repeated gruffly and steered him towards the hall. 'If you want to survive, you know the first rule of Griswold.'

As Xavier turned, he noticed, or did he just sense it, a flicker of movement, a shifting curtain and a fleeting glance, cold and distant. It came from Principal Ratchet's flat on the third floor above the dining hall.

'What is the rule?' Gabe asked.

'Never be different.'

'But that is rather boring,' Gabe said as he looked up at Ms Ratchet's window. 'Or should I say, *that's* rather boring.'

Ethan grinned. 'That's better.'

Xavier nodded. 'I think you're right.'

'For now,' Gabe conceded.

* * *

Old Tomkins wheeled his squeaky trolley into the maths classroom while Xavier craned his neck along with thirty-odd boys, to see what was on the menu. Six blueberry tartlets scattered on a white china plate glistened with a light sugary frosting. Xavier's stomach gurgled at the heavenly aroma of freshly brewed coffee and hunger pangs gripped him so fiercely, he felt queasy.

The maths teacher, Eric Phineas paused from his pacing in front of the blackboard. 'You're late,' he accused his assistant, Tomkins, while tapping his hand rapidly with his whip-like stick. Crankier than usual, Phineas obviously needed sugar.

Although he couldn't taste the coffee or tarts, Xavier was grateful that at least they might ease Phineas' bad mood. It would also distract him from launching into another tiresome lecture about how lucky they were to be at Griswold or inflicting cuts across their knuckles with his switch.

'Sorry, sir, new kitchen staff,' Tomkins muttered while dropping sugar cubes into a cup. After stirring the coffee, he transferred the plate of pastries from the trolley to Phineas' desk, but one tart slid and fell from the plate. Thirty pairs of hungry eyes watched it fall to the floor and roll wheel-like, leaving a faint sugary trail until it came to rest beside the bookshelf near the window. Phineas missed the action and Tomkins ignored it, but every boy was obviously plotting to claim the sweet prize.

'Am I interrupting anything?' a raspy voice asked from the doorway.

Phineas had popped a tart into his mouth, so when he hurriedly tried to swallow it whole, he choked and coughed. Boys smothered giggles at the sight of Phineas spluttering and red-faced. Without an invitation and ignoring Phineas, Ms Ratchet swept into the room.

Xavier was glad Phineas was humiliated; however he quickly sobered at the sight of the withered crone. Lizard-like, Ratti's eyes flicked right and left, monitoring each boy. He half-expected a curled tongue to dart between her jagged teeth to snatch a fly from the air.

'I'm visiting classrooms today to make some important announcements.' She stared and pointed at the floor near the window. 'What's that rubbish?'

No one answered.

'Go and fetch it, Tomkins.'

The old servant shuffled towards the window and in slow motion, bent forward to retrieve the offending pastry.

'Disgusting!' Her upper lip curled as she watched Tomkins hawkishly. 'No, don't put it in the bin. Next we'll have rats in the classrooms.'

Xavier could sense the disappointment of every boy watching as Tomkins slipped it in his pocket.

Ratti turned to the boys. 'Now back to my announcement. It gives me great pleasure to name the boy who has been selected from your class as one of the chosen ones,' she said, although she didn't look particularly pleased.

Since returning from Ravenwood, Xavier had dreaded this moment. 'No, no, no,' he whispered without moving his lips.

Gabe leant forward and pretended to fiddle with his sock. 'Shh, she'll hear you,' he said under his breath.

And as if on cue, the old woman paused and looked over her glasses towards the back of the classroom where Gabe and Xavier were sitting.

Xavier suppressed a shudder. His concern over her announcement made him forget for a moment she was a witch.

She cleared her throat. 'As I was saying, the fortunate boy who has been selected for this wonderful opportunity is Ethan Klee.' A commotion at the front of the room caused her to pause again. Ethan had fallen from his chair and Felix, one of the boys sitting nearby, was poking him with his foot.

'He's fainted, miss,' Felix said.

Ethan groaned.

Boys stood to catch a glimpse of him sprawled on the floor.

'Yep, I'm pretty sure, miss.' Felix sounded pleased with himself for making the diagnosis.

'Sit down,' Phineas snapped.

Knowing it was safer to remain unseen, no one dared to help Ethan.

'Quiet.' Ratchet's restrained tone instantly silenced the boys.

'Obviously the wonderful news has overwhelmed Mr Klee. There's more,' she continued, oblivious to Ethan's moans. 'This year we've decided to add a few more names to the list, not so much due to the boys' test results but rather as encouragement for what we consider potential. These boys are Gabriel Shepherd and Xavier Jones. Well done, boys.' She half-smiled to reveal a row of small sharp teeth.

'Look excited.' Gabe patted Xavier on the back while boys turned and stared at them with envious expressions.

Xavier wanted to be sick, but he grinned and nodded at the boys until they had stopped looking at them. 'She knows, doesn't she?'

'Maybe not, although I believe she's curious. We'll have to convince her otherwise.'

'I'm also here this morning to let you know we're introducing regular assemblies but at no set time. In future when the chapel bell rings thrice, all boys are to report to the quadrangle, no matter what time of day or night. Are there any questions?'

Xavier was too afraid to glance at Gabe in case he had his hand in the air, so he was relieved when Ratti continued. He wondered if all the boys understood what thrice meant. Sometimes she used ancient words as though they were ordinary.

'There's one last announcement. The boys selected for special classes are to assemble outside the chapel on Wednesday at four o'clock sharp for their first class.'

Once again, boys turned and stared enviously at Xavier and Gabe.

Xavier longed to trade places with them.

Ms Ratchet looked at Phineas, who was discreetly trying to nudge the pastry trolley out of her sight to the other side of his desk. Her interruptions to classes and formal announcements were more frequent and even teachers like Phineas seemed rattled by them. 'Please resume whatever it was you were doing, Mr Phineas.' She eyed him disdainfully, gathered her black, layered skirt and then rustled from the classroom.

'Good riddance.' Gabe turned to Xavier, who was now pale and silent. 'Don't despair. We'll come up with something special for her.'

Several weeks had passed since they first climbed over the wall to escape Griswold College and flee through Mourn Forest to Rosegrove. The bus trip through the Southern Lands and the terrifying train journey through the Northern Lands were now unpleasant memories. Since Phineas and Grubner had caught the boys in Ravenwood and brought them back to school, Xavier had been plagued by nightmares. He dreamed of the beautiful Boundary Land and its keeper, only to be woken by visions of moths, demons and the Darklaw. He wondered if they would ever meet Artemis and Sarah again although they were only a short car trip away in Rosegrove. And then there was that strange angel, Raphael and poor Nisroc, who he feared had met a terrible fate. Artemis should have received the ledger, so perhaps he would know the purpose of that peculiar book. And what about Beth? He could not bear to think too long about her out there alone. Where was she now? Thinking about her inevitably led to the most painful thoughts of all, those about his family and that pain was too much to endure. What if he never saw his parents and little sister, Allie again?

The boys had been back at school for only a few weeks since Phineas and Grubner had dropped them at the front door of Griswold College, but it seemed an eternity. Each day he had expected detentions or punishments and had lain awake at night imagining them. Now he knew. Their punishment as chosen ones wasn't going to be predictable like a flogging from Kennedy but rather something far worse. The frightening part was simply, not knowing.

CHAPTER 2

* * *

Mr Pittworthy's natural history

Ethan, Gabe and Xavier filed into the natural history classroom. Sunlight streamed from the windows through the row of jars holding Mr Earnest Pittworthy's pickled specimens on the ledge. On weekends over many years, he had ventured alone into Mourn Forest to trap and collect animals. Bloated or puckered, piglets, cats, rats, hares and birds floated side by side in their liquid worlds. Some with surprised expressions had obviously been caught unaware while others slept peacefully. The afternoon sunlight bounced and reflected gold rays around the room, catching specks of dust sinking in the air onto the wooden benches where boys sat waiting for class. Drawn to the macabre display, boys like Felix sat close to the bottles, but Xavier always selected a bench near the far wall.

'The chosen classes will be fun,' Ethan said as he sat beside Xavier. 'We'll be fine.'

'Then why did you pass out when Ratti told us the news?' Xavier said.

'I hadn't been named in seven years. She got me by surprise, but I'm not worried. What can a shrivelled lizard do to us?'

'You know what she is. Have you forgotten her detentions and how she made Ugly whip Gabe?'

'But we're in the chosen class now,' Ethan said.

In high spirits, Ethan was almost bouncing off the walls, which irritated Xavier. 'You know, I think you're happy to be back at Griswold.'

He looked at Xavier strangely. 'What are you talking about? I want to escape from here just as much as you.'

'Do you?'

'Enough,' said Gabe, who was sitting opposite the boys. 'You two haven't stopped fighting since we returned.'

Xavier felt guilty. Ever since they had been brought back to Griswold by Phineas and Grubner he knew he had been depressed. Seeing Ethan more at ease and happier only made him feel worse. He hated Phineas for dragging him from his home in Ravenwood back to this awful place. He was angry he had no rights and was powerless to leave. Why hadn't he just run from them? Why hadn't he fought for his freedom? He was so weak. What made the Boundary Keeper believe he could ever be a leader?

'Focus on how we'll deal with these special classes,' Gabe said. 'We need a plan.'

Both boys looked at him blankly.

Lugging a large cardboard box, Pittworthy, the natural history teacher lurched into the classroom. 'Settle down, boys.' As usual he was dressed in an oversized suit, looking like an ancient turtle with a wrinkled neck protruding from its shell. He waited until they were seated and quiet. 'Open your textbooks at chapter four,' he said in a mechanical voice. After depositing the box, he meticulously arranged and rearranged pens and books on his desk.

Xavier flicked through the pages of his ancient textbook as he tried to forget being chosen by Ratti. Colour printing hadn't reached Griswold, so the pages of dreary text were interrupted only occasionally by tiny grey illustrations.

Pittworthy looked up from his text. 'Who can tell me about the origins of man?'

Xavier rested his book on the desk and listened. His parents had been interested in topics like this.

Ethan whispered from the seat behind him, 'Pitt should know. He's so old, he was probably there.'

Tentatively, Xavier raised his hand.

'Mr Jones?'

'We descended from apes—from the old planet, sir.'

Pittworthy chuckled. 'Earth apes? An interesting notion, but I don't think so.'

'My parents ...,' Xavier began.

His eyes sparked. 'Yes?'

'Um, I mean, my parents taught me that, sir.'

The spark dimmed. 'Mr Jones, we're your family now.'

Stung by his response, Xavier breathed through a swirl of anger and bitterness as his hands shook and his heart thumped. Were all the teachers brainwashed? He blinked away tears. 'My parents are scientists,' he said defiantly.

Pittworthy flicked imaginary fluff from the sleeve of his suit.

Xavier wanted to scream, you stupid, old man, but instead he clenched his fists.

'Man was created by a divine force. Everyone write that down.'

Xavier continued to stare at him angrily while the boys scratched Pittworthy's declaration in their notebooks.

'Do you know what the divine force is?' Pittworthy glanced at Xavier. He whistled the word force between his false teeth, which made some of the boys giggle.

Xavier focused on the bench.

'Hmm, I didn't think so. Why you have been selected among the chosen ones, I'll never know. Can any boy help Mr Jones?' He looked around the classroom, but no one offered to speak. 'In the beginning was the Maker and he made heaven and hell, the sky and earth, mountains and oceans, man and beast and ...'

Xavier raised his hand.

Pittworthy stared at him.

'What if the Maker created the apes, sir?' Xavier said.

Ignoring him, Pittworthy continued his ramblings until most of the class appeared comatose.

As he droned on, Xavier tried to remember details of his parents' research. Mostly they spoke of genetics and their conversation was complex and dull. Although one evening he recalled them both being excited after receiving a package. He remembered it because it was the first time his father had smiled and laughed since the new university science dean had fired him. He kept himself busy though with his microscope in a secret room in their basement, which he kept locked.

'These are special cells,' his father had said to his mother.

When Xavier had asked them what made them special, they both startled and his mother said he must have misheard them. They never spoke of the cells again—at least as far as he knew.

Ethan jiggled a foot and yawned. 'I can't take too much more of this,' he whispered.

Xavier caught a flicker of movement at the edge of his vision. Gabe had raised his hand.

'Yes?'

Gabe stood slowly. 'I have a question about the history you describe. It concerns demons, sir.'

Pittworthy flinched. 'You may sit down, Mr Shepherd.'

'Thank you, sir.' Gabe resumed his seat but didn't take the hint and continued his questioning. 'They weren't always on our planet, were they?'

A buzz grew among the boys. Some had heard of demons through the kitchen staff, but only Xavier, Gabe and Ethan had seen them in the flesh.

Pittworthy was silent.

'They're out there, sir.' Gabe looked at him steadily. 'We all know.'

Although flustered, Pittworthy recovered enough to speak. 'I don't know where you got this nonsense.'

'Where do you suppose they came from?' Gabe said.

'Demons, phh,' Pittworthy said. 'If there were such abominations, it would require a very great evil for them to be drawn to our world.'

'Oh, so you think they travelled to Kepler? Me too. They couldn't fly, seeing as there's no air in space. Do you think they travelled here in spaceships like we did? It makes sense, doesn't it?'

'I didn't say that,' Pittworthy said in a constricted voice.

'What about the Darklaw?' Gabe said.

Thrilled by the topics and Gabe's daring, the boys murmured excitedly to each other.

'Enough,' Pittworthy thundered.

Gabe persisted. 'Mr Phineas told us these were dark times. Is that what he meant, Mr Pittworthy?'

Pittworthy slammed a book on his desk and then in a quiet voice said, 'You're cocky and insolent, Mr Shepherd, but believe me, you wouldn't be so brave if you had the wisdom of experience. Don't speak anymore of this fantasy—for your own good.' He glanced at the small viewing window set in the door as though he sensed someone watching and then turned his gaze to the class. 'And that goes for all of you.'

Xavier was worried. If Gabe continued to push Pittworthy, he would only attract attention. After their capture in Ravenwood and with the special classes coming up, he was begging for trouble.

'Take an assignment sheet from the box near the door as you leave. You're to complete it before our next class.'

While boys filed noisily out the door, Xavier watched Pittworthy's shoulders twitch as he studied Gabe. He wished his friend had been more careful.

After leaving Pittworthy's class, Xavier, Ethan and Gabe trailed the other boys while walking along the Great Corridor.

Beneath the guard of gargoyles, Xavier remained silent. Once they had turned the corner, he said quietly, 'Why did you push Pitt? I don't understand.' He glanced behind. 'He'll be suspicious. We're starting special classes this week and it's the last thing we need.'

Gabe answered in a low tone, 'I did it because I want to know him. I think there are teachers oblivious to what's going on. Then there are those like Ratti and Ugly.'

'Who are rotten to the core,' Xavier said.

'Like bad apples?' Gabe said, obviously distracted by the saying.

'Yes or just plain evil.'

'That's the word I would have selected, but humans have strange expressions. I need to learn more, so I do not ... I mean ... don't stand apart.'

'Don't worry, your speech is almost perfectly average now,' Xavier said.

Gabe frowned. "Average?'

'Yeah, how come you're suddenly talking like us?' Ethan asked.

'Because I choose to. I can speak any language in any accent. Test me if you want.'

'You're speaking just right,' Xavier said reassuringly. 'Anyway, what about Pitt?'

'Maybe Pitt's just turning a blind eye, 'cause he doesn't want to get involved,' Ethan said.

'He's different. I've watched him. He lives on the outside,' Gabe said. 'But I'd like to be sure.'

'Outside of what?'

'You haven't noticed, have you?' Ethan said to Xavier. 'You're a typical rabbit.'

Xavier ignored him.

'He walks and eats alone and isn't violent—telltale signs.' Gabe said. 'He also warned us not to speak about demons and the Darklaw.'

'When Pitt left Ratti at the altar, I reckon she pushed him to the outer,' Ethan said. 'I'm sure she'd be the type to hold a grudge.'

'I wonder if there are any good teachers at Griswold,' Xavier said.

Ethan skipped along avoiding cracks in the stone floor. 'It's a hive. Ratti's queen bee, and Phineas and Kennedy are soldier bees. Kennedy came to Griswold as an outsider, but he pleases her. Pitt's got a broken wing and crawls in circles. Though Ratti must care a little for him 'cause she hasn't chucked him out, even though he's damaged.'

'Beehives don't work exactly like that, but I enjoy your analogy. Perhaps evil has warped this hive,' Gabe said.

'Rabbits, bees—it's too confusing.' Xavier sighed. 'How do the other teachers fit in this zoo?'

'Crowley and Matron are worker bees,' Ethan said.

Gabe frowned. 'Grubner's a curious one. In Ravenwood he didn't tell Phineas I had wings.'

'Don't be so sure,' Xavier said.

Gabe raised an eyebrow.

'I willed him not to feel them.' Xavier noticed Gabe's look of disbelief. 'What? You don't think I could do that? Don't you remember me warding off the demons during the First Strike?'

'That's what you told me, although I was unconscious at the time.'

Xavier grinned. Gabe was obviously not convinced that as a half-angel he could possess such power. Xavier wasn't sure the magic or power had sprung from himself, and it certainly wasn't something he could conjure or control at will. He knew this because he had tried several times since returning to Griswold and failed.

'What?' Gabe said.

'Never mind.'

* * *

CHAPTER 3

Ready or not

From the window of his room, Xavier watched a flock of dark birds soaring in sleek formation over the school. They skimmed the shadowy treetops of Mourn Forest and then vanished in the twilight. Knowing that demons attacked men and rabbits, Xavier wondered if they ate birds too. Were they waiting in the deepening darkness ready to pounce and snatch them? It was just as well demons only hunted at night otherwise they would have delighted in plucking tasty morsels from the playgrounds of Griswold College.

'There's something I need to tell you, Ethan,' he said, fingering the arch of his tightly-bound right wing.

Ethan looked up from the essay he was writing for Pittworthy.

Xavier took a deep breath. 'I'm an angel too.'

Blinking a few times, Ethan laid his pen on the desk.

'Well, half-angel and half-human, I suspect.' Unable to read Ethan's expression, Xavier continued, 'I think I'm ready to learn to fly.'

Gabe, who was lying on his bed, opened his eyes. 'Really?'

'So, how long have you known?' Ethan asked quietly.

Xavier sensed Ethan was trying to control his emotions. 'I found out just before the First Strike. They've grown quickly since then.'

'But you didn't think to tell me?' Ethan turned to Gabe. 'Did you know?'

'It wasn't like that,' Xavier said defensively. 'I felt something sticking into my back on the train and Gabe found them.'

Ethan tapped the desk agitatedly with a couple of fingers. 'But you waited a few weeks to tell me.'

Xavier couldn't tell Ethan the real reason. He was worried about his friend's murky aura and the Boundary Keeper's talk of him being an ancient soul who had once fallen. 'I'm sorry. I suppose I wanted to be certain,' Xavier said.

'Of the wings—or me?'

'The wings, of course.' Xavier wondered if Ethan could tell he wasn't being honest. 'I just know I'm ready to fly now.'

Gabe sat up. 'That's exactly what happened to me.'

Ethan sighed and closed his book. 'I'm going for a walk.'

After he had gone, Xavier said, 'I don't blame him for leaving.'

'It's not our fault.'

'I know, but think how you'd feel.'

Gabe frowned. 'I would—I mean I'd feel the same way. It's not our fault he's physically incapable.'

'Gabe!'

'I meant incapable of flying,' Gabe said.

'If he's a fallen soul like the Boundary Keeper said, he might have once been an angel too,' Xavier said.

'Perhaps,' Gabe said. 'So when do you want to test your wings?'

'As soon as possible.'

'Good, we'll go tonight when Ethan's asleep.'

'Without him?'

'You know it's safer that way.'

'I don't care. If Ethan can't come, I won't go either.'

* * *

Xavier woke with a start after sleeping through the night and realised it was only an hour or so until dawn. He shook Gabe and Ethan, who both grumbled but eventually flung their blankets back and got up.

After the boys crept downstairs, they slipped out the side door in the light of a full moon. In the deep shadows of the western wall they ran to the back of the school and along the northern wall to the small oval near the burial plot where they were less visible from the school buildings.

'Are you going to give me some expert tips?' Xavier asked Gabe.

Wearing only a singlet and cotton trousers, Xavier crossed his arms to keep his body warm in the cool spring air. Taking a breath he closed his eyes, relaxed and let them drop. Slowly, he stretched and raised his arms wide, unfurling his wings at the same time. Blood rushed and tingled to the tips of his fingers. It felt good. Muscle and feather crunched and crackled as he stretched and reached for the dark sky.

'Not bad,' Gabe declared as he examined Xavier's wings.

'Not bad?' Although he fought to control it, Xavier's voice sounded peevish.

Ethan groaned. 'Not you too? Are you all vain?'

Blushing, Xavier was grateful it was too dim for them to notice.

'Try to flap,' Gabe directed.

Xavier struggled to hitch his shoulders up and down.

'No, not with your shoulders.' Gabe grabbed the bases of Xavier's wings and moved them up and over his ribs. 'Can you feel the muscles? Try to help me and that will teach your brain the movement.'

Xavier repeated the action several times until he felt the synchrony of muscles about his shoulder blades and could flap without his help. 'Yes, I get it now!'

Ethan climbed the mulberry tree in the corner and scrambled onto the eastern wall where he perched to gain a better view of the boys' antics.

'And flap and lift and flap and lift,' Gabe called, making Ethan laugh.

Xavier sprinted across the oval a few times but couldn't coordinate flapping with running. Soon he realised he wouldn't be flying that night.

After a few attempts, he lay face down on the grass exhausted. 'Just let me die for a few moments.'

Gabe stood over him with his hands on his hips. 'You're obviously not ready. You can't be very fit.'

Xavier pulled on the elastic binding Gabe had given him as he no longer needed it because he could now morph his feathers into skin cells when he wasn't using them. Embarrassed at having to wear the binding, Xavier longed to learn his amazing trick. It would also help him escape detection if he were ever searched again like Grubner had done in Ravenwood.

'Come and see this,' called Ethan, who was looking over the other side of the eastern wall.

Xavier and Gabe jogged to the mulberry tree and scrambled up its trunk to join Ethan on the wall.

'It's a building site,' Ethan said, 'and it's going to look just like Griswold College. See, they've nearly finished the second floor.'

As the sun breathed the first pink of dawn over the horizon, the boys heard a heavy droning coming from the front of the building site. They lay low on the stone wall behind the mulberry branches and watched an ancient bus trundle down the gravel drive and veer left down a side road towards the back of the site. When it stopped on what appeared to be a new quadrangle, the driver opened the passenger door. He blew a whistle draped around his neck and a file of men and women carrying work tools streamed down the steps from the bus. A few minutes later, another bus arrived with more workers. When all the passengers had left the buses, they stood in orderly rows until the whistle man waved his hands and barked instructions. Once dismissed, the workers hurried to designated areas. Some scurried up scaffolding while others on the ground carried bricks or mixed concrete. After working for several minutes, a bricklayer wearing red overalls climbed from the scaffold, dropped his trowel in the dirt and stood staring at the eastern wall. One of the supervisors marched up behind the man staring at the wall and whacked him across his back with a stick.

'Wow! He's asking for it,' Ethan said. 'Bet there'll be a fight.'

But the man turned with a calm expression as though he'd only been lightly tapped on his shoulder. He walked back to his trowel, picked it up and resumed work as though nothing had happened.

'Lower order human,' Gabe murmured.

'Slave, you mean.' Ethan pointed at a separate white building with a padlocked gate and fence around it. 'I wonder what's in there.'

Gabe climbed onto a branch to get a better view. 'I'd like to know what the main building is for.'

'Probably more classrooms,' Xavier said.

'Or more boys,' Gabe said.

Xavier spotted a man on the other side of the site restraining two large dogs on leashes. 'I think he's the dog-man who bailed me up outside the kitchen.'

'Watch out, he's looking our way,' Gabe said.

The man jogged across the building site towards them with the dogs snapping at the air and dragging him as though they had detected a scent.

'Get off the wall!' Gabe ordered.

The boys scrambled down the mulberry tree back into the school grounds.

In his haste, Xavier skinned an ankle while sliding down the tree trunk. 'Do you think he saw us?' He wiped a trickle of blood from his leg.

'If he did, he couldn't have recognised us from that distance,' Ethan said. 'We'd better go.'

As the boys headed towards the dining hall for breakfast, Xavier shook and inspected the watch Artemis had given him, but as usual it wasn't working. It was now a habit. Since he received the watch, it had worked during the First Strike although only the second-hand had moved. Artemis had told him when the watch struck the hour it would be time to act, whatever that meant.

* * *

'What are you ordering?' Ethan asked as the boys trekked into the dining hall.

'Poached eggs with mushrooms and a cappuccino,' Xavier said.

'I'll have two of that,' Ethan said.

Hayley walked behind the boys carrying a pile of plates. 'Sorry, we're out of coffee and the chooks are on strike. Why don't you try the porridge?'

'Chooks?' Gabe said.

'Chicken,' Xavier said.

The boys laughed and turned to greet Hayley. Xavier noticed she was wearing her blue dress and white apron and had pulled her dark hair from her face with a floral-patterned band.

As the boys collected breakfast and walked to their table, the sun was just filtering into the dining hall from the high windows on the eastern side.

Xavier stirred the porridge in his bowl. 'Ah, it's good to be alive.'

'Trust you boys to be here first—always thinking of your stomachs.'

The boys turned their heads at the same time. 'Beth!'

'What are you doing here?' Xavier said in a voice registering his delight and relief. He wanted to jump and hug her to make sure she was real.

Beth's fiery hair was restrained in a single plait, accentuating how pale her face appeared. Even her freckles seemed faded.

'Are you okay?' Xavier asked.

She glanced around and although the dining hall was empty, didn't dare to sit beside the boys. 'I'm fine. I'll have to speak quickly.'

'What happened to you?' Xavier asked.

'When you were taken in Ravenwood, I went to your neighbour's house.'

'Mrs Creedy?'

'Yes, she was lovely. I know it was a risk, but I had to find help. She was so worried because she hadn't seen your family for months, so I told her what happened.'

Dejected by her news, Xavier could only nod.

'But how did you get here?' Gabe asked.

'She gave me money to buy train and bus tickets.'

'What about the border guards near Lanoris?' Gabe said.

'I didn't go that way. I took a train to Clearview and a bus to Rosegrove.'

Gabe raised his eyebrows. 'You took great risks.'

'I wasn't afraid. I can sense danger.'

'What if you were wrong?'

Beth eyed Gabe directly and with a quiet confidence said, 'I haven't been yet. Anyway, I could ask you the same question. What if your wings failed?'

'They wouldn't ...,' Gabe's voice trailed off as though conceding the logic in her argument.

Xavier was in awe of her bravery because he couldn't imagine facing a journey across Clanarde, especially alone.

Beth turned to Xavier. 'I remembered you talking about Sarah and her cafe in Rosegrove. It wasn't hard to track her down and she helped me find Artemis, who took me to Hayley's home, where I'm staying now. Hayley's father managed to get me work as a kitchen hand.' With tears welling in her eyes, she smiled. 'I'm just so glad to see you all again. I want to hug each of you, but I'd better not.'

Xavier told her how Phineas and Grubner had driven them back to school and how they had expected punishment but instead were chosen for special classes.

'Isn't that what you feared?'

Xavier nodded. 'But at least we know you're okay. We can plan our next escape together—all of us.'

'Ugly just entered the room,' Ethan warned. 'He's looking this way.'

The boys continued eating their porridge while Beth wiped the table with her back to the sports teacher, Mr Kennedy, who was standing at the servery scanning the dining hall.

Xavier lowered his voice. 'Did Artemis receive the ledger?'

'Yes, but he didn't understand it, so he sent it to someone he thought might,' Beth said. 'There's one more thing—I've been having dreams. I need to tell you about them.'

'Ugly's coming,' Ethan said urgently.

'We have to meet away from here,' Beth said quickly.

'Now you're here, we'll see and talk to you every day.' Knowing Beth was alive and safe elated Xavier. They could begin to plan again. For once he dared to feel hope.

* * *

CHAPTER 4

Don't close your eyes

The afternoon shadows were long when Gabe, Ethan and Xavier gathered with a handful of boys at the entrance to the chapel. They waited nervously with the silence broken only by a few buzzing flies. In the distance, Xavier could see boys racing around the oval. He wished he were there too. Listening to Ugly bawling insults at them had to be better than worrying about the chosen class. Searching the faces of the other boys standing with him, he wondered why they had been selected. A door from the east wing slammed and drew his attention to Ratti scurrying towards them with a tall, thin man loping after her.

'I'd like to introduce Dr Arnold Hortense,' she said when she reached the boys. 'You're the first pupils at St Griswold to have the privilege of meeting our new Etiquette and Ethics teacher.' Her look was so acidic that the boys' desire to snigger evaporated.

A chill prickled Xavier's skin when he met the gaze of the towering man. He was middle-aged with mousy hair so greasy that it appeared deliberately tamed with oil. Every aspect of his body was ridiculously elongated, especially his bony fingers, scrawny neck and pasty face. Only his thick moustache and furry, brown vest with its faint yellow stripes countered the vertical appearance of his body. He tried not to imagine what Hortense was carrying in the leather satchel tucked firmly under his armpit.

'Good morning, boys,' he said in a crisp and distant tone.

'Good morning, Dr Hortense.'

As he bowed slightly, he hooked his spidery fingers under the satchel and lowered it until it dangled and rested against his thigh. The bag's movement released a mothball whiff and a decidedly more unpleasant odour that Xavier couldn't identify.

'Dr Hortense will be taking your first class in one of the new buildings,' Ratti said after she had checked the boys' names off her clipboard list. Some boys appeared puzzled because they obviously hadn't heard about the construction site next door.

'Where did that come from?' Xavier whispered after Ratti marched the boys behind the chapel to a new opening in the eastern wall that had been fitted with a gate.

'The key to this gate could come in handy,' Ethan murmured.

Ratti unlocked the gate and ushered the boys through. 'As you can see,' she said and waved her hand. 'We're expanding the school.'

'Excuse me, Ms Ratchet,' Gabe said in a bright voice. 'Who'll be using the new buildings?'

'That's not your concern, Mr Shepherd.'

'Yes, miss, but I was wondering, will we be getting new boys?'

She didn't seem to hear as she turned and walked briskly towards the small white building at the back of the site while the boys and Dr Hortense hurried to keep up. Someone had already opened the outer padlocked gate which led to another path. When Ratti reached the building, she rummaged through her keys and unlocked the door. 'Please go in and find a seat.'

An antiseptic mist identical to the one that permeated Griswold College's foyer greeted Xavier and as he stepped into the room, the smell grew stronger. While the other boys eagerly found seats, Xavier, Gabe and Ethan hung back. Xavier breathed a sigh of relief when he saw the room was arranged like an ordinary classroom with desks and chairs. Apart from the old-fashioned blackboard at the front and the odd smell, it could have been a classroom in his old school at Ravenwood.

Xavier stood behind Ratti and Hortense in the doorway.

'Did you get them?' Ratti asked discreetly.

Hortense patted the satchel.

'Excellent,' she replied. Ratti turned to see Xavier, Gabe and Ethan hadn't found seats. 'Hurry along, boys, sit down.' She nodded at Hortense, who stepped onto the raised platform at the head of the classroom.

Smoothing his vest and straightening his tie, Hortense waited for them to settle. 'It's a pleasure to meet you, boys. First, I'd like to tell you a little about myself because I want us to be friends.' As he looked around the room he smiled, but it didn't reach his hooded eyes.

'I was raised in a large family on a farm south of here near Laurendale. We were poor, so I understand how tough you boys have had it. From the age of twelve, I'd get up at four and pick tomatoes. After a couple of hours of labour in the fields, I'd eat breakfast and study before catching the school bus. I didn't complain or blame anyone because I knew that was life. Every day I worked and studied hard. Eventually I was rewarded with a scholarship.' He paused and looked around again. 'Just because you're an orphan or abandoned, doesn't mean you can't become special. What I want you boys to understand is that with hard work and integrity, you can make something of yourselves too.' He glanced at Ratti, who nodded approvingly.

Although the doctor sounded educated and cultivated, his words sounded hollow and false. Xavier wondered if Hortense was a soldier bee.

Gabe had his hand in the air.

'What is it?' Ratti asked, not waiting for Hortense.

'I wanted to know how Dr Hortense found the tomatoes.'

'What?'

'How did he find them in the dark?'

Ratti looked ready to bite, but Hortense shook his head slightly. 'Why, I carried a lantern of course.'

'Tomatoes only grow in summer, don't they? So did you sleep in over winter?'

Ratti folded her arms while Hortense regarded him with narrowed eyes. 'We had winter crops too, like spinach.'

Gabe nodded. 'I see, thank you.'

'Any other questions?' Hortense asked. 'Right, good. Today we're going to start with something I'm sure you'll enjoy.'

Xavier wasn't convinced. He couldn't think of a single activity he had enjoyed at Griswold.

'I want you to settle back in these fine new chairs.'

As he leant back, Xavier found it difficult to find any comfort in the unpadded wooden seats.

Hortense reached into his pocket and withdrew a timepiece on a shiny, silver chain. It flashed and spun as he dangled it in a shaft of sunlight coming through a small, high window. 'We're going to start off at an easy pace,' he said in a low tone and half-smiled. 'All you need to do today is relax. Focus on the watch and relax—just relax.'

Xavier watched the light bounce off the spinning watch and twisting chain. This wasn't too hard. Perhaps the other kids were right. Maybe these classes weren't to be feared.

'Keep watching.' The timepiece flashed and spun. 'That's good. Just relax. Let your body sink and your muscles go loose.'

Xavier's body grew limp. He couldn't remember the last time he had felt so comfortable. For a few moments he floated and it felt good. Should he fight or surrender? He tried to resist the urge to follow Hortense's voice, which was now smooth, soft and on the outside—yet on the outside of what? He struggled to move his limbs, but they were separate and asleep. Focusing on his eyelids, he managed to open them a fraction. The light had changed. The room now smelled musty and old. At the edge of his vision, he noticed a line of guards in metallic armour standing to attention before a row of arched windows with a heavy tapestry between each one. It was happening again, but this time he was powerless. He closed his eyes until something brushed against his leg. Forcing his eyes open a crack, he saw Ratti's grey cat tip-toeing over the weathered timber floor. Wasn't the floor concrete before? Once again he closed his eyes and drifted until he became aware of buzzing at the periphery of his consciousness. The buzzing morphed into mumbling followed by a sudden rapping on the door. Xavier jerked into awareness just as the door opened.

'Good afternoon, Ms Ratchet and Dr Hortense. So sorry to interrupt,' Father Augustine called in his fat, jovial voice as he held the door open. 'We have a distinguished visitor.'

As a brown-haired, lightly-built man in his mid-thirties entered the room with the priest, Xavier wondered if he had been dreaming. The tapestries and armoured men had vanished. He checked Gabe and Ethan who seemed undisturbed and relaxed.

Ratti stepped forward quickly. 'Ah, James, how lovely to see you again. It's been a while.' She turned to Hortense. 'Arnold, this is James Griswold, the grandson of Philip Griswold.'

James extended a hand. 'Pleased to meet you.'

Hortense shook it. 'Thank you.'

'Mr Griswold is most keen to inspect the new building site. The classroom is jolly good, isn't it, boys?' Father Augustine was speaking a little quicker than usual and Xavier noticed the sheen of sweat on his upper lip. Maybe he was overheating in his dark, priestly robes, or was he just nervous?

James Griswold paced backwards and forwards as though he had an excess of energy to discharge. 'Good afternoon, class.' He smiled warmly at them. 'It's wonderful to see you here. I hope you're enjoying your new classroom.'

Xavier noticed Ratti was bristling, obviously disturbed by James' presence. Xavier however, instinctively liked James' open face and cheerful smile. Friendly adults at Griswold College were rare.

'So, what are we learning today, Dr Hortense?' James asked.

Hortense slipped his silver watch in his pocket and cleared his throat. Before he could answer, Ratti stepped forward. 'Dr Hortense has just commenced work with our special boys, who were selected after a recent exam.'

'Well done, lads. That's very pleasing to hear. What are you learning?'

Ratti intervened again. 'Today they're being instructed on the value of positive thinking. We believe happy boys will perform better academically.'

'Wonderful! Are we enjoying ourselves?' James looked directly at Xavier when he asked the question.

James Griswold was so close. Xavier wanted to tell him, but he was overwhelmed. He wanted to grab his hand and plead with him, to beg for his help to find his parents and to tell him everything, but as he looked at the man he wondered. He couldn't be sure. Did his smile conceal evil? It was better to be safe. 'Umm, um, yes, thank you, sir.'

James raised an eyebrow as if he sensed his uneasiness. 'I wish I had teachers like yours when I was a lad. Times have obviously changed.' He winked and smiled at Xavier and then turned to Ratti. 'I plan to return soon for the grand opening. I trust all the boys will be attending?'

'Of course,' she said. 'We're all looking forward to it.'

Xavier was repulsed by her attempt to smile.

'It was great to meet you, boys.' He turned to go but paused. 'I was thinking, Ms Ratchet, if you'd like to select two boys, I'll send a car on Monday and they can come to dinner at Griswold Manor. In fact, we might make it a regular event, so eventually we'll get to meet all you boys. You see I'm planning on having a much greater involvement with the school now I've returned to Rosegrove.'

Ratti flinched but without missing a beat replied, 'Thank you. That would be lovely.'

Xavier could see her jaw clench when she said lovely. She was obviously not happy.

Ratti folded her arms and surveyed the boys. She pointed at Ethan. 'I think you ...' she studied the boys' faces again, 'and you, Mr Jones can go on Monday.'

'That's settled then.' James smiled at the boys. 'I'll look forward to seeing you at the manor.'

Xavier's stomach churned as he wondered why Ratti had chosen him and Ethan. He didn't want to go to a stranger's home, no matter how kindly and decent the man seemed. He just wanted to blend.

* * *

Later that evening, Xavier, Gabe and Ethan sat in the dining hall surrounded by noisy boys wolfing down their meagre meals.

Xavier picked listlessly at the gristly chunks of grey meat on his plate.

Carrying his meal, Alex Johnson paused at their table. 'Did you hear the n-news?'

'No,' Xavier said.

'I heard Ratti's turning some dorms into a c-classroom and boys are gonna be shuffled into different rooms. A list's g-going up about who's getting new roomies. You g-guys have a spare bed. Reckon you'll get one.' Ever since Alex had attempted to escape with them over the wall, he no longer bullied Xavier and seemed to want to please the boys. 'I'll catch you later.'

That's all they needed, Xavier thought; a new roommate to stop their night flights.

Ethan stabbed at his meat. 'I wonder what we'll have for dinner at Grissie Manor. I can't wait.'

'Matron said the family's cursed,' Gabe said as he chewed happily on his last piece of gristle, 'all the way back to Arthur Griswold.'

Xavier remembered Hayley telling them he was the man who converted an old castle into Griswold College. 'So does James own the school now?'

'No, Matron said his grandfather, Philip has all the money,' Gabe said.

Xavier could see Gabe was just warming up to the subject, so he put his fork down.

'James' father died of the plague ten years ago and his mother died in a car accident between here and Rosegrove last year.'

'I remember. Police came and questioned staff about the accident. There were rumours it was deliberate—something about the car's brakes, though they didn't catch anyone,' Ethan said. 'James went overseas after that.'

'So who's the saint of St Griswold?' Xavier asked while he watched Gabe lick his plate clean.

Ethan burst into laughter.

'What?'

'It's a joke. Most kids reckon they just like the sound of it. Why don't you ask Ratti?'

'I'd rather not,' Xavier said.

'Doubt he's Philip. Anyone who's met him says he's mean. Anyway you've got to be dead to be a saint, don't you?' Ethan looked at Gabe for confirmation.

'On Monday, maybe you could tell James about what's been happening here,' Gabe suggested as he eyed a chunk of meat Xavier had left on his plate.

Xavier caught his glance and offered it to him. 'What if he's evil? Dinner might be a trap. Ratti could've been pretending she was upset by James' visit.'

'I trusted him,' Ethan said.

Gabe speared the meaty chunk with his fork. 'Me too.'

'Why?' Xavier asked. 'You barely met him. Just because his eyes weren't close together and he didn't have a tail.'

Ethan frowned.

'You know what I mean,' Xavier said. 'He could be a shape shifter.'

'Whichever side James is on, it was just as well he entered the classroom when he did,' Gabe said.

'Why?' Xavier asked.

Ethan laughed. 'Cause Hortz nearly had you.'

Xavier looked puzzled.

'I'm guessing you're easily hypnotised,' Gabe said.

'I didn't fall for it, but you and the other kids slipped under his spell straight away. If it weren't for James G, you'd be Hortz's zombie slave,' Ethan added.

'Did you see it?' Xavier asked.

'What?' Ethan asked.

'The guys in armour, the arched windows and ...' Xavier's voice tailed off as he saw the boys' puzzled expressions. 'Don't worry, it must have been a dream.'

'We'll have to watch you in future.' Gabe ran a finger around his plate to capture the last stewy remains. 'I wonder what Ratti and Hortense were up to.'

Xavier watched Gabe lick his finger. 'I think if we could look inside Hortz's satchel, we might find a clue.'

'That moth-eaten, old thing?' Ethan said.

'He didn't let it out of his sight and clutched it like it was precious.'

Ethan grinned.

'What?' Xavier said.

'Now I have to know what's in it.'

CHAPTER 5

* * *

Spelling beetles and minding manners

Xavier opened his eyes as he tried to make sense of a scratching sound outside the window. While he puzzled over it, fluttering moths invaded his mind. Please, not again, he thought. Sweating and tangled in his blanket, he struggled to free himself.

Ethan was curled up asleep facing away from him while Gabe was lying on his back snoring.

Xavier crept to the window and surveyed the empty quadrangle. Why was he always the first to hear strange noises and see weird things? Maybe he had overheated and the scratching was only a dream.

When a tiny, red and black beetle scurried across the window, he startled but then felt embarrassed by his reaction. It was just a tiny insect on the other side of the glass, yet he watched curiously as two identical beetles emerged and scuttled across the window pane to join the first. Outside, he saw the moon shimmer of many tiny beating wings approaching. Memories of the moth-face loomed in his mind. Unable to cope with the thought alone, he shook Gabe. 'Wake up,' he pleaded in a whisper.

Gabe grunted and was slow and disoriented for a few moments.

Xavier returned to the window and watched spellbound as at least twenty beetles scurried across the glass. 'Look, it's happening again.'

Gabe sat up and rubbed his eyes. 'Just insects,' he mumbled yet climbed from his bed.

More beetles gathered, and the boys could now hear their frenetic scratching through the closed window.

Horrified, Xavier watched as Gabe brought his face closer to the beetles. They massed and crawled together as though arranging their positions for a group photo.

'It appears to be a dance,' Gabe said.

Xavier held his breath.

'Look! They're forming a pattern. Fascinating!'

Of all the Griswold rooms, Xavier wondered why the animal world had chosen his window. Were they seeking him?

'That's a funny looking V. Hurry, write the letters down — I, S.'

Xavier searched for a pencil and paper in the semi-darkness but could only find a pencil stub, so he scrambled to scribble the letters on the desk.

'O—and a letter I can't decipher. Have you got that?'

Xavier copied the shapes carefully.

After a while, the beetles dispersed and then regrouped lower down the window.

'They're moving again,' Gabe said excitedly just as a clump of beetles fell from the window. 'What's happening to them?'

'A white vulture's hovering out there,' Xavier said.

'Bizarre.' Gabe pressed his nose against the window. 'It's flicking and scraping them with its wing.'

The vulture struck the window with its beak. Catching sight of its crazed eyeball, Xavier jumped backwards. In that instant, a vision flashed in his mind of children, sad and huddled in a dark place. He slumped on the bed as the bird attacked the last few beetles so viciously it left a fine crack in the glass. Xavier was terrified the glass would shatter and the vulture would find its way into their room, but instead it turned and took off into the night. Half-awake, Ethan grumbled.

'You missed the action,' Gabe said.

'What?' Ethan said.

'Beetles that could spell—well, sort of. It was most strange.'

'Shut up,' Ethan mumbled and rolled over and went back to sleep. Gabe chuckled.

'How can you be so flippant?' Xavier said.

'They couldn't have harmed you through the window.'

'What about the vulture? I'm sure it was evil. Look how it cracked the glass.'

'Perhaps.'

'I'm sure the vulture was trying to stop the beetles telling us something.' He didn't mention the vision as he thought Gabe would probably blame it on stress.

Gabe stood up and examined the letters on the desk:

VISO88WVZ

'It doesn't spell anything. Maybe it's a code or perhaps they can't spell—their brains are small.'

* * *

'What are you doing?' Ethan had just woken and sounded groggy. 'You don't look too well.'

Xavier was sitting at the desk, pondering the letters on its surface. 'I haven't slept much.'

'You've got bags under your eyes.'

'Thanks.'

'What were you and Gabe up to last night? You woke me.'

'Sorry about that, but masses of strange beetles were making strange patterns on the window—spelling out letters. A vulture cracked the glass trying to get at them.'

'You're turning into a Gabe.'

Xavier pointed at the letters on the desk. 'Okay, how do you explain these?'

Ethan crawled from under his covers to the end of the bed and peered at the symbols. 'Whatever you do, don't leave them on the desk for Ratti or a teacher to see.'

Xavier ran his fingers through his hair. 'Maybe they had more to say. Perhaps they'll come back to finish.' He left the symbols on the desk but covered them carefully with a book.

'Forget your beetles 'cause today we've got something to look forward to for a change,' Ethan said happily.

'More to worry about, you mean.'

Ethan bounced on his bed. 'Don't be so negative. It'll be fun being picked up in a fancy car and having a proper dinner. I can't wait.'

Gabe stirred in his bed. 'Wish it were me.'

A sharp bang at the base of the door interrupted their conversation and without waiting for a response, Felix barged in. 'Hortz's teaching us first period instead of Kennedy, but it'll be in the new classroom,' he said as he chewed something. He then turned and sauntered off down the hallway to kick on another door and repeat his message.

Xavier rubbed his temple and sighed.

'Don't think about it,' Ethan said as he collected his clothes for the shower. 'Who knows it might be something fun.'

'If not, we'll endeavour to make it so,' Gabe said.

* * *

The boys filed into an unfamiliar classroom on the first floor of west wing before the stairwell. In addition to the chosen classes, Hortense was now also taking the first three forms for *Ethics and Etiquette* classes and this was their first class with him.

Xavier sat by the window overlooking the sloping roof that extended over the outside walkway and was surprised when he spotted a gargoyle not encrusted with layers of grey-green lichen. It had to be new unless Grubner had scrubbed it recently. He stood and surveyed a few of the others; but they were grimy as usual and perched at a different angle to the newcomer. Unlike the other gargoyles looking east towards Ratti's lair, this one focused on the western wall. Xavier felt as though it was looking at him from the periphery of its stony vision. He realised this classroom wasn't too far from Ratti's lair on the third floor; however, an awning prevented her from seeing directly into the classroom.

'What are you looking at?' Ethan asked.

'A new gargoyle,' Xavier said.

'He was planted there a couple of days ago.'

'He?'

'Kids are calling him Stinky Eye. He's a big brute, bigger than the others. They would've used pulleys to get him up there. Saw Ratti standing on the quad yesterday, gazing lovingly at him. Reckon he's her favourite now.'

Xavier grinned. 'Love at first sight?'

Hortense strode swiftly into the room, reaching the teacher's desk with three elongated steps. 'Good morning, class.' His face appeared fuzzy as though he hadn't time to shave that morning or comb his bristly eyebrows.

'Good morning, sir,' the boys responded mechanically as they sat up straight.

Xavier noticed he was carrying a bag with his right hand and the mysterious satchel snugly under his left armpit. After dropping the bag on his desk, he arranged the satchel on his chair. He reached into the bag, removed a red, cloth-covered bundle and opened it to reveal a pile of cutlery and napkins. 'My name is Dr Hortense. In future my *Ethics and Etiquette* class will be replacing Mr Kennedy's sports class in second period on Wednesday mornings.'

None of the boys appeared disappointed with the news.

Hortense continued, 'Today I'm going to share some basic dining customs, which I suspect most of you won't have encountered. Please gather around the front bench.'

Intrigued, the boys jostled for position, surprising Xavier with their eagerness. Even Gabe and Ethan craned their necks, leaned in and pushed forwards. Realising the class might be distracted enough for him to peek in the satchel, Xavier stood behind the boys and edged closer to it.

Hortense placed the cutlery on the table and then added a plate, napkin and glass that he took from the bag. 'Knives to the right and forks left,' he said as he laid them out. 'Soup spoon goes to the far right. Now, if it's an informal meal, the dessert cutlery is placed above with fork facing right and spoon left. However in a formal setting, the spoon is placed here and the fork to the left. Everyone got that?'

Xavier was amazed to see some of the boys taking notes. With the back of his legs resting against the front of the teacher's desk, he edged left while watching Hortense's oily hair in case he turned and caught him.

'Which tool do you use, sir?' Ethan asked.

The boys waited keenly for his answer.

'I think you mean utensil. You use them all—just not at the same time.'

Ethan glanced at Xavier. 'Which do you use first, sir?'

Xavier realised he was trying to distract Hortense, so he moved quickly to the back of the desk.

'Always begin on the outside. If you're having an entrée, use the first pair of utensils. The next pair will be for main course. If there's soup, the spoon will be on the right,' Hortense said.

The boys looked confused.

Ethan stood on the tips of his toes. 'What's an entree, sir?'

'A small meal before the main one.'

'At the same dinner?'

'Fascinating,' Gabe said aloud.

Xavier smiled but then realised he was serious. What was the attraction of this nonsense, he wondered as he stepped backwards, closer to the satchel.

'Glasses to the right,' Hortense continued.

Ethan fiddled with one of the napkins. 'What do we do with the little towels, sir?'

'Napkins,' Hortense corrected him and then spoke in a manner that suggested he thought Ethan was dim-witted. 'Sit down and I'll demonstrate the correct way to use it.' He plucked the folded napkin from Ethan's grasp, snapped it open and laid it across his lap.

'I get it, sir. It captures the food that misses or falls out of my mouth.'

With an expression of distaste, Hortense said, 'Hopefully if you chew with your mouth closed that won't happen. The napkin captures the odd crumb or drop of liquid but not your entire meal.'

'Are there any more tricks, sir?' Ethan said.

Hortense groaned. 'Does anyone else have any questions before we move on to the next point?'

No one said anything.

'Right, can anyone tell me what this is for?'

'A child's plate, sir?'

Hortense ignored Ethan and when no one offered a suggestion, he answered his own question. 'It's a bread and butter plate that sits to the left of your dinner plate and this is a butter knife.' He held it up. 'The knife is never used to cut bread. Do you understand? One always breaks bread with one's fingers during a formal dinner.'

Xavier reached for the satchel flap, but as he tried to lift it, he realised it had a small lock fastening it shut.

'What's the little knife used for then?' Gabe asked.

'Why to butter the bread, of course.'

The boys nodded with puzzled expressions.

Hortense sighed and regarded them as though they were a horde of small savages. 'We will spend the rest of the class practising with the utensils. I don't want to overload you with too many details.'

'But we've no food, sir,' Gabe said.

'That's why we have imaginations,' Hortense said.

'Did you use yours on the tomato farm, sir, when you were a boy?'

Ignoring Gabe, Hortense said to Ethan, 'I trust you've absorbed sufficient information, so you can properly represent the school this evening?'

'I hope so, sir,' Ethan said earnestly.

Hortense then turned around and with narrowed eyes looked directly at Xavier, who had just pulled his hand away from the satchel in time.

'Yes, sir, we won't let you down,' Xavier replied automatically.

'Remember, chew your food with your mouth closed and keep your knife and fork pointed downwards at all times when you're using them,' Hortense said as the boys filed from the classroom at the end of the lesson. 'And don't slurp your soup!'

'Humans are more complex than I imagined,' Gabe said as they walked to their maths class. 'Did you observe these fine customs in Ravenwood?'

Xavier shook his head. 'Since the war, most people are lucky to just eat every day.' He couldn't blame any of them for believing this was how normal people behaved. As an angel, Gabe was not familiar with human customs and like most of the boys, Ethan's experiences and memories were now related to Griswold.

'What's their purpose then?' Gabe said.

Xavier shrugged. 'They died out long ago.'

'Are you quite sure?'

'Definitely.'

'Then why are Ratti and Hortense so insistent we learn them?' Gabe asked.

'I think they're stuck in a time warp. Maybe they don't want us to let down St Grissie's reputation this evening,' Xavier said, 'whatever that is.'

'Did you look inside the bag?' Ethan asked Xavier.

'It was locked.'

Ethan grinned. 'A key challenge—excellent. He must be hiding something special to carry it around and keep it locked.'

* * *

CHAPTER 6

Dinner at Griswold Manor

After inspecting their hair and fingernails, Mr Crowley waited with Xavier and Ethan on the front steps of the school. Ratti had warned them to be on their best behaviour and said she would be checking with Mr Griswold to make sure they represented the school in a fitting manner. For the occasion, the boys had each been given a freshly laundered uniform, a navy jacket bearing the school crest on their pocket and a pair of shiny, black shoes. Although they looked fine, Xavier's shoes pinched his heels.

'Why the glum face?' Crowley asked Xavier.

Xavier shrugged.

'Nothing to worry about—Griswold Manor's an amazing place and James Griswold's a great host. Forget about school and enjoy yourself.'

'I'll try.'

At five o'clock, a sleek limousine cruised up the Griswold College driveway, softly crunching and compressing the gravel until it came to a halt a few metres from the boys.

Xavier shoved his hands into his pockets to stop them shaking.

The front door of the limousine opened and a grey-suited driver stepped out. Without speaking to the boys, he tipped his cap and opened a door for them to climb in the back.

As Xavier followed Ethan, he noticed scores of boys like pale statues standing and watching from the windows of the school. He could see their envy and feel their longing to be a part of the chosen pair. Every boy standing at the windows wanted nothing more than to be him or

Ethan. He knew they were imagining a stately manor with carpets, staircases and waiting butlers. He knew also, they were fighting to ignore the dream of clinking cutlery and crystal and the taste and smell of glorious food.

Xavier turned from their wistful faces and climbed into the car. He gingerly patted the deep-red velvet upholstery and touched the lacquered wood panelling.

Ethan grinned as they drove out the gate and whispered, 'I can't hear any road noise or feel any bumps in the road.' He pressed his nose to the leather seat. 'Smells like money.'

The car glided through Mourn Forest as Xavier strained to see any signs of demons or wraiths amongst the trees, but it looked like any other forest. Yet he knew it wasn't. As the twilight fog descended; trees, bushes, ferns and vines wrapped and curved around each other to create strange shapes and shifting shadows. He was relieved to be in the car but still checked the door was locked. By the time they reached the open road, he relaxed and enjoyed the ride. When they drove into the main street of Rosegrove and past Sarah's café, Xavier craned his neck to see if she was at the counter, but it was dark inside. He hoped she was safe. The limousine glided through back streets and past houses with boarded windows. Had their owners lost faith and fled north? He smiled when he saw in some of the homes, small lights burning bravely through chinks between boards.

They drove uphill on a dark, narrow road until the fog thinned enough for Xavier to notice flickering lights between the trees and a pair of open gates appearing from the gloom. After passing between two winged-horses guarding the gateway and up a winding driveway, the driver suddenly braked to avoid a herd of dark creatures tearing across their path.

'Deer,' Ethan exclaimed.

'Master likes to hunt.' It was the first time the driver had spoken.

'Who's the Master?'

'Mr Philip Griswold, of course.'

'I wouldn't have thought he'd need to hunt for meat,' Ethan said.

The driver chuckled. 'He doesn't. It's his sport.'

Although he hadn't met Philip Griswold, Xavier disliked him already. When the limousine stopped under a balcony projecting beyond the front steps, Ethan quickly jumped out, but Xavier remained in its velvety cocoon.

'Come on,' the driver said and held the door open until reluctantly Xavier climbed out. He ushered the boys up the front steps to where a man was waiting. 'Mr Bellows will take you from here. I'll be back later to return you to school.'

The boys followed Mr Bellows, who was dressed like an old-fashioned butler, through one of the open front doors inset with stained-glass. Ethan reached out to touch the colourful glass, which depicted children dancing among flowers and butterflies before a fiery sun. After the butler pulled a tasselled cord dangling near the door, a bell rang in an adjoining room. While they waited, the boys stood in the entrance and gazed at the paintings on the wall and at the golden handrails of the stairway spiralling to the floors above.

A door burst open and James Griswold strode out to greet them. 'Welcome, boys. So, who do we have here?'

Ethan introduced himself and turned to Xavier, whose mouth dried with nervousness making his reply a struggle.

'Wonderful! Come and meet my grandfather.'

'The Master's attending to business, Mr James. He'll be delayed.'

'Thanks, Bellows. I'll show the boys around while we're waiting. Would you let me know when he gets in?'

Bellows nodded and left them.

'Come along, boys.' James smiled and held the door open to another room. 'Come and see our art collection.'

Inside the room, a small circle of chairs and a couch, upholstered in rich red and gold fabric, looked out over a garden. James switched on the lights and drew the curtains. The walls were covered with paintings and small tables held vases and ornaments.

Ethan stepped forward and ran his hand over the back of the couch. 'It's nice and slippery.'

'They're covered in silk,' James said.

'Silk? I don't know it.'

James pointed at the paintings on the wall. 'These are family portraits of old Griswolds. Even as an adult, they still make me uneasy. The large one in the centre is my grandfather, Philip.'

Xavier examined the portrait of a severe-looking man in his seventies, wiry-thin, small-mouthed and white-haired. With his hair parted down the middle and wearing thick-framed glasses, Philip also stared angrily at him from a smaller yellowing canvas. 'Why is your grandfather in fancy dress in this painting?'

James chuckled. 'No, he's Arthur Griswold, another relative in the clan. I know there's a strong family resemblance. He's the oldest hanging here. I've heard he was a good and amazing man, but he's pretty scary looking, isn't he? He came from a very wealthy family and converted a crumbling castle into St Griswold College. He also built the girls' school on the other side of Rosegrove.' He pointed at a blue and gold banner with a crest on it. 'That's our family coat of arms. It's very old—from when the Griswolds lived in the castle.'

'You own so many things,' Ethan said.

'Too many actually,' James said. 'Don't tell Grandfather I told you, but he's a hoarder. You should see his book collection; he has enough books for several lifetimes. I'm working on bringing a few boxes of them to the school.'

'Who owns this room?' Ethan asked from another doorway.

James strolled over to his side. 'You can go in. It's my old room; the one I had as a boy. The manor is so large that we all lived here with my grandfather.'

On one wall, a scene was painted of boats sailing on a wild ocean, and on another, shelves brimmed with books and games. A wooden ladder led to the top of a double-bunk bed, which was covered in a bright patchwork quilt. In the corner was a small fireplace surrounded by chairs covered in cushions and more books.

'It's an amazing room,' Ethan said quietly as he bent forward to peer through the eyepiece of a large telescope standing before the window. 'And no one uses it?'

'Not now.'

'This has to be the best bedroom ever.' Ethan inspected a cluster of framed photographs. 'Who are these people?'

James glanced at the doorway before picking up the closest photograph. 'My parents,' he said and sighed, 'but they're no longer with us.'

'I'm sorry.' Ethan picked up another frame.

'They're my uncle, aunt and baby cousin, but they've gone too.'

Xavier wanted to ask him more about his family, but he didn't because James looked so sad. 'So only you and your grandfather live here now?'

'Yes, but that's enough of our history. Come and we'll see if Grandfather has arrived.'

The boys followed him to a room where a long table with place settings at one end stretched almost its entire length. Beyond the table was a fireplace, which housed a roaring fire lit no doubt to heat the large, high-ceilinged room.

Although the room was warm, Xavier smelled a hint of sour damp. His attention was drawn to the hissing and crackling fire where he noticed a hunched figure seated before it. As they drew closer, Xavier waited for him to turn around.

'Grandfather, you're back,' James said brightly. 'Our guests have arrived.'

Philip Griswold turned to reveal a cold, pinched face highlighted by the flames. Instantly, Xavier's throat constricted as voices, thoughts and sensations flooded his mind. There was no doubt. He already knew the man was evil.

'Good evening,' Philip said with a half-smile. He appeared exactly how the painting depicted. 'Who are you?' he asked in a raspy voice and leaned forward to gain a closer view like a cat inspecting prey. He blended with the dark fabric of the lounge chair apart from his pale bony hands, which were draped over the armrests and twitched when he spoke as though they had a life of their own.

'Xavier Jones and Ethan Klee,' Xavier said and tried to relax.

He fixed them with his stony eyes. 'Tell me about yourselves.'

Xavier tried to ignore the rattle of the old man's breathing and the ticking of a large clock in the corner while he wondered what he shouldn't tell him.

'Well?'

'I was brought to St Griswold about four months ago, but Ethan has lived at the school since he was six.'

'So you've recently arrived at St Griswold College, Xavier. Why is that?' Philip asked.

'I don't know. It was my parents' decision.'

'I see.' As Philip clutched at the armrests and struggled to stand, the tendons of his hands flicked and twitched under his pale, papery skin. 'I'm hungry. We'll have dinner. Where's Bellows?' he asked irritably.

James rushed to ring a bell to summon the butler, who appeared within seconds as though he had been listening at the door.

'We'd like to eat now, thanks, Bellows,' James said.

Bellows bowed. 'Very well, sir.'

He disappeared and soon after staff entered the dining room bearing platters of food. James ushered the spellbound boys to their seats while the servants placed plates of steak, potatoes, carrots, pumpkin and peas on the pure white table cloth in front of them. A woman brought a jug of steaming gravy and poured it on Xavier's steak. His stomach growled at the sight and smell of the vision. Another servant moved a crystal bowl overflowing with white blossom to make room for more plates with extra potatoes and bread rolls while James filled the boys' glasses with ginger beer.

When Xavier noticed that the plates and cutlery were set out in the same manner Hortense had shown them that morning, he grinned at Ethan and pointed at the cutlery.

Philip must have noticed their exchange of expressions. 'What's the matter?'

'Oh nothing, sir,' Ethan said. 'It's quite funny actually. We just learned about etiquette at school—using cutlery and napkins and such. This'll be our first practice.'

Philip said nothing, but Xavier noticed the fleeting curl of his lip.

'That's great, then,' James said encouragingly. 'After this dinner, you'll be experts.' Before he sat at the table, he placed a record on a player, and soon strains of light music filtered across the room.

Despite the fact he was seated next to Philip and could hear his rattling breath, Xavier was determined to enjoy his meal. He revelled in the tastes and textures of real food and could see Ethan was enjoying them too.

'Turn that confounded music down. Sounds like a clowder of mewling cats,' Philip said without looking at James and then struggled with a fit of coughing.

As James turned the dial down discreetly, Xavier wondered if Philip had something wrong with his lungs.

'So, tell me about your teachers and classes,' the old man said.

'What do you want to know?' Ethan asked. He didn't seem fazed by him as he bit a large chunk of steak from his fork.

'Who's your favourite teacher?' James asked brightly, although he seemed on edge.

Ethan chewed and looked at the ceiling for inspiration. 'Hmm.'

'Too many to choose from?' James teased and then laughed heartily. 'I was like you when I was a lad. School wasn't my favourite place.'

Ethan grinned. 'I like Lily and Matron, although I suppose they're not really teachers.'

Philip stopped chewing, put his knife and fork on the table carefully and then like a spider watching and plotting from its web, said, 'What a lovely name. Tell me more about Lily.'

Xavier wanted to kick Ethan under the table but couldn't reach. Why was he so trusting of Philip? Next thing he'd be telling the man Lily was a spirit. Xavier couldn't understand Ethan because usually he was careful and aware. Perhaps the food was distracting him.

'She helps out in the library sometimes,' Ethan said slowly in a changed tone that suggested he was now wary of Philip's curiosity.

Philip leaned forward. 'Does she now? Is she new?'

'Probably,' Ethan said.

'That's interesting. I must meet her.'

James' smile faded. 'That isn't necessary, Grandfather.'

Philip gave James a look that chilled Xavier.

'I'll meet her next time I visit the school,' James said in a worried voice.

'No, I will,' Philip snapped. 'Tell me more about your teachers.'

Xavier was losing his appetite. 'We have Mr Phineas for maths.'

'Fine teacher. Are you a good student?'

'Umm, I try. I'm average, I suppose.'

'Average? Perhaps you're not trying hard enough?'

Xavier blushed.

'Well? Do you try?' Philip persisted.

'I think so.'

'They must be promising students, Grandfather because they're in the special class, aren't you boys.'

'Is that so?' Philip said.

Ethan nodded.

'Interesting.'

'What subjects do you enjoy, Xavier?' James asked.

'History with Mr Crowley.' He frowned as he tried to think of another subject that might satisfy Philip. 'I was reasonably good at science when I was in Ravenwood, but the subject's a bit different at St Griswold.'

Philip fixed him with a stare. 'How so?'

Xavier's mouth was dry. 'It has a different name. It's called natural history. At home we worked on ideas rather than identifying things like we do with Mr Pittworthy.'

'You're very lucky to have such an experienced teacher. Forget your old ways. Embrace the privilege of the fine education you've been gifted, young man. Be grateful and accept your new life,' Philip said.

Xavier bent his head and focused on his potatoes.

At that moment, the music stopped and the room became unnaturally quiet apart from the scratching needle on the vinyl record. The atmosphere of the evening descended into gloom, although Ethan seemed unaware as he delightedly devoured the chocolate mousse and ice cream. Despite the dessert being one of Xavier's favourites, he struggled to eat a few mouthfuls. Every angel instinct was screaming silently and although he thought he could trust James, he knew Philip was evil. Xavier was exhausted. All he wanted now was to go back to school.

Just before they left the manor and when they were out of Philip's view, James handed them a large paper bag each.

Ethan opened his immediately. 'Oh, sweets, thank you, Mr Griswold.'

'Please call me James. You can share them with your friends. I know you don't get to enjoy much.' He looked at them with a sad expression and then whispered, 'Take heart, I'm working to improve your lot.'

Xavier smiled at James. Suddenly he felt certain he could be trusted.

* * *

CHAPTER 7

Painting over the cracks

Ethan burst into the dorm room, where Gabe and Xavier were dropping their books before going to lunch.

'Quick! You've got to see them. Come with me.'

Xavier and Gabe followed him downstairs and discovered pots brimming with leafy ferns and palms and colourful paintings adorning the first landing and the foyer.

'Unbelievable,' Xavier said as he examined an oil painting of yellow daffodils hanging near the front doors. 'Has Ratti cracked?'

Standing in the doorway, Ethan watched curiously as a van pulled up outside and a man jumped from the driver's seat. 'Hello, Mr Griswold.'

Whistling, James Griswold bounded up the steps. 'Hi Xavier, Ethan! How are you?'

Xavier was surprised he remembered their names. 'Hi, Mr Griswold.'

'Please call me James. So who's your friend?'

'I'm Gabe.'

'Pleased to meet you, Gabe. I remember your face from the special classes,' James said. 'I was hoping I might run into you, Ethan. I brought something for you.' He returned to the van and the boys followed. 'Here it is.' He handed a paperback with a bright cover to Ethan.

'Thank you,' Ethan said and read the title, 'Adventure in the Craggie Mountains'.

'My dad wrote children's books. He wrote this one for me. Actually I do it for a living now too.'

Ethan pulled a photograph from between the pages.

'That's a picture of the bedroom I had as a child—the one I showed you,' James said. 'I want you boys to know I'm looking at ways to improve your rooms. Perhaps you could help me choose paint, furniture and decorations. Hopefully the photo will inspire you. We won't be able to do it all at once, but it could be a long-term project. What do you say?'

Ethan grinned as he looked at the photo. 'Thanks, I'd like that very much.'

'How will you afford it?' Gabe asked. 'Will your grandfather help?'

James chuckled. 'I inherited money from my parents and my books are starting to pay off.'

Gabe looked at him curiously. 'I'd like to read them.'

'I'll bring a few when I visit next.' James smiled at Gabe. 'Right, now I need some assistance—if you're free?' James slid the side door of the van open to reveal boxes filled with books, plants, tablecloths and paintings. 'These are for the dining hall.' He handed the boys some paintings. 'I thought the place needed brightening and these were just crowding our walls at the manor. Grandfather will never miss them!' He winked at Xavier. 'Don't worry, I didn't bring any pictures of old Griswold men.'

As the boys helped him carry the paintings, James asked them how their classes were going.

'Good,' Xavier said.

'Come on, you can tell me. Grandfather's not around. I know he can be intimidating.'

Xavier grinned wryly.

James laughed. 'Don't let him bother you. His bark's worse than his bite.'

When they walked into the dining hall, the boys noticed the room was warm for a change and the air sweet. A large portable heater stood near the front servery and another on the back wall. Bowls of apples and oranges sat on every table and potted flowers were scattered near the windows.

'What do you think?' James asked the boys.

'Incredible,' Ethan said.

'Once we get these paintings up, you won't know the place. Now go and see what's for lunch.'

The boys rushed to the servery and were stunned to see slices of pizza warming in the trays.

James followed them. 'I popped into town and ordered them early this morning.'

'Thank you. It's brilliant what you've done,' Xavier said.

'I plan to do more around the school, and meals and heating are high on my list of things to do. Next winter I'll be looking at more blankets and warmer clothing for you boys too,' James said. 'Go ahead; enjoy the pizza and thanks for your help. I'll see you when I next visit. And Gabe, hopefully you'll come and visit the manor soon too.'

When James had left, the boys took their plates of pizza and found a table.

'It can't last,' Gabe said.

Ethan stuffed an apple in his pocket. 'Of course it can. Just enjoy it.'

Alex passed their table, chewing on a slice of pizza. 'List's out. Howard's your n-new roomy.'

'When's the move?' Xavier asked.

'In a few days.'

'I knew everything was too good to be true,' Gabe said when Alex left them. 'Howard's annoying.'

'Not much we can do about it. You heard Ratti. We have to share,' Xavier said.

'We could swap him for someone more agreeable,' Gabe said.

'I don't think it works like that,' Xavier said. 'Maybe once we get to know him, he'll be okay.'

'He's such a know-all and so vain,' Gabe said. 'I just don't understand how someone could be so insufferable.'

Ethan and Xavier grinned.

'What?' Gabe said.

'Howard's only been at school for a couple of weeks. How do you know what he's like?' Xavier said.

'I've heard boys talk about him and since then I've watched.'

'Sounds gossipy for a ....'

Gabe straightened. 'You'll see.'

'We've only got a few days, so I need to practise flying tonight. I don't know how we'll do it once he moves in permanently,' Xavier said.

Gabe's expression changed. 'Maybe he's one of us?'

Ethan rolled his eyes.

'What?' Gabe said.

'We've enough already.'

'We could go around midnight, but before lights out, I want to see Lily to make sure she's okay,' Xavier said.

'I don't know why I told Philip about Lily at the dinner,' Ethan said apologetically. 'I'd like to come too, but I've got detention with Phineas this evening.'

Xavier knew how guilty Ethan felt. 'Don't worry about Lily. We can warn her.'

'Are you sure?' Ethan said.

'Matron told me Ratti has been searching for her for years. She's heard the rumours but has never been able to track her down, so I think Philip will have difficulty,' Gabe said.

'Matron told you?' Xavier tried to control the surprise in his voice.

'Yes, we get on rather well. She also told me not to attract Philip's attention,' Gabe said. 'Go to your detention, Ethan and we'll visit Lily.'

* * *

After dinner Xavier walked with Gabe across the quadrangle towards the library. 'I'm sure they're looking at me.'

Gabe turned around to check. 'Who?'

Xavier tilted his head and said in a quiet tone, 'Them.'

'The gargoyles?'

'Shh.'

'Yes, I agree.'

Xavier's heart missed a beat.

'Since we spoke of them during the snowfall, I've researched their function. The gargling grotesques have many purposes. You know how rainwater runs through their mouths?'

Xavier nodded. He particularly hated the snarling and spitting sound they made spouting water after a heavy downfall.

'It keeps water from the building and stops the mortar between bricks wearing away.'

'You said they had other purposes?'

'Gargoyles were designed to ward off evil spirits, but over time many have come to view them as evil themselves.'

'Do you think ours are evil?'

'I believe they're like watchdogs. Perhaps they answer to Ratti,' Gabe said matter-of-factly.

'You sound so calm.'

Gabe shrugged. 'They cannot, I mean can't touch you. Unless I suppose someone could cast a spell to animate them, but why would a person do that? It's unlikely. You just need to be more logical—like me.'

When they reached the library it was empty. There was no sign of old Mrs Bayou, the day librarian, who had probably returned to her first floor room in the east wing, where most of the teachers' rooms were located.

As they walked to the back of the library in search of Lily, Xavier relished the smell of the polished wooden floors and musty books. He found the library still and restful, the most comforting place in the school.

'Why are you here?' Lily asked in a thin, high-pitched voice from the basement. She loomed from the shadows of the stairwell, elongated and ethereal, up the stairs and towards the ceiling. 'It is late. You must go.' She faded and then reappeared overhead, chilling the air around her and frosting the closest books and shelves. She ushered them with her outstretched arms.

Curious, Xavier felt tempted to reach and touch her misty form but was too afraid.

Suddenly she brought her face so close to Xavier's that he yelped in fright. 'You must go!'

'What's wrong?' Gabe asked Lily.

'Get out! Get out while you can!'

Xavier stood flat-footed and uncomprehending. 'Why?'

'The dark is coming. It will catch lingerers.'

Gabe started to back up. 'Who's the dark?'

But Lily didn't answer.

'Lily, please be careful,' Xavier called as loudly as he dared. 'Philip Griswold's looking for you.'

'It's here!' Lily's voice was now thin and shrill, and her words echoed in their heads.

Scratching sounds emanated from the shadows. Cockroaches dropped from bookcases to the floor. They spilled from cracks and crevices in the walls. From ceiling vents, they fell onto the boys' heads and down their necks. Others scurried over their shoes and up their legs. Frantically, Xavier and Gabe scraped and batted them away.

'Run!' Gabe yelled.

The boys rushed towards the entrance of the library, which now seemed far away. Crushing their brown shells with each step, the boys left a slimy trail of oozing roaches. Panicking, they slipped and skidded as they dodged trolleys. Soon the floor was a sea of crawling and scuttling roaches. Darkness had turned the library to a tomb. Forced to slow, the boys walked the last few steps with hands outstretched.

Desperately Xavier tried to ignore the roaches scratching and scurrying over his face and fingers. Finally he spotted a dim light. 'The door,' he gasped and spat a roach from his lips.

They jumped over the last mass of dark bodies, tore through the exit and slammed the door shut behind them.

Peering through the window in the door, Xavier was horrified to see creatures crawling over it, totally obscuring his view. Repulsed by a few roaches crawling inside his sleeve, he shuddered as he flicked and stamped on each one. Eventually he removed them all and then slid down a wall to the ground, exhausted. 'What just happened?'

'I don't know,' Gabe said as he nonchalantly flicked a roach from his collar. 'At least we know Lily hasn't been harmed—assuming you can harm a spirit. We also got to warn her about Philip.'

'What have you got in your hand?' Xavier asked.

'Not sure. I grabbed this to swat the bugs.' He flicked one from the book and examined its cover. 'This looks inspiring: *The Golden Rules of Etiquette.*'

Despite their ordeal, Xavier couldn't help laughing. 'Look, it's written by Hortense.'

As they hurried back to their room, Xavier felt comforted Lily was safe and they had warned her of Philip. As for the roaches, they were only another horror to worry about. He wondered where and how it would end. There was no way they could risk flying tonight. When they reached the Great Corridor, they slowed and tried to walk casually beneath the gargoyles, but once out of their stony sight, the boys sprinted all the way back to their room.

CHAPTER 8

* * *

Howard Linnaeus

'Actually, my father's a high flier in the Ambrosian Government—very high up. He's won medals.' Howard deposited his books and bag on the spare bunk. Unexpectedly, he had decided to visit the boys' room before he was due to move in permanently. After testing his mattress by bouncing on it several times, Howard sniffed and pushed his thick glasses up the bridge of his nose. 'He's very important,' he said in a softer voice as though confirming it to himself. 'I'll show you his business card,' he added and rummaged in his bag.

'That's great. You must be proud.' Xavier felt Gabe flinch beside him.

'I am.' Howard handed Xavier a white card, which read, Senator Charles Linnaeus, Department of Security, Ambrosian Government.

'Is that a beetle beside your father's name?' Xavier asked.

'It isn't just any beetle, it's a scarab,' Howard said in a proud tone.

Puzzled, Xavier ran his finger over the raised text and insect. He didn't want to sound stupid asking why a scarab was superior, so he just nodded.

'Is Ambrosia big enough to have a government?' Ethan asked.

He looked at Ethan as though he were simple. 'Of course.'

'Why did he leave you here?' Ethan asked.

'Security. My father's business is top secret. I've been left here for protection, so he can travel.'

Ethan frowned. 'Protection from ...?'

'Spies from other countries. I'm not allowed to know the details.'

Nodding with a vague expression, Ethan looked as though he couldn't decide whether to laugh or believe him.

'We all come from pretty ordinary backgrounds,' Xavier said, 'but you're very welcome here.'

'Thanks,' Howard replied. 'I'm sure I'll adjust.'

Xavier spotted Ethan's upper lip quivering but quickly looked away. 'I suppose we should head off for class.'

'Actually I might pop back this afternoon and do some study here, just to get to know you better,' Howard said.

On the way to Hortense's class, Xavier noticed Grubner and Phineas standing outside the open library doors. Holding a mop, Grubner grumbled loudly and pointed to the slurry of dead roaches coating the library floor. Phineas seemed stunned by the sight, and Xavier caught a snatch of him saying something about boys taking food into the library. Xavier smiled at the unlikelihood of a Griswold boy having any spare food to drop on the library floor. When they reached the classroom, they discovered Hortense busy scratching notes on the blackboard.

'Please take your seats,' he said in a crisp tone. 'Without the chatter, thank you.'

The boys straggled into the room while he stood next to the blackboard with his chalk poised, and when they had settled, he wrote 'etiquette' on the board. Xavier and Gabe settled into seats in the back row while Howard and Ethan sat in front of them. Hortense paced down the aisle towards Howard's desk and peered at him with a severe expression. 'You, young man, what is etiquette?'

With a vacant expression, Howard gazed at him as if it hadn't occurred to him to be intimidated. 'Umm ...,' he scratched an armpit, 'eti-cut, sir, is something to do with first aid, I'd imagine.'

The teacher sighed and moved to the next boy.

'Me sir?' Felix said anxiously. 'I don't really know about eti-cets.'

Hortense closed his eyes as though in pain. When he opened them, he looked around the room.

Gabe raised a hand and Hortense nodded at him. 'Etiquette, sir is a group of social rules that help us get along with each other, for instance, covering your mouth when you sneeze.'

'Excellent, give the boy a hand,' Hortense said.

Some of the boys clapped half-heartedly.

'Without etiquette, we're savages. Etiquette is about good manners and being graceful and polite, respectful and clean,' Hortense said.

Some of the boys looked puzzled, but Xavier felt like laughing in disgust. When you were cold, hungry and away from your family, etiquette was bizarre.

'Take a partner and we'll practise role plays. Imagine you're sitting down for dinner. I want you to consider all the ways in which you might express good manners.'

After they had paired off, Xavier asked Gabe, 'Would you care to sit down or shall I chop off your legs to make it easier?'

Gabe raised an eyebrow. 'You're too kind.'

'We'll be serving dinner soon, sir. We're having a lovely aged fish. I wish to apologise in advance for the putrid stench. I do hope it's to your liking.'

'Exotic flavour.' Gabe coughed. 'Pardon me. Is it usual for your throat to close over while consuming this delicacy?'

'Quite normal, sir, please enjoy.' Xavier watched Hortense as he walked from pair to pair and listened to their role plays.

Peals of laughter and clattering chairs disrupted the class as boys enjoyed the comic side of etiquette. Hortense clapped for attention, but the laughter and commotion had gained too much momentum. Amid the uproar, the back door of the classroom suddenly swung open. Ratti stood in the doorway with a thunderous expression. Behind her was the cadaverous form of Philip Griswold accompanied by the portly Father Augustine.

The boys fell into stunned silence and shrank back in their chairs.

Hortense's elongated face burned crimson as he slowly lowered his hands to his sides. 'I do apologise, I ...,' he said, but Ratti turned her back on him and ushered Philip and Father Augustine into the classroom behind the back row of desks. She invited Philip to sit, but he shook his head and folded his arms.

'Philip, this is our new *Etiquette and Ethics* class. I hope you'll excuse any teething problems.' Ratti spoke in a low tone, but in the silent room most of the boys could hear her clearly.

Xavier and Gabe were in the back row, so they could see her glaring at Hortense.

Father Augustine smiled placidly, but Philip scowled as he scoured the room with his beady eyes.

Xavier flinched when Philip paused after catching sight of him. He forced himself to breathe slowly and deeply until the panic and scrutiny passed.

Hortense repeated the earlier part of the lesson as though his mind had frozen and he couldn't remember what he had planned. 'Without etiquette, we're s-savages. Etiquette is about good manners and being graceful and polite, respectful and clean.' He stumbled on for the next ten minutes until just before the bell rang when Ratti stood and interrupted the class.

'Excuse me,' she piped.

The boys turned around to listen.

'Mr Philip Griswold will be here for the next two days before the new school opening. So please make him welcome if he chooses to join you in the dining hall.'

When she dismissed the class, the boys filed quickly and quietly from the room, obviously glad to escape.

Xavier, Gabe, Ethan and Howard waited to exit through the back door behind Ratti. She turned to Philip and the priest and talked to them in soft tones and then chuckled in a hollow way like dry bones scraping together. Philip didn't look as old and hunched as Xavier remembered from Griswold Manor, and his face seemed less drawn and pinched. Perhaps it was the different light. His evil aura, however, was unchanged and made Xavier feel nauseated and dizzy. Beside him, Gabe, who was obviously having a similar reaction, wiped sweat from his forehead. Just when Xavier felt he was going to black out, Philip turned and without warning strolled to the door and left the classroom with Ratti and Father Augustine scrambling in pursuit.

'So that was Philip Griswold,' Howard said as he watched the teachers walking towards the east wing. 'Creepy, isn't he?'

* * *

After spending the afternoon running laps around the school perimeter goaded by Kennedy, Ethan and Xavier lay on their beds nursing their sore and blistered feet.

Howard sat at the desk and opened a notebook. 'You must have covered at least twelve kilometres today—maybe more.'

Ethan groaned. 'How come you didn't have to run?'

'I picked up a clipboard and offered to record times and Mr Kennedy was agreeable.'

Gabe laughed. 'That's odd.'

'Of me or Mr Kennedy?'

'Ugly Kennedy, of course,' Ethan said.

Howard shrugged and returned to his writing.

Xavier was surprised he had escaped the run, but as the boy was well-rounded and wore thick glasses, Ugly probably didn't expect too much of him athletically. 'What are you writing now?'

'My private diary,' Howard said and closed his notebook.

Ethan chuckled. 'Got up, ate gruel, went to classes, ate more gruel, went to more classes, got a whipping, ate more gruel and went to bed. That about sums it up.'

Howard ignored him. 'By the way, what's Zambrosia?'

'Why?' Xavier said.

'Because of the writing here on the desk—it's a code, isn't it? It took me a while to work out, but I like this sort of puzzle.'

Xavier sat upright. 'A code?'

'Mmm, I reversed the word first, like this.' He scribbled the letters on his pad to show Xavier.

ZVW88OSIV

'I don't understand it.'

'So, it's not yours?' Howard said. 'See, you have to turn it upside down.' He wrote the letters and figures quickly on the pad. 'Look.'

ZAM88OSIA

'Zambrosia. That's what it says. Who made up the puzzle?' He looked at Gabe and Ethan. 'Did I read the Z wrong? Is it a number two?'

Startled, Xavier wondered if Howard had stumbled on the answer to the beetles' message.

'No, it was a Z,' Gabe said quickly.

'Oh, so it's your puzzle,' Howard said.

'It's just a game. It didn't mean anything.'

'Do you have any more?'

Gabe shook his head.

Of course, that's what the beetles had been trying to tell them. Xavier had assumed Howard was dim-witted and odd, but perhaps he was actually clever. He wondered if there was more to this kid than they knew. But what did *2 Ambrosia* mean, or could the beetles have meant *to Ambrosia*? Nisroc had spoken of Ambrosia and Beth had come from there. Maybe it was a sign that something was going to happen in the town. He had so many questions that he wished he could talk to Artemis or the Boundary Keeper.

* * *

CHAPTER 9

Boys can fly

Standing in the middle of the oval, Xavier shoved his hands under his armpits in an attempt to keep them warm. Under the spotlight of the moon, he felt exposed and inadequate. In the shadows of the trees nearby, Gabe and Ethan were quietly urging him to fly. Although Xavier knew time was running out for him to perfect his flying skills because Howard was due to move in permanently the next day, he struggled to overcome his fear.

With Philip staying at Griswold, they decided to stuff sheets under their bed covers just in case there was a sudden room check. The thought of Philip sleeping in one of the rooms at the school made him shudder, but thankfully none of the windows had a view of this oval. Even so, they would have to be more careful than ever.

Gabe stared at the sky. 'It's magnificent isn't it?'

'The moon?' Ethan said.

'Yes, I wish Kepler had a few more—two aren't enough. I never tire of them. I believe the planet Earth, where humans originated, only had one, but it too was beautiful.' He sighed. 'What a glorious gibbous moon.'

Xavier stifled a grin. 'Yes, that's what I was going to say.'

'Are you laughing at me?'

He was growing used to Gabe's fascination with stars, clouds and moons. 'No, of course not.'

'A gibbous moon is one that has begun to lose its fullness. It's waning.'

Ethan rocked from one foot to the other. 'Enough moon talk. Are you guys going to fly?'

'Ready?' Gabe said.

Although scared, Xavier squeaked, 'Yes.'

'The lesson today begins with the flap and step and flap and step,' Gabe said.

Ethan and Xavier tried not to laugh while watching him demonstrate the action.

Xavier stuck his tongue out with the effort of trying to concentrate on the flapping motion. He saw Gabe smiling at one stage and turned around to see Ethan cross-eyed and with his tongue protruding as he copied and exaggerated his attempt.

'Thanks,' he said in a huffy tone. 'It's not as easy as it looks.'

'Actually, it's not that hard,' Gabe said. 'I found it rather instinctive.'

'Yes, we know.' Xavier knew Gabe didn't say it to make him feel bad; he was simply pleased with himself and his talents.

'Well show us then,' Gabe said.

Xavier stood at the end of the oval with his fists clenched. He charged halfway across the oval to get to full speed and with all his might flapped both wings in what he imagined perfect synchrony. For a split second, he felt an uplifting sensation as his feet left the ground but just as quickly his knees banged together and he rolled and cartwheeled until he came to an embarrassing conclusion in the manure pile beyond the oval. He heard stifled laughs behind him.

Ethan coughed. 'Ah, the manure pile, the downfall of many an angel.'

Gabe said nothing. He had sat in the same manure only a few months earlier when he misjudged a landing over the wall.

After dragging himself from the manure, Xavier headed back to the oval. Waiting for the headwind to drop, he bounced on his toes a few times. When it finally died, he ran.

'Pick it up,' Ethan urged.

Xavier pumped his arms and lifted his knees to accelerate and just before the end of the oval, leapt into the air. The shock of lifting off the ground made him forget to use his wings for a few beats. He flapped but failed to lift and crashed to the earth. After a few more unsuccessful attempts, Xavier returned to his starting point. 'What am I doing wrong?'

'I think you're trying too hard.' Gabe rubbed his chin. 'Why don't you ask the voices for help?'

'That's not a bad idea.' Xavier closed his eyes and focused.

Turn arms out. Relax.

He faced the oval again, breathed deeply and shook his fingers until they were loose. Taking a run up, he carefully turned his arms out before taking off. This time he hovered for several seconds before landing once more on his bottom.

'Better,' Gabe said.

Xavier stood and rubbed his backside. 'Do you think so?' He retraced his steps, turned and faced the oval again. 'Please, I need more help,' he said aloud to the voices.

Lift head. Think and see.

Before starting his run up, Xavier mentally rehearsed the action several times. He took a deep breath, ran with his wings outstretched and rapidly accelerated. In the middle of the oval, he plunged forward and leapt into the air while driving his wings toward the earth. When they reached their full arc, he strained and lifted them powerfully. He was giddy with elation and excitement as the air rushed across his face. Finally he was airborne. He was flying! Once he had made the breakthrough, he wondered why it had taken him so long. When he landed beside the boys after several short flights of increasing complexity, he asked, 'Well? What do you think?'

Gabe examined his fingernails. 'I told you it was straightforward.'

Ethan laughed.

'That's it?' Xavier said.

'Would you like a ribbon?' Gabe said.

Xavier grinned. He was buzzing with confidence and joy. 'I think that's enough practice for today.'

After Xavier pulled his binding and jumper on, the boys jogged towards the west wing. Birds cawed and fluttered in the trees as the first rays of light stirred them into life.

'Trouble coming,' Ethan murmured.

Ratti and Kennedy emerged from the chapel entrance.

Xavier could almost hear his heart thud as they neared the pair. 'What should we do?'

'Don't panic,' Gabe said.

Ugly eyed them with a curious expression. 'Where have you come from, boys?'

Ratti casually rearranged the cobweb-like shawl draped around her neck.

Gabe stepped forward. 'We've been running. After cross country the other day, we decided we needed to get fitter.'

'I struggled in the class run, so Gabe and Ethan offered to come with me this morning to train.'

Ratti folded her arms slowly. 'Where did you run?'

'We did a few laps of the back oval. It's such a nice morning, blue sky and all,' Gabe said.

Ratti's lips tightened. 'Did you ask Mr Crowley for permission?'

'No, we didn't think of that,' Gabe said with an innocent expression.

Ugly sneered.

'What time did you leave your dormitory?' Ratti asked.

'Just before dawn, but I'm not sure of the exact time. We wanted to avoid the heat,' Ethan said.

'What heat? How did you get out of the building when the doors were locked?' Her questions were coming quicker and her tone was sharper.

'They weren't when we left.'

Xavier could see she didn't believe Ethan.

'Turn around, Mr Jones,' Ratti demanded.

Xavier had tried to hide the manure stain on his pants. How did Ratti know? Slowly he turned and waited for her response.

Ugly sniffed at the air. 'It's manure.'

'Umm, I took a detour to run up a small hill out the back. I didn't know it was manure until I slipped.'

Ratti eyed him curiously. 'I would have thought you'd have fallen forwards?'

'Umm, no, um, I was actually coming downhill and skidded and fell on my backside.'

'In future if you need extra activity, seek permission from Mr Crowley. I don't want you wandering around the grounds before dawn. Do you understand?' Xavier could hear her black, layered skirt rustling in the breeze as she stood waiting for their response. He looked at the ground with a contrite expression.

'Yes, miss,' Gabe said politely.

'If you boys enjoy exercise so much, perhaps you can put in a few kilometres every afternoon before dinner.' Kennedy smiled in a repulsive way.

'Go now, return to your dormitory. I do not, do you hear me, want a repeat of this behaviour again.' Ratti's tone was now freezing. 'Go and get ready for the opening ceremony.' Without any further niceties, she and Ugly turned and left them.

As they walked in silence towards the west wing, Xavier waited for his heart to stop pounding before he could think to speak.

'No detention? Something's up,' Ethan said.

'They're probably distracted with the opening ceremony,' Xavier said.

'No, it doesn't make sense,' Gabe said.

On the way back to the dorm, Xavier detoured to the laundry to scavenge fresh clothes and then rushed to the showers before anyone could see his stained pants. After showering, he discovered Howard approaching their door with another bag. Xavier was amazed at the number of possessions he had compared to other Griswold kids.

'My first official day as a roommate,' Howard said after Xavier held the door open and welcomed him.

Gabe was peering into the small mirror mounted on the cupboard combing his hair, but he stood back to allow Howard to deposit his bags. 'I've parted my hair on the other side for a change. What do you think?'

'What do you mean?' Howard asked.

'Is my physical appearance satisfactory?'

'You look fine,' Xavier said quickly.

'Ordinary, I suppose' Howard said. 'I don't know.'

Gabe glowered. 'What do you mean by that?'

'You're not extra ugly or strange.'

'I'm not like one of us,' Gabe said indignantly.

Xavier could tell he was still dwelling on the word 'ordinary'. 'You're fine.'

'I didn't mean to offend you,' Howard said, yet as he turned away from Gabe, Xavier noticed his brief smile.

The boys heard Mr Crowley calling from the corridor and the assembly bell ringing. They headed downstairs to where most of the students were already waiting for the teachers. Silence fell over the quadrangle as Phineas strolled to the front of the assembly. 'Line up.' He stood with his hands joined behind his back and watched as the boys quickly joined their year groups. Once they were in place, he directed the first form line, which included Xavier, Gabe, Ethan and Howard, to march in single file to the eastern gate. The other forms followed in order.

Ugly opened the gate and directed the boys through. 'Keep it down. Hurry up.' He clipped ears and pushed boys who lagged, talked or looked him in the eye.

To Xavier it seemed peculiar to be allowed to step out beyond the wall again.

Ugly led them up the path, but where it divided, he veered right towards the main building.

Clutching his satchel, Hortense however, slipped down the left path towards the white building.

When the boys reached the new school quadrangle, the first form boys formed two rows, so Xavier, Gabe and Ethan chose the second row to avoid scrutiny.

It was a parallel universe to Griswold, Xavier thought as he gazed up at the windows of the building, except there were no faces there yet. He felt sorry for those destined to fill the new rooms.

Ratti followed the last boys to the quadrangle but continued towards the front of the assembly. A man and woman were waiting in the shadows under the overhang of the first floor which resembled the Great Corridor of Griswold College. Xavier felt his breath catch when he realised they were Philip and Mrs Oakshof, or Beauty as they called her when they had first seen her before the ceremony for Jordie. He felt sick as he recalled Gabe and Ethan being captured by her in Lanoris and how she had murdered Harold Eastly. He wondered where she had hidden her pet beast. As he watched, Hortense crept up behind them to also skulk in the shadows—without his satchel.

Gabe ducked and looked at the ground. 'Did you see her?' he whispered.

Xavier nudged Ethan. 'Beauty.'

'I see her,' Ethan murmured. He was standing directly behind a taller boy out of her view.

Beauty was smoothing her hair and smiling at Phineas, who had joined them.

'Watch out, Phineas,' Ethan said. 'She'll eat you.'

Ratti tapped at a microphone planted in front of a large sash tied between two columns. Philip stepped forward and took the microphone without asking Ratti, who appeared stiff and awkward.

'I'm sure Arthur Griswold would be pleased to see his legacy continued today. I'm delighted to carry the Griswold tradition into the future; honoured to provide for those less fortunate and proud to guide the youth of today,' Philip began in a grating voice.

Ethan made a squeaky sound as though stifling a giggle.

'I hope each of you in turn will honour the Griswold name and focus on how you can contribute in a meaningful way to shaping our bright new world,' Philip said.

Ratti nodded her approval as the speech meandered and boys shifted and yawned.

Philip's voice rose in tone as he took a pair of scissors from Ratti and cut through the ribbon. 'It gives me great pleasure to declare the new St Griswold College buildings open.'

'Finally,' Ethan murmured.

'Where's James?' Xavier whispered as he scanned the teachers' faces. 'He said he was coming.' A tick of concern was echoed by a flurry of soft chattering in Xavier's mind. There were so many whispering voices that he couldn't decipher any message, but their tone troubled him.

The teachers clapped, and Ugly waved at the students to join the applause.

Ratti stepped forward. 'Thank you, Mr Griswold. The school is deeply indebted to you for these wonderful buildings,' she gushed. 'I'm

sure the new students will enjoy living and learning here. I know they'll
think of you when they take up residence here.'

While Ratti spoke, Philip appeared uninterested and aloof,
scrunching his nose and peering at the archway of the overhang as
though checking its architectural detail. When Ratti stopped speaking,
he bowed stiffly, turned and walked towards a door in the building with
her in pursuit. His manner was abrupt and strange and he obviously
didn't care what anyone thought.

'Well that was short and sour,' Ethan said. 'What a letdown.'

'You'll return to St Griswold in order. First form, lead the way.
Now!' Ugly bellowed.

'We can't go,' Gabe said suddenly as the first few students marched
off the quadrangle.

'Why not?' Xavier asked.

'Beauty's at the gate. She might recognise me and Ethan.'

'What are you going to do?' Xavier said.

'Ethan, come with me.' Gabe slipped to the end of the line with
Ethan in pursuit.

Xavier watched as they ducked across to a gap between two
buildings and disappeared. He then followed the line of first formers to
the gateway where the teachers were clustered.

'Where's that friend of yours—the blonde pest?' Ugly asked in an
unusually playful way. He was obviously trying to impress Beauty, who
seemed bored although she glanced at Xavier.

'He's already gone through, sir.'

'I didn't see him,' Phineas said in a flat tone as his focus skimmed
across the faces of the boys behind Xavier.

'Yes he did, sir. I saw him with the first few boys who went through
the gate.'

Phineas looked at him doubtfully for a few seconds, but Xavier held
his nerve.

Xavier walked back to the dorm by himself and checked to see if he could see Gabe or Ethan from the window. It was then he noticed Howard emerging near the chapel with Grubner and Phineas. He froze. What was he doing with them? Was he a spy? Perhaps that's why Ugly had given him the clipboard instead of making him run cross country. Or had he only been asked to stay behind to help? Xavier didn't know what to think.

Just then Gabe and Ethan burst through the door talking and laughing loudly.

'How did you get back in?' Xavier asked.

'Circled the building and climbed over the west wall out the front. No one saw us,' Ethan said.

'You hope.'

A few minutes later, Howard returned to the room.

'Where have you been?' Ethan asked.

'Stopped at the library for a book.'

First lie, Xavier thought. He would be watching Howard very closely now. 'Did you find what you were looking for?'

'No, why?' Howard said without missing a beat.

* * *

'Not rocks, please no.' Ethan groaned and put his head on the desk.

Pittworthy's natural history classes could be dry, but this promised to be particularly so. In his usual manner, the teacher had lined up samples of rocks in small groups according to colour, each in perfect order of size while others he discarded in a box because they didn't fit his ordering scheme. Xavier watched as he covered the box with a lid and poked it under the bench as though the misfits bothered him.

'Over the years, I've collected these rocks from the grounds of Griswold and Mourn Forest. I want you to come up in groups of three or four and try to identify them. You'll need to make sketches and take notes. While you wait, please read chapter seven of the text I've left on each of your benches.'

Howard poked at one of the moth-eaten books and flipped the cover open. 'Look at the date. They're ancient.'

Xavier carefully turned the yellowing pages and peered at the sepia illustrations of rocks and their descriptions.

'Actually, they're rather fascinating. Rocks are rocks and although these books are old, what's written still rings true,' Gabe said.

'Rings true? What are you on about?' Ethan said.

Gabe continued unfazed. 'Lily directed me to geology books on this region and I found them instructive.'

'Who's Lily?' Howard asked in a sharp and penetrating voice.

Gabe paused for a moment. 'Lily's my sister. She used to work at a bookstore and she'd bring books home for me. I miss her. Actually I miss all my siblings. Do you have siblings, Howard?'

'None.' Howard flicked over the pages of his text. 'How many do you have?'

Gabe sighed. 'Too many actually. That's why I'm here.'

Howard examined the rock illustrations. 'Where did you live before Griswold College?'

But Gabe had turned to Ethan to discuss a football game scheduled for the next day.

'So where did he come from?' Howard asked Xavier in a low tone.

Xavier shrugged. 'I don't know. I'm not familiar with this part of the country, so the names of towns don't mean much to me when I hear them.'

'You boys,' Pittworthy was pointing at their group, 'come out to the front bench. Hurry up. I expect punc-tu-ality.'

The boys reluctantly filed out to the demonstration bench.

'Okay, Gabe, what are the answers?' Ethan asked as Pittworthy wandered off to his desk to collect a clipboard and pen.

'Gabe picked up a rock from the first group. 'Limestone.' He selected another. 'This one has a fossil in it—a Trilobite, which would make the rock over 500 million years old.'

'What's a Trilobite?' Ethan asked.

'You have to pay attention,' Gabe said. 'As I said, it's a fossil.'

'Of?' Ethan asked.

'A marine arthropod.'

Howard listened with his mouth half-open. 'You're joking, right?'

'No, he's just smart,' Xavier said.

Gabe nodded his head in agreement.

'Tell me about marine arthro ...,' Howard said.

'Arthropods.' Gabe sighed. 'An arthropod's an animal without a backbone. It has a segmented body and jointed legs, like a spider.'

'What's this rock, then?' Howard asked.

'Gneiss. It's metamorphic.'

Howard picked up the rock and when Pittworthy returned, he said, 'Is this gneiss, sir?'

Pittworthy seemed surprised. 'Yes, very good, Howard.'

Howard replaced the rock and when the teacher was distracted by another student, turned to Gabe. 'How did you know that?'

'Gneiss is common around here,' Gabe said. 'If you were born in this region, you'd know that.'

'So you were born near Griswold?'

'Close enough.' Gabe strolled to the other end of the bench to a different group of pink rocks, but Howard followed him.

'What's this?' Howard asked.

'Feldspar—very common,' Gabe said and moved away again.

'He's a genius,' Howard whispered to Xavier.

'He enjoys reading about rocks,' Xavier said in the hope of making his knowledge seem more normal.

At the opposite end of the bench, Ethan picked up a lump of sandstone but dropped it immediately.

Xavier noticed his reaction and sidled over to him. 'What's wrong?'

Ethan didn't answer. He put one finger on the stone gingerly but withdrew it quickly. He repeated this several times. 'I can see colours when I touch it.'

'Touch the other stones.'

Ethan carefully fingered the other stones in turn. He shook his head.

Xavier examined one of the sandstone pieces. He wondered if Ethan's experience was similar to the one he'd had with the bird bones.

CHAPTER 10

* * *

New horizons

Xavier and Gabe perched on the back wall of the school after sneaking from the west wing before dawn. The two Kepler moons cast a ghostly hue down the rocky slope in front of them and over the tree tops in the valley below. Even though they had been warned by Ratti and Kennedy, Xavier knew he desperately needed to practise flying. Ethan had offered to cover for them if Howard woke early. They had each brought a spare T-shirt with them to change into after flying in case they got sweaty even though it was a cool spring morning.

Xavier pitched a stone into the valley and watched and listened as it hit an outcrop of rocks, tumbled and disappeared into a tangle of moonlit grey and green. 'What do you think of Howard?'

'I'm inclined to think he's a small, annoying human. He gives them a bad name,' Gabe said.

Xavier threw another stone. 'I'm not sure I trust him.'

'Yes?'

Xavier took a deep breath and blurted, 'I've also been thinking about the beetle message and I think we need to go to Ambrosia.'

Gabe raised his eyebrows. 'Why—because Howard guessed the message was about Ambrosia? That's impulsive and un-Xavier like of you. What if he's wrong? If you don't trust him that's another reason not to go to Ambrosia.'

Xavier chuckled.

'What?'

'Nothing, it's just that wanting to stay here is not very Gabe-like of you.'

'Nonsense. I rely on logic and facts.'

'Nisroc said we needed to go to the Ambrosian Forest.'

'That's not exactly how I remember it. Nisroc said we were to tell the six they'll be needed for the final battle, and that one of them lived in the wilds of the Ambrosian Forest and another on Green Isle. He also said to keep their identities safe.'

'Well how do you suppose we're going to get a message to someone in the wilds of a forest on the other side of the country without going there?' Xavier had no desire to go to Ambrosia, but he knew if he were ever to escape Griswold or see his parents again, he had to. 'I have this feeling and the voices are whispering about Ambrosia. They're bothering me.'

'I hope your voices are valid.'

'You don't hear them?'

'I hear them,' Gabe admitted. 'But as a guardian angel, I'd need more than whisperings before considering such a journey.'

'If only Beth were here. She's from Ambrosia and might know. She's smart.'

'I need more information,' Gabe said.

'I'm not sure how we'd get there though.'

'If we were to fly, you'd need more practice,' Gabe said as though considering the idea.

'I just assumed we'd catch a bus like last time.'

'Would you choose to wander through Mourn Forest and to catch a bus in Rosegrove again? Too risky. Anyway they'd be ready for that. We'd need a better plan this time.'

Xavier grinned. 'Yes, I suppose you're right.'

'Of course I am,' Gabe said. 'Enough talk. Today you need to fly outside the school.' He took off his jumper, folded it and laid it on the wall behind a thick branch with the spare T-shirts.

Xavier's heartbeat quickened because the drop over the northern wall they were overlooking was steep and treacherous. On the positive side, the larger of the Kepler moons hung full and bright in the predawn sky, so there was enough light to make a flight.

He peeled off his jumper and left it with the other clothes on the wall. After stretching his back from side to side, he flexed his knees a few times. As he slowly unfurled his wings, he listened to his feathers and tendons creaking and crackling as they protruded through the long slits he had cut in the back of his shirt. Unlike Gabe, who now took his wings for granted, they were still a fascinating novelty to Xavier. He had begun to take pride in his abilities and the fact he was improving in Kennedy's classes meant he wasn't as physically pathetic as he had been when he came to Griswold. He wondered whether his parents would recognise him when they finally met again.

'What are you waiting for?'

'Nothing,' Xavier fibbed. 'I'm ready.'

'Okay, all you have to do is dive, but keep your head up,' Gabe said as though he were instructing him on how to take a lazy plunge into a swimming pool.

Feeling dizzy from over breathing, Xavier held his breath. When his head finally settled, he tested his wings by flapping them several times and was relieved they still seemed to work.

'Come on,' Gabe urged and sprang into the air to show him how easy it was.

'Do it, do it, do it,' Xavier chanted softly as he closed his eyes and flexed his fists. When he opened his eyes and hands, a slow wave of calm descended upon him and he knew it was time. He lifted his arms and leapt off the wall into space. For a moment all he felt was a confusion of rushing air through his fingers, hair and up his nose and then—he was falling. He thought he heard Gabe screaming but couldn't decipher his words.

Use your wings.

With a jolt, Xavier realised he wasn't actually flapping his wings. Quickly and powerfully he pumped them, yet it seemed an eternity before he gained control over his descent.

Gabe flew close by. 'What were you doing? I thought you were going to crash.'

With his heart still banging and legs limp from the scare, Xavier called feebly, 'Forgot to use my wings.' He didn't admit that the voices had just saved him from plummeting into the rocky slope.

Gabe shook his head.

Xavier hovered close to Gabe. 'I'm fine now. It's easy.'

'Are you sure?'

'Yes.' Now he just felt embarrassed.

Gabe pointed and between wing-beats called, 'Fly to that hill.'

Xavier felt a growing sense of elation and freedom as they flapped and glided in unison towards the horizon, which was now a paler shade of night sky. The air whooshed past his ears and streamed over his face as they gathered speed. Suddenly he felt a violent tugging pulling him upwards.

'Just an updraft,' Gabe explained. 'Relax. Go with it.'

It was like body surfing an air current. When they reached the hill, they touched down on a cleared patch of land and Xavier turned to see how far they had flown. It was difficult to see Griswold amongst the forest trees, but eventually he spotted the chapel spire and the roofline above the dormitories. There it was like a scene from medieval Earth, a stern grey stain amongst the forest greenery. Although they had journeyed through the southern aspect of Mourn Forest a few weeks ago, the rest of the forest was still a mystery. He was curious to know what lay below the tree canopy between the hill and school although he suspected creatures like wraiths and crazy Jacob lurked there.

'It was strange to have an updraft before sunrise. I wonder what caused it.' Gabe turned to see the washed-out horizon now tinged with gold.

Xavier didn't want to think about the updraft, worrying it was connected to something sinister within the forest.

Gabe stretched his wings. 'We need to go.'

For a moment Xavier was tempted to turn his back on Griswold and continue flying in the opposite direction, but he couldn't.

By the time they had returned to the school grounds, the sun was just rising, but being Sunday, the boys knew most of the school would still be sleeping.

'I want to check something before going to the dorm. Are you interested?' Gabe asked.

Xavier picked up the spare shirt and jumper he had left on the wall. 'Depends.' He shook his clothes in case spiders had crawled inside.

'Don't change your shirt yet. I want to check the white building. It will only take a few minutes. Follow me.' Gabe jogged to the eastern wall and scrambled up the mulberry tree. 'Wait here.' He then flew into the new school grounds.

Xavier regretted having mentioned to Gabe he had seen Hortense enter the building with the satchel before assembly. As he waited on the wall, he glanced in the direction of where they had last seen the dogman, but in the dim light, the new school site appeared deserted.

Gabe stopped at the back of the white building, which was enclosed by wire fencing. Without a word he flapped a few times and cleared the fence.

Xavier wanted to object yet was fearful someone might hear, so he crouched shivering on the wall in the early morning air waiting for Gabe. When he heard a dog bark near the main school building, he hissed at Gabe and hid behind a branch. 'Hurry up,' he said as loudly as he could. Within seconds he heard a fluttering and then a thump followed by dogs yelping. Someone was approaching. Gabe had made it back over the wire fencing, but was now hiding behind trees in the new school yard. The dogman followed his straining hounds as they homed in on the sound and scent of Gabe. Paralysed by fear, Xavier could only watch from the wall as the dog handler ran past him. He recognised him as the large, heavyset man who had bailed him up outside the kitchen a few months earlier. Xavier was so close that in the dim light, he could see his wild uncombed hair, a rifle slung over his shoulder and even the heavy tattoos circling the wrist of his hand holding the dog leashes. The man released the dogs and they tore off into the thicket of trees towards the back of the new school. He was surprised they only smelled Gabe and completely ignored him crouching above them on the wall.

Xavier waited to hear the hounds discover Gabe, but instead a crack of gunshot split the air. He then saw a flash of movement on the wall to his left. Gabe suddenly appeared next to him.

'Quick, jump,' Gabe urged.

Too surprised to speak, Xavier obeyed him instinctively by leaping from the wall and gliding to the ground.

'Bloody demons!' the dogman yelled. 'Next time I'll get you.'

The boys sprinted towards the burial plot where they pulled their clean shirts on, hid their flying shirts in a hole and covered it with rocks. They then headed towards the dining hall and moments after reaching it, the doors were flung open by kitchen staff.

'Safe,' Gabe said and strolled nonchalantly into the hall.

Xavier followed but as he reached out to collect his porridge, noticed his hand was shaking. 'I hope you're right.'

Soon groups of boys filtered into the hall for breakfast.

When his heart had slowed sufficiently, Xavier asked, 'Did you see anything in the white room?'

'There were two rooms, the larger one was where we had the chosen class and another smaller one appeared to be a medical room.'

'A sick bay?' Xavier said.

'Perhaps. I saw what appeared to be Hortense's bag on a shelf. So you were right.'

'Why would he leave it there?'

'With locks on the door, bars on the windows and resident guard dogs, I'd imagine because it's safe,' Gabe said. 'There was also a microscope, tubes in a rack and a small refrigerator.'

'You guys were up early. I didn't hear you leave,' Howard said as he and Ethan joined Xavier and Gabe.

'We didn't want to wake you,' Xavier said.

'You must have flown out of the room. I didn't hear any footsteps,' Ethan added as he spilled some of his gruel on the table. 'Oops.'

Xavier was careful not to glance at Ethan, who he knew would be smirking.

Just then the chapel bell rang.

'Why's the bell ringing?' Howard asked.

No one answered as the boys counted.

'Too many rings for an assembly,' Xavier said after they counted six.

'And too early for services.' Ethan stood and looked out on the quadrangle. 'I can't see anyone about. Maybe they're just cleaning the bell.'

Hayley emerged from the kitchen followed by Beth. Xavier watched as they picked up the odd dirty dish while heading towards the boys' table.

'Have you heard the news?' Hayley asked in a breathless voice. 'Mr Griswold died.'

A cold joy burst and spread through Xavier's veins. He pictured the old man sitting in his armchair before the fireplace at Griswold Manor and imagined Philip's bony fingers twitching as he took his last breath. He felt no sympathy or guilt for enjoying the thought.

'It's just so sad,' Hayley said. 'So young.'

Xavier's head spun. 'You're talking about Philip Griswold, aren't you?'

Hayley shook her head. 'James,' she said quietly.

Xavier didn't need to ask anymore. The voices were now singing in his head and when he looked at Gabe, he knew that he heard the same chorus: Philip Griswold. He started to shake and wanted to cry. He thought of James' smiling face, his record player, his warm laugh and his final words to them. It was too much.

Hayley glanced at Ethan, who had buried his face in his hands. 'What do you suppose happened to him? I wouldn't have minded if his horrible old grandfather had died. It would've been good riddance to him. But James? He was a saint. Look at what he did here in the dining hall. You'd never see the old weasel do that, ever.' She placed a hand on Ethan's shoulder, who was now trembling.

'We only had dinner with him a few nights ago. Even though we had just met him, he was a good person,' Xavier said in a choked voice. 'He cared.'

* * *

Later that morning, Ratti called a special assembly. As the boys lined up in their year groups on the quadrangle, Ratti assumed her usual vantage on the platform with her henchmen, Phineas and Ugly standing either side.

'It's my sad duty to inform staff and students that the grandson of St Griswold's benefactor was involved in an unfortunate accident at Griswold Manor last night. Mr James Griswold was a much loved and respected member of our school community and will be sadly missed.' She paused and glanced over her glasses as though assessing the boys' reaction. 'Mr Pittworthy has gone to town to assist Mr Philip Griswold organise the funeral. I'd like you all to remember James in your prayers.' She dabbed the corner of her eye with a handkerchief as though pretending to catch a tear.

Xavier swore he could see acid steaming from her lips when she said the word 'prayers'.

'As a tribute to dear James, we've decided to name the new building in his honour.'

Ratti and Philip deserved to be struck by lightning, Xavier thought. He gazed at the sky, but all he saw were a pair of white vultures circling high overhead.

Ethan kicked at the ground.

Xavier hadn't mentioned that the voices had told him Philip was the culprit. Ethan had been affected greatly by the news of James' death, so telling him would only make it worse. Focusing on the insect scratching sound of Ratti's voice, he felt it was obvious she didn't care by the way she switched seamlessly to the next topic.

'There's one final matter.' She paused to pluck at something caught in the web of her shawl. 'As we will be quite busy organising our new school, all special classes will be cancelled for this month. Instead of sport this afternoon, I expect you to remain in your rooms to do private study.'

* * *

Numb with grief, Xavier and Ethan lay on their beds while Howard wrote in his notebook and Gabe sat on the window sill. Ethan had poked the book James had given him under his mattress, too upset to finish reading it.

'Looks like the teachers are having a meeting in the chapel,' Gabe said. 'Even Grubner's going.'

Xavier didn't want to hear about them. His mind overflowed with questions about Philip, James and the beetles' message. These questions only added to his ever growing list of obsessive worries like whether he would see his parents and sister again or if he would ever get to go home.

'I'm thinking of volunteering to go to James Griswold's funeral next week. They're taking a busload of kids. How about you, Xavier?' Howard asked.

What was he up to? 'I hadn't thought about it.' But Xavier knew he had to decide. He knew there was a chance Artemis would be there given Rosegrove was such a small town and James was a popular figure. It might be an opportunity to meet him and tell him about their journey to Ravenwood and everything that had happened since. Artemis might also know what to do about the beetles' message. No matter how unbearable the thought of the funeral, he knew he had to go. 'Actually, yes, I might go.'

'What about you, Ethan?' Howard said. 'You knew James too, didn't you?'

Xavier shook his head at Ethan without Howard noticing. There was a possibility Beauty might attend the funeral, so he couldn't go.

'Not me, I hate funerals,' Ethan said and rolled over to face the wall.

CHAPTER 11

* * *

Shells

'What happened to the paintings and plants?' Ethan asked in a crestfallen tone as the boys entered the dining hall for dinner the next day.

'The heaters have gone too,' Xavier said.

'I knew this would happen,' Gabe said. 'Philip probably found them missing from the manor.'

'Shouldn't Hayley be on kitchen duty today?' Xavier asked. Seeing her was always the best thing about breakfast. Cold porridge certainly wasn't a high point, but Hayley's big dark eyes and bright laugh always helped to compensate.

'That's odd,' Ethan said as they queued with their empty bowls. 'I don't recognise any of the staff today.'

With a vacant and faraway gaze, the woman spooning out dollops of gruel didn't greet the boys at the servery.

The boys took their bowls and headed to their usual table.

'They're shells,' Howard said as he sat down.

Xavier slid his bowl along the table and sat beside him. 'What?'

'Haven't you heard? Felix overheard Hortense telling Phineas. Everyone's talking about them. They're shells—replacements for the old staff.' Howard licked the porridge from his spoon. 'Someone sucked their brains out.'

Gabe, who had sat on the opposite side of the bench next to Ethan, twitched.

Xavier's throat tightened with fear as he thought of Beth and Hayley. 'What happened to the usual staff?'

Howard shrugged and stood. 'I'm going to see if the shells will give me more porridge. Maybe they're not as stingy as the last lot.'

When Howard had gone, Gabe turned and squinted at the closest shell and spoke in a low tone. 'They seem to be in a trance like the man who was taken by that Darklaw agent on the bus. I'm guessing these people have been treated the same way. Ratti or Philip probably brought them here as free labour.'

'Just like the workers on the building site,' Ethan said. 'Remember the man who was hit with a stick and didn't react? What Howard said makes sense. What do you think they did with Hayley and Beth?'

Xavier didn't want to think about it. He knew Beth especially was resourceful and brave, so if she had a chance to get away she would. Even if they knew where the girls were, there was nothing they could do to help them. Overwhelmed by the thought they might end up shells too, he pushed his uneaten bowl of porridge to one side.

The boys lapsed into a miserable silence until Gabe said quietly, 'We'd better go to Crowley's class.'

Xavier straggled behind the boys as they trudged from the dining hall to the class via the Great Corridor. For once he was oblivious to the gargoyles.

* * *

Xavier had never been to a church funeral before. In Ravenwood when an important person had died, he remembered seeing a long, slow procession of cars following the dark car bearing the coffin. He knew where the cemetery was and hated passing the fields of white crosses and statues. It made him feel sad for the people who had lost those they loved.

He and Howard sat in the church waiting with the other Griswold boys. The mood inside was quiet and sombre as people filed in from the various entrances until every seat was taken. It was obvious, Rosegrove had cared for James.

As Father Augustine began the service, Xavier remembered James' dinner at Griswold Manor. Feeling sad and powerless, Xavier stared at the brown coffin near the altar and the back of Philip Griswold's head in the front row. He noticed the coffin was draped in the blue and gold banner James had shown them at the manor. When Philip rose from his seat and walked to the pulpit to say a few words, Xavier felt an intense need for air. He stood, sidled past those seated in his row and excused himself as he made his way to the aisle.

'I'm going to be sick, sir,' he whispered to Phineas, who was seated at the end of the row.

'Very well, go and stand at the door, where you can get some fresh air.'

Xavier must have appeared sufficiently green in the face for Phineas not to question him. He made his way down the aisle and through open doors. The foyer was empty apart from a stand with books and pamphlets, a receptacle for holy water and a few empty plastic chairs. Xavier sat on one and dipped his head between his knees as he tried to ease the nausea and dizziness.

'Are you alright?' a voice asked. 'Don't look up.' He patted Xavier on the back.

'Artemis!'

'Shh, be careful,' Artemis whispered. 'Stand up.'

Xavier stood but swayed slightly.

'Come on.' Artemis took him by the elbow and guided him to the open front door where a burly man in a dark suit stood as if on guard. 'The lad's not feeling well, he needs some fresh air.'

The suited man stared at him with an unreadable expression but nodded.

Once they were in the car park, Xavier felt his head clear instantly.

He sat on the stone steps but continued to pretend he was unwell in case he was being watched. 'There was so much evil in there.'

'I know. I felt it too,' Artemis said. 'It's so good to see you again. Every day since you boys left Rosegrove, I worried until Sarah visited. She told me Beth had come to her and that you were taken back to school.'

'Beth and Hayley were working in the kitchen, but they're gone just like most of the staff.'

'Yes, I heard about the staff, but don't worry, the girls are safe.'

Xavier brightened. 'You know where they are?'

'Hayley's father, Henry was taken by the Darklaw, but they sent Hayley to the Griswold girls' school.'

'What about Beth?'

'She wasn't on duty when the Darklaw came for the staff. She had a vision of what happened and went to Sarah's cafe instead.'

Xavier managed a smile with the thought the girls were safe. 'Do you know what the Darklaw did with Hayley's dad and the kitchen staff?'

Artemis sighed. 'I assume they were taken to one of their camps.'

'We saw a Darklaw agent use a collar on a man to control him,' Xavier said.

'I'm familiar with their method. The minds of some people break. All they are useful for then is simple tasks and slave labour.'

'Shells?'

Artemis nodded. 'Those who don't break are persuaded to join them, the rest—I don't know.'

One of the church doors opened and the guard strode out onto the porch to scan the car park.

Xavier groaned.

The guard retreated into the church but left the door ajar.

'Have you ever met Raphael?' Xavier asked.

Artemis shook his head.

'He's a messenger angel, who appeared on the train before we reached Ravenwood.' Xavier told him about the terrible battle between the angels and demons. 'Raphael called it the First Strike.'

The guard appeared at the entrance again.

Xavier stood, leaned over a bush and pretended to heave and dry retch.

After the guard finished surveying the car park and had returned inside the church, Xavier spoke as quickly but as quietly as he could. 'I didn't know whether to trust Raphael, but he sent us to Nisroc, another angel. He was the one who kept the ledger. Did you get it, the ledger I mean?'

'I sent it to the Boundary Keeper. I thought it would be safer with her.'

'Nisroc said that it was the ledger between good and evil.'

'I had a good look at it, but the pages were blank. It could be bound by spells.'

'I'm worried about Nisroc. When he disappeared, the tally in the ledger increased by one and it showed a time and place which might have represented him.'

Artemis looked at him thoughtfully. 'I don't believe the nature of the ledger is that simple. There may be many chapters, and some may not reveal themselves to casual readers.'

'I haven't much time, but we need your help, Artemis.' Xavier quickly told him about the beetles' message. 'Nisroc also spoke about Ambrosia yet didn't make a lot of sense. He was dragged away and we didn't get to ask him any more questions.'

Artemis rubbed his chin. 'Your destiny may lie in Ambrosia. I'll need to think about how you might get there. Perhaps Gabe could fly there.'

'Well there's something else you should know.'

Artemis looked at him curiously and then smiled.

'You already know, don't you?'

'The Keeper told me about her suspicion. Can you fly yet?'

'Yes,' Xavier said proudly. 'Well, the basics I mean.'

'Well done!' Artemis then added as though thinking aloud, 'If you were to fly to Ambrosia, you'd need a good reason to be absent from Griswold for a few days.'

'Perhaps Gabe and I could fly to Rosegrove one night and we could work out a plan.' Xavier couldn't believe he was offering to do something so daring, but he knew their Ambrosia plan had to be perfect for them to succeed.

Once again the guard emerged from the church and stood on the veranda.

'If you choose to fly to Rosegrove be very careful,' Artemis whispered as he made a show of helping Xavier to stand.

A few people filed out the door and stood around in groups waiting for the coffin to be carried from the church. Beauty, wearing a navy pillbox hat with a short black veil shadowing her face, strolled out with Phineas.

'What are you doing here, boy?' Phineas glared at Artemis.

'I was feeling ill, sir. Don't you remember?'

'You look fine now. Go and join the other boys.' He mumbled something to Beauty, who glanced at Artemis through her spotted veil.

The afternoon was grey and unusually cool for spring. Shivering, Xavier watched the coffin being carried by dark-suited men as a mournful dirge was piped ghostlike from inside the church. It was six months now since Xavier had come to the Southern Lands. His world continued to change and grow ever stranger, but he had no control over it. The joy of knowing Beth and Hayley were safe was tempered by the loss of James. As the men struggled to load the coffin into the dark hearse, he felt sad for the man who had been so different from those he had encountered at Griswold.

CHAPTER 12

* * *

Messengers

'Why are we having maths here?' Xavier said to Gabe as he looked around the new classroom on the first floor of east wing where the wall between two rooms had been removed to make one large one. 'And why are we crammed into half the space?'

Phineas stood by the teacher's desk tapping his palm with the switch at a quicker rhythm than usual. 'Quiet!' he yelled angrily as the boys grew restless. 'Start working on the problem.'

Xavier opened his exercise book and carefully copied the graph on the blackboard. *Write an equation to describe this graph using x and y.* He sighed as he stared at it, wondering where to begin. From the outside corridor, he heard growing sounds of footsteps echoing and high voices chattering. Above the noise, a woman clapped and yelled, but he couldn't decipher her words.

'Girls!' a boy said excitedly. Heads swung as a line of girls wearing lettuce-green uniforms filed in through the back entrance of the classroom.

'Quiet!' Phineas shouted at the boys. 'Quickly take a seat, girls. I want as little a disruption to my class as possible.'

'Hayley!' Xavier said quietly to Gabe. He grinned, for at last he could see for himself that she was safe.

When all the girls were seated, Phineas closed the door. 'I'd like to welcome the students from our new school who'll be with us temporarily until a teacher is hired. If you work hard and behave, you'll succeed in my class. If you don't then we will not get along and as the boys will tell you, I don't tolerate bad behaviour.' He pointed at a large cardboard carton of worn texts on his desk. 'Felix and Xavier, distribute the texts to the new students.'

Xavier grabbed an armful and strode to the back row where Hayley was seated.

'Great to see you,' he whispered. 'I'm sorry about your dad.'

Hayley took the book Xavier handed her. 'I'll give you a note at the end of class.'

He nodded discreetly while keeping an eye on Phineas, who was putting his switch in the teacher's desk drawer. He obviously didn't want the girls to see it.

'Beth's gone too,' Hayley whispered.

'I know. She's with Sarah in Rosegrove.'

Xavier could see the relief in her expression.

When Tomkins made his usual delivery of tea and pastries, Phineas inspected the two fat chocolate éclairs stuffed with whipped cream lying on the china plate.

A ripple of comments, chatter and laughter burst from the back half of the classroom where the girls sat.

Phineas put the plate down and scanned the room. 'Does anyone have something to say?'

The girls went quiet, but Hayley put her hand up.

'Yes?' Phineas said.

Be careful, Xavier thought.

'Sir, I don't think it's fair you should eat pastries in front of us kids when most of us are hungry.'

Xavier didn't dare look at Phineas, but in his heart he cheered for Hayley. He wished he had her courage as she always spoke her mind and never seemed afraid. The room was silent and Phineas, who was now pink-faced and ruffled, took an age to respond.

'What's your name?'

'Hayley Robinson.' She looked around at the class. 'I had an aunt who ate too many sweets. She got fat and got diabetes.'

'I don't believe I asked for your medical opinion, Miss Robinson.' He glared at her and she met his gaze defiantly. 'I don't abide impertinence in my classroom. As you'll discover, you don't have rights at St Griswold College. You're here because of the generosity of the college benefactor, Mr Griswold. While you're in my class, you'll show respect, obedience and humility. Do you understand?'

'But sir,' she tried again. 'I was only ...'

'And self control.'

'But ...'

'Do you understand?'

Xavier held his breath.

'Yes.' Hayley said, although she sounded annoyed rather than frightened.

'Yes?'

'Yes, sir,' she said in a reluctant tone.

'Count yourself as fortunate this is your first class, Miss Robinson as I won't be lenient next time.' He turned to the rest of the class. 'Open your books at page 17. Mr Zhou, please read the first three pages.'

Jian, who was sitting in the back row read the chapter heading, 'Graphing lines from a table of values: equations as relationships ...'

As the boy read about points, lines and graphs, Xavier's mind slid away.

Phineas was licking sugar from his fingertips and gazing curiously out the window.

Xavier signalled to Ethan, who was sitting by the window, for him to see what was attracting Phineas' attention.

Ethan nodded and half-stood to gain a better view.

'Sit down, Mr Klee. Focus on Mr Zhou's reading,' Phineas snapped.

Just before the end of class, Phineas ordered Xavier and Ethan to collect the books. When Xavier took Hayley's book, she slipped him a folded note which he opened and read as soon as he sat down:

> *Beth had a vision about you and Gabe in a forest.*
> *She said you need to speak to Lily.*
> *If I can help, let me know.*

Xavier screwed the note up into a ball and held it in his hand.

After Phineas dismissed the class, the girls filed out the back while the boys left via the other door.

'What were you reading?' Phineas asked Xavier loudly as he approached the door with Gabe behind him.

A sudden crashing noise diverted everyone's attention. Ethan had tripped and knocked over a desk and two chairs.

'Eat it,' Gabe whispered urgently behind Xavier.

Xavier stuffed the note in his mouth, hurriedly chewed and then swallowed it whole. He almost choked as it felt as large as a tennis ball.

Phineas turned back to him. 'What are you eating?'

'Porridge stuck in my teeth from breakfast.'

Phineas glared at him. 'Turn your pockets out. You too, Mr Shepherd.'

The two boys stood with their pockets hanging out.

Ethan sidled towards the door.

Phineas pointed at Ethan. 'And you.'

An empty cotton reel, an odd shaped stone and a handful of almonds fell to the floor as Ethan emptied his pockets.

Phineas' lip curled as he snarled, 'Pick that rubbish up.' He returned to the teacher's desk to write on his detention pad. 'You must think I'm stupid.' He handed each boy a slip. 'I'm watching you.'

* * *

'Okay, what did I deliberately bang my shin for?' Ethan asked as the boys walked to their history class with Crowley.

'That was a deliberate diversion?' Gabe said. 'Masterful.'

'Thanks, Ethan.' Xavier patted him on the back. 'Hayley gave me a note.'

'So where's the note?' Ethan asked.

Xavier grinned. 'I ate it.'

Ethan raised his eyebrows.

'She said Beth had a vision about me and Gabe in a forest and that we needed to see Lily.'

'So where was I in this vision?' Ethan's voice had an edge.

Xavier shrugged. 'It was only a dream. I wouldn't worry. What was Phineas looking at out the window?'

'Just some of those creepy visitors wearing black clothes like those who came for Jordie's ceremony.'

Xavier's skin prickled.

'They might be having another ceremony,' Gabe said. 'I've tried to ask the voices, but lately they've been faint.'

'You too?' Xavier said. 'I haven't been able to hear them either. I thought it was just me.'

'We need to talk to Lily tonight while the teachers are distracted with their visitors. Ethan, could you keep Howard busy for us?' Gabe said.

Ethan grunted.

Xavier could tell he was annoyed at being left out again.

A few hours later Gabe and Xavier pretended they were going to the library to return books while Ethan convinced Howard to help him with his homework. Xavier tried not to think too hard about cockroaches as they walked along the deserted corridors.

'So why do you think Beth said we should talk to Lily?' Xavier asked as he followed him into the library.

'Shh.' Gabe checked the aisles.

The cold air swirled around them creating a haze of dust infused with a whiff of lavender.

'Why are you here so late?' Lily floated from the dark end of the aisle the boys were standing in.

'Hello Lily, it's us—me and Xavier,' Gabe said.

'Shouldn't be here. Should never be here. Not sssafe. I warned you,' she said in a rapid monotone. 'He's here, they're here and more are coming. They keep coming, staying, going—forever.' She sounded distressed and confused.

'Philip Griswold?' Xavier asked curiously.

'All of them,' she moaned and stared into space.

'I'm sure they're gathering for a ceremony,' Gabe said.

'Death, sadness, on and on ...,' Lily said.

'I think it's for James Griswold,' Xavier said.

'No!' Her voice stretched and echoed and her form rippled and shimmered. When it settled, Xavier could hear weeping.

'You knew him?' Xavier said.

'Knew them all.'

'We don't know what you mean,' Xavier said.

'Learn!' She moved swiftly to the end of the aisle and Gabe and Xavier followed hurriedly.

'Wait. Talk to us,' Gabe implored.

Just as the boys reached her, a book fell to the ground distracting them. When they looked up she had vanished.

Xavier watched Gabe pick up the book. 'Now what do we do?'

It was a small notebook with a green and black, floral fabric cover. Gabe flicked through its pages which were covered in old handwriting. 'Hide it until we get a chance to see what it's about. Until then, we can't tell anyone about it.' He concealed the notebook under his shirt.

'Even Ethan?'

'Yes.'

CHAPTER 13

* * *

Night flight

'I don't want to waste any more time. We have to go to Rosegrove,' Gabe said. 'Ethan, you'll need to cover for us.'

Ethan looked at the ceiling.

'Ethan?' Xavier said in a soft tone.

'It's always about what you want. You've not even told me what you're up to.'

'I need to practise flying and to see Artemis to tell him about everything that's happened. He might have some ideas about what we should do next. If you could fly we'd absolutely want you to come too.'

Ethan sighed.

'You wanted to pay the new gargoyle a visit. How about we do that soon?' Gabe offered.

'You mean Stinky Eye?' Ethan said. 'When?'

'Name the day.'

He regarded Gabe with narrowed eyes. 'Wednesday night.'

Xavier had noticed Ethan's recent restlessness and suspected he was hatching a plan. 'Is it more than a visit?'

'Of course, but it's a surprise, so don't ask. You'll see on the night.'

Gabe turned to Xavier. 'Do you really think you're ready to fly to Rosegrove?'

'I'm fit and fast now,' Xavier said defensively.

'But not as fast as me,' Gabe said matter-of-factly.

Ethan groaned. 'What night will you vultures go airborne?'

Xavier knew Ethan was battling to sound light-hearted.

'Tonight at midnight,' Gabe said. 'Once Howard's asleep, we'll bunch clothes under our blankets, so it looks like we're still in bed. If he discovers us missing, will you make up something to cover for us?'

Ethan nodded, although Xavier knew he was disturbed they had left him out of their plan.

'Could we borrow your west wing door key please?' Xavier asked.

Ethan fished under his mattress where he had stowed his small horde of possessions, such as pens, photos and safety pins, until he found a small brass key which he handed to him. 'They changed the locks to the west side door a week ago, but it was the same as another we've had before. They just swap the locks around—it's always the cheapest option at Griswold.'

'That's a real talent you have,' Xavier said.

'Crowley labels all his keys, so I borrowed the key from his room and found it matched a key from my stash. If they ever get new ones, we'll be in trouble. I almost got caught getting the original back to his room. When I heard him coming, I sat on his chair and pretended to cry. I told him I wanted to go home—that I couldn't take it anymore. In the end he made me a cup of tea. Crowley's okay. He completely forgot I'd been in his room in the first place.'

From the window, Xavier noticed the white vultures had returned and were circling over the vegetable patch. Beneath them a small boy was walking across the quadrangle towards the path to the gardening shed. 'That's Howard,' he said aloud in surprise.

'What about him?' Gabe asked.

'He was on the garden path and just went into Grubner's shed.'

'Did he have detention?' Ethan asked.

'I don't think so.'

'Grubner isn't exactly a warm person you'd drop in on for a chat,' Gabe said.

The boys continued planning for the night flight as Xavier kept an eye on the path. 'Howard just left the shed.'

The three boys watched as one of the white vultures dived at Howard, but he just picked up a sizeable stick and swung it at the bird. Eventually after a few more passes it gave up and Howard walked back towards west wing.

'That's odd,' Xavier said. 'He obviously stayed long enough to talk to Grubner—but why?'

* * *

Later that night, Gabe and Xavier skirted around the front of the school from the west wing door and ran along beside the eastern wall under the cover of trees and bushes to the back wall. It was the only way they could be sure they would avoid the watch of the gargoyles. They climbed the trellis onto the back wall behind the compost heap to launch off where they couldn't be seen from the school.

Xavier peered at the top of the wall. 'What's that?'

'Coils of wire with sharp bits.'

'A nice homely touch. I wonder who put it there.'

'It could have been Grubner,' Gabe said. 'I saw him with a ladder headed here after lunch.'

The boys jogged to an apple tree which they scaled to reach a clear section of the wall.

'Something's moving by the shed,' Xavier whispered.

They both withdrew instinctively behind the tree branches.

They crouched motionless behind the branches until Gabe spotted a white vulture beside the shed that stopped to peck and pluck at the ground. 'Very strange. How many birds do you see wandering around at this hour?'

Xavier tried to control his alarm. 'We'd better go before we're caught.'

Both boys sprung off the wall above the rocky slope that plunged to the valley below. They caught an updraft and glided up and over the treetops yet made sure they kept close enough to drop into the forest in case they encountered a demon or wraith.

'See where the far moon is? Below it you can just make out the outline of a mountain range. If we fly towards the highest peak, we'll reach Rosegrove,' Gabe said.

Xavier baulked at a white object hurtling out of the forest.

'It's just an owl,' Gabe said.

'I know. My night vision's much better than it was.'

'It's an angel thing,' Gabe said. 'You'll need it.'

They skimmed over the dark leafy canopy under an inky sky noisy with brilliant stars and moons. The wind rushed through their hair, over their faces and across their limbs. Despite the danger, Xavier loved every moment, but after flying for forty minutes or so he began to tire. 'Could we stop and rest?'

Gabe scanned the ground. 'The trees are thinning. We're getting close to the Keeper's territory. There's the boundary between the forest and farmland.'

Xavier felt a longing to fly lower in search of the Boundary Land. In his mind he could see the blue sky, wisps of cloud and the white buildings beyond the archway. He wondered if the Boundary children were playing under the canopy and strained to see their blue light in the shadowy trees.

Minutes later the boys landed gently in a paddock of bare earth that felt loose and soft through their canvas shoes. At the edge of the field, Xavier retracted his wings and sat on a tuft of grass to catch his breath. He was grinning. 'That was fun. I wish we could just take off and leave the school for good.'

'Where would we go? Where's safe? Just because there are people we don't trust at the school doesn't mean it's the worst place to be for now.

At least we have food and shelter. A Darklaw camp could be a lot worse. And remember, we've others to think about.'

Everything Gabe said was right although the bit about helping the others scared him. It brought back what the Keeper and Raphael had said about him becoming a leader, yet once more he pushed it to the back of his mind alongside thoughts of his parents and sister. It was getting crowded in there.

'We'd better keep going,' Gabe said.

Xavier got to his feet reluctantly as he was worried about flying in the open space over the farms. They both ran over the grass until they had sufficient speed to take off. Once they were airborne, they skimmed over the paddocks with enough height to avoid being seen. In the distance they could see a small collection of lights.

'Rosegrove,' Gabe said.

The air was colder in the open and despite the fact he was pumping his wings hard and fast, Xavier was shivering. They would need warmer clothes if they were to fly to Ambrosia in the next few weeks.

A dark shadow soared across the sky ahead of them after dropping from a low-lying cloud. 'What's that?' Xavier asked.

Gabe pointed to a cluster of trees between the paddocks. 'We'd better land.'

They tipped their wings to the left, glided silently in an arc to the ground and after they touched down, ran to the cover of the trees.

'A demon,' Gabe whispered. 'It's hunting.'

Xavier shrank under the foliage as close to the trunk as he could. When he heard sudden flapping, he stifled the urge to scream. Peering between the leaves, he saw the silhouette of a demon diving and then pulling up to land. Moments later, the squeals of a struggling animal pierced the silence of the night, but the demon flicked it hard until it was limp and lifeless. The boys watched from the shadows as the demon leapt into the air and arced across the night sky with its dinner.

'Lucky it's going in the opposite direction,' Gabe said.

Xavier was too horrified to speak for a while.

The boys took to the air again but checked compulsively while making the final flight to Rosegrove. When he spotted the first few houses, Xavier exhaled a long, slow breath. They had made it.

'Remember, there's curfew,' Gabe said. 'We must be careful.'

They drifted to the ground again, retracted their wings, and pulled on the jumpers they had tied around their waists before running to the town centre. The streets were deserted with only the occasional barking dog breaking the stillness and the few they saw were housed in heavy duty, padlocked cages. No doubt the demons had a taste for them too. Tonight, not even the Darklaw were about, so the boys walked unchallenged along the streets. Once they reached the lane that Artemis' house backed on to, they ran swiftly and quietly.

Gabe looked around furtively before unlatching Artemis' gate. They crept up the garden path, but unlike last time, there was no sign of Mano, Artemis' large black dog.

Xavier tapped on the door. 'Hurry up,' he whispered as he glanced at the dark shadows in the garden, which seemed to loom and grow the longer he stared at them. He knocked again, slightly louder. 'Did you see something over there?' he muttered as he tilted his head towards a massive gnarled tree in the back corner of the yard. 'Don't turn too quickly.'

The back door opened suddenly, startling the boys.

'Quick, come in,' Artemis said as he searched the darkness behind them.

The boys rushed past Artemis, nearly tripping each other in their haste.

'It's so good to see you again. Did you travel safely?' Artemis locked the door carefully.

Xavier blocked the memory of the hunting demon. 'We're fine.'

Artemis guided them to his workroom. 'Warm yourselves by the fire while I make tea.'

'Mano!' Xavier put a hand out to pat the Doberman that was stretched out on a woolly grey rug in front of the crackling fire. The dog closed its eyes as he scratched behind its ears and looked around the room. The mechanical birds and papery butterflies lay at one end of the workbench in a brilliant mosaic as though asleep while more toasters, jugs and mugs cluttered the other end.

After Artemis brought the tea, he listened to the boys tell him about their journey to Ravenwood and of the changes at Griswold since they had returned.

'You were lucky to survive,' Artemis said in a sombre tone once he had heard the full story. 'You took great ...' He was interrupted by a knock on the front door. Immediately he guided the boys to a bookshelf in the room and waved his hand. Xavier heard Artemis hum a few odd notes and saw a swirl of bright particles flying from his hand towards the shelf. The bookcase swung around to reveal a small room. 'Go in there and wait. Darklaw patrols are lurking about the town tonight and may have decided to visit.'

'We didn't see any,' Gabe said.

'They are always around.' Artemis pushed them in as the banging on the door became more urgent.

After the bookshelf swung back to its original position, the boys sat in darkness listening to doors opening and closing and muffled conversation on the other side. Terrified, Xavier wondered if they had been spotted flying into Rosegrove and whether they would start searching Artemis' home. So fearful they would be caught, he didn't even ponder witnessing Artemis' magic.

Suddenly the bookshelf swung back open and Xavier blinked in the bright light.

'Relax, boys,' Artemis said. 'We have welcome visitors.'

'Beth!' Xavier exclaimed. He jumped to his feet and hugged her. A short, well-rounded woman stood behind Beth. 'And Sarah!' Xavier felt awkward as the middle-aged woman hugged him too.

'It seems so long ago that you boys came to my cafe. Every day since I've wondered what happened to you until Beth found me,' Sarah said.

'Why are you here tonight?' Gabe asked.

'I had a vision and knew you'd be here, so we took the chance and walked over,' Beth explained.

Artemis shook his head. 'With curfew, that was very risky.'

'We had to come, Artemis,' Sarah said. 'Tell them about your visions, Beth.'

'I tried to tell Hayley what I knew, so she could tell you, but since then I've seen more.'

'Sit down,' Artemis cleared a space on the bench to set out mugs for tea.

Beth sat on a chair near the couch. 'In my dreams I've been seeing Xavier and Gabe in a forest. Now I know it's the Ambrosian Forest.'

'Are you sure?' Artemis said.

'Initially I wasn't, but lately I've seen them visit Ambrosia, which I can easily recognise. They then go to the Ambrosian Forest and meet a woman on a hill. I don't know her name, but she claims to be a Farseer.'

'I think we must go there,' Gabe said.

Xavier nodded.

'What? Because of a dream?' Sarah said.

'We met an angel called Nisroc in Ravenwood. He said we must find six for the final battle and that we have to keep them safe,' Xavier said, yet once the words had escaped his mouth, he wondered if he should have spoken. Although he trusted everyone in the room, he was aware the more his friends knew, the greater the risk to them.

'Are you sure you want to go?' Artemis said. 'You've seen how dangerous it is out there.'

'I don't think we've a choice if Beth's visions are true,' Xavier said.

'What do you know of the Farseers?' Gabe asked Artemis, who was pouring tea into the cups.

'Come and help yourselves to the tea,' Artemis invited them. 'Like Beth, I've never visited the Ambrosian Forest, but I know a little about the Farseers' traditions and beliefs. They're an old magical tribe, one of the Ancients, the true natives of Clanarde.'

'Who are the Ancients?' Gabe asked as he poured milk into his tea.

Artemis sat on the couch by the fire. 'There are four tribes native to Clanarde: Farseers, Shay, Karn and Chanshi.'

'We've met the Shay and Craig from the Karn. They are fighting their own battles against the Darklaw and demons. I wonder if the other two tribes are also facing them,' Xavier said.

'Perhaps we could align with them and defeat them together,' Gabe said.

Artemis rubbed his forehead. 'Perhaps together, but evil's a cunning worm. It draws on kindred beings and gorges on neutral brains.'

Xavier shuddered at the thought of worms and brains.

'Evil operates with direction and some magic folk are easily led,' Artemis explained.

Xavier was finding it difficult to breathe. Artemis' talk worried him.

'So is there someone or something directing the evil?' Gabe said.

'The Overseer,' Sarah said softly.

'Who's the Overseer?' Gabe asked.

'One they all answer to,' Artemis said quietly.

'And you've seen him?' Gabe probed.

Artemis looked away.

Xavier's skin prickled.

Gabe eyed Artemis coolly. 'Then how do you know he exists?'

'Everyone knows of the Overseer,' Sarah said.

Gabe switched his scrutiny to her. 'So you've seen him?'

'No, but I've heard plenty. Some think he's a fallen angel while others say he's a shape shifter gone astray. There are endless stories about his twisted origins and foul deeds.'

Gabe raised his eyebrows.

'Trust me, he exists.' Artemis stared into the fire.

Sarah stood, stretched and tapped Beth's shoulder. 'We need to go home.'

'No, it's too dangerous for you to return tonight. You can stay here.'

Gabe stood. 'We must return to school.'

'I'll see you to the door,' Artemis said. 'Sarah, Beth, you stay by the fire and help yourselves to more tea.'

'Good luck if you decide to go,' Beth said to the boys. 'I'd go with you, if I could.' She hugged them again. 'Please be careful flying back to school.'

Xavier knew what she said was true and wished he was as fearless. 'Thanks. We'll see you soon.'

Artemis walked the boys down the hallway to the back door. 'How do you propose to reach Ambrosia?'

'Isn't it obvious?' Gabe asked. 'We'll fly of course.'

Artemis shook his head slowly. 'It will be dangerous.'

'I suppose it's our only option.' Xavier wished he could sound as brave as Gabe.

As they stood in a huddle at the door, Artemis sighed. 'I thought you might say that. The only plan I could come up with is complicated and risky.'

'That's alright,' Gabe said. 'I am sure I can, I mean *we* can ensure its success.'

Artemis disappeared into a side room and returned with a tiny, green stoppered flask. He placed it in a drawstring bag and gave it to Gabe, who strung it over his neck. 'Whatever you do, don't open it yet.'

'Why not?' Xavier asked.

'The flask contains a potion. When you return to school, you must each drink from it.' Artemis plucked a bottle from a pocket in his robe. 'When you become ill as inevitably you will, the town doctor, Angus Magin will be called. He'll have the antidote, but you won't get it until you reach the hospital.'

'And if he isn't called?' Xavier asked.

'Then you must exaggerate your symptoms until the teachers worry it might be contagious. Once Angus is called, he'll send an ambulance to bring you to Rosegrove and place you in quarantine.'

'Is it dangerous?' Xavier asked.

'It's not lethal, but it will make you quite ill.'

Xavier ran his fingers through his hair. He wasn't keen on the plan.

'The antidote will work straight away. You'll have about a week to reach Ambrosia, find the Farseers and get back to Rosegrove without being missed. In the meantime, I'll see if I can find someone for you to contact in Ambrosia.'

'Do you trust Dr Magin?' Xavier asked.

'Most definitely. Now you must return to Griswold before you're missed.'

* * *

CHAPTER 14

Crazy

'Did you hear that?' Xavier jumped from his bed, rushed to the window and pushed it wide open. 'What's that kid doing?' Wearing only underwear, a boy was running in circles on the quadrangle, yelling one minute and doing cartwheels, the next. Although a few white vultures were gathering on the western wall, he was oblivious to them. Thrilled by his daring or insanity, boys were hanging out of their windows and jeering, whooping and clapping.

Gabe looked over his shoulder. 'It's Ethan.'

Xavier called Ethan to come inside, but he ignored him. 'We've got to get to Ethan fast, before a teacher catches him or the vultures attack.' Xavier dashed out the door and down the corridor with Gabe in pursuit. They tore down the stairs, burst through the west wing doorway and sprinted across the quadrangle. After each grabbing one of Ethan's elbows, they dragged him frantically from the quad, away from the view of the boys laughing and waving from their windows. When they reached the doorway of the west wing they shoved Ethan into the stairwell.

Xavier sat on the bottom step and heaved as he tried to regain his breath. 'I swear I saw Stinky Eye move—huh—he was watching.'

Deflated, Ethan slumped to the ground as though he suddenly realised what he had done.

'You said gargoyles and demons sleep by day, Gabe. How come Stinky Eye's awake and how did it move?' Xavier said in a panicky voice.

'He must be different,' Gabe said.

'What if it tells Ratti about Ethan's craziness on the quad?'

Xavier turned to Ethan and said gruffly, 'What were you thinking?'

'Not a lot.'

'Then you're an idiot.'

'What does it matter?' Ethan said.

'What does it matter?' Xavier repeated angrily. 'You're drawing attention to yourself, which means we'll be watched too before we've had a chance to escape.'

'I'm just sick of it all.'

'We all are,' Xavier said in unsympathetic tone, 'but we're working on a way to get out of here and we don't want you to stuff it up.' Xavier had been so rattled by the sight of the moving gargoyle that he was still shaking. 'Go and get dressed, and stay out of sight until classes start. Do you hear me?'

Ethan got up and dragged himself up the stairs without talking to them.

They watched him until he disappeared from view.

'Has he cracked?' Xavier asked.

'No, he's intact,' Gabe said.

'Cracked—crazy, I mean.'

'I knew that.'

'Did he tell you why he did it?' asked a voice.

They turned around to see Alex Johnson leaning up casually against the doorframe with his hands in his pockets.

'It's not hard to see he's feeling down,' Xavier said.

'There's more.'

Gabe and Xavier looked at him questioningly.

'It's his b-birthday.'

'Oh,' Xavier said suddenly feeling small.

'Well, according to his imprint.'

'His what?' Gabe said.

'He's got an imprint, j-just like me.' Alex pulled up his sleeve to reveal a small tattoo on his forearm.

'I've seen Ethan's,' Gabe admitted. 'Jordie had one too. I presumed it was a human custom to have flesh engravings.'

Alex shook his head. 'Nope, not this sort. Those k-kids who came here when they were really young didn't know their b-birth dates, so teachers chose a date for them and t-tattooed it on their arms.'

'But why? They never celebrate our birthdays,' Xavier said.

'I know, but years ago one of the t-teachers told me that it was to k-keep track of our ages.'

'That's sad,' Xavier said.

'Can I see yours?' Gabe asked.

Alex stretched his arm towards him. 'Knock yourself out.'

'What?'

'He means go ahead,' Xavier murmured.

Gabe examined the tattoo. 'It's really just a label.'

Xavier saw them exchange looks.

'Do you know what?' Gabe said brightly. 'I've read many accounts of how humans celebrate birthdays. I think we should organise something special for the occasion.'

'Do you mean a party?' Xavier said. 'We'd get caught.'

'Maybe or maybe not, but I think we need to do it anyway.' He turned to Xavier. 'You have the most recent experience of birthdays. What would constitute a memorable celebration?'

Xavier scratched his head. 'Well, I suppose a present would be good. Decorations, party food, games and drinks would be bonuses.'

'We'll spread the word and see what everyone can contribute to the cause,' Gabe said. 'The party will be after lights out.'

'Where will we have it?' Xavier asked.

Gabe turned to Alex. 'Do you have any suggestions?'

Alex looked at the ceiling and grinned.

'What? Go on,' Gabe said.

'Tell us,' Xavier said.

'It's not your usual p-party place, but we've used it a handful of times over the years.'

'Yes?' Gabe said.

'The chapel,' Alex said with a mischievous grin. 'After lights out, of c-course.'

'What? Are you mad?' Xavier said.

Gabe slapped Alex on the back. 'Lovely!'

Xavier looked at the boys as if they were possessed. 'Even if we manage to get in there without being detected, we'll need to switch the lights on. They'll be spotted.'

'No, most of the windows are south-facing, apart from t-two windows on the west, and I can take care of them,' Alex said. 'Think about it. It's p-perfect. Augy won't be here until Friday. The walls are thick. As long as we keep reasonably q-quiet.'

'Who's Augy?' Xavier asked.

'Father Augustine.'

Xavier couldn't believe what he was hearing. It was as though both boys were obsessed with a shared vision of something they had never enjoyed but had seen in books or heard about second-hand.

'Decorations, I can do,' Gabe declared.

'Put me down for f-food and drinks,' Alex said. 'I've ways of getting into the k-kitchen, and like I said, I'll fix the chapel windows.'

They both turned to Xavier.

'You can find a gift,' Gabe said. 'The party begins at midnight. Spread the word.'

* * *

Xavier peered at the lower branches of the apple tree but couldn't see any fruit, so he began to climb to see if there were any higher up. Apples were a sub-standard birthday present, but he was desperate. The only other option was to steal something from the library or the dining hall. In Ravenwood he would have slipped down to the main street and dropped in to Devons, the department store. As he climbed, he imagined buying a book, poster or even a T-shirt and then choosing wrapping paper and a funny birthday card. Everything had been so easy, yet he had taken it for granted.

'What the blazes are you doing up there?' exclaimed an angry voice. 'Get down here now!'

Startled, Xavier nearly fell out of the tree. There was no place to hide and he couldn't run away, so he slid down the trunk. When his feet touched the ground, he turned around slowly.

Grubner was standing with his arms folded. 'Well? What were you doing up there?' He didn't wait for Xavier to reply. 'You could've fallen and broken your neck and then it'd be my fault. You know if Ms Ratchet or Mr Phineas were to catch you up there, they'd send you to the dungeons.'

Xavier blinked. 'What dungeons?'

'Well, what've you got to say for yourself?'

'Um, I wanted an apple.'

'You risked getting caught for an apple? Are you hungry?'

Xavier looked at the ground.

'Well? I'm speaking to you, boy. I expect an answer.'

Xavier raised his face. 'It was to be a present, sir—for my friend's birthday.'

Grubner gazed into the distance while rubbing his chin. 'A birthday, you say?'

'He's been here a long time. He has a date stamped on his arm. It's his birthday and he was sad,' Xavier rambled nervously. 'He can't remember what a birthday should be like. I just thought if I could find a present, it would help.'

'Stay there,' Grubner said gruffly and disappeared into the gardening shed.

Xavier was tempted to run, but he knew it would be useless. Grubner would tell Ratti and his punishment might be worse if tried to escape. No doubt Grubner was collecting a detention booklet to give him a slip. All the teachers carried them. He wondered which teacher Grubner would choose to send him to for detention. Please not Ratti, he thought. When Grubner emerged he could see that he was carrying something.

'Here,' he said and held it out.

Surprised, Xavier stared at him. He wasn't sure what he was supposed to do.

'Take it.'

Xavier held his palm out and Grubner placed a small wooden box in his palm. Examining it closely, he saw it was carved with images of clouds and birds.

'The lid slides off,' Grubner explained. 'Now you'll have to keep it hidden. Do you understand?'

Speechless, Xavier nodded.

'If you or your friend is caught with it, you're to say it's yours. You must never tell them I gave it to you. Do you understand?'

'Yes, but why are you giving it to me?'

'I was young once.' He picked up his spade. 'Now get back to school.' As Xavier walked away, Grubner growled, 'But if I ever catch you up a tree or lurking about here again, I'll give you detention.'

'It won't happen again. Thank you for the box.'

Xavier jogged back to the west wing, delighted he had something special to give Ethan but puzzled by Grubner. While he ran, something in the box rattled and although he wanted to discover what it was, he was too wary to stop.

* * *

'Well? How did you go?' Xavier asked Gabe, who pulled a pillowcase from under his bed and tipped its contents on the floor. A number of toilet rolls spilled out, along with tape, scissors and a few old magazines.

'I know it doesn't look much, but I've managed to make a few lanterns and paper chains using pages from the magazines.'

'How did you make them?'

'There are all sorts of books hidden in the library basement. Months ago, I found this book about having a merry Christmas on a shoestring budget. When I saw the cover, I felt an urge to know more about shoestring budgets and the like. It taught me many useful skills,' Gabe said earnestly. 'I can't wait to hang the paper chains in the chapel. I think we'll need to get there about twenty minutes before the rest of the boys.'

The door burst open. 'You should see what I g-got!' Alex boasted.

'Shh.' Xavier was afraid the boys were getting crazier by the second.

Alex carried two pillowcases. One was stuffed with bread, a tub of butter and two plastic flagons of juice.

Xavier knew the juice had to be from the teachers' stock. 'If Ratti finds out, she'll ....' Worriedly, he imagined the scene.

'She won't. If you're going to steal from the k-kitchen, the first thing you have to do is f-find the inventory of the food they have in store. Sometimes they're not very smart.'

'Why's that?' Gabe asked.

''Cause they write the number of each food item in p-pencil.'

'And?'

'I have an eraser.'

Gabe grinned.

'You altered the numbers!' Xavier said.

Alex shrugged. 'They were b-begging for it.'

Peering in the other pillowcase, Xavier gasped when he saw scores of red and blue lollies. 'Where did you get them?'

'For the p-past year I've collected a small handful from c-Crowley's lolly jar every week. I don't like them, but I trade them for stuff with k-kids.'

'How did you get them from Crowley?'

Alex patted his pocket. 'I have a k-key.' He picked up one of the packets of bread. 'B-bread's basic, but most of the kids are so hungry they won't complain.'

Xavier extracted a small jar from his bag in the cupboard. 'This might help.' He handed the jar to Alex, who held it up to the light and shook it several times.

'What are they?' Gabe asked curiously.

'Sprinkles. They're pieces of coloured sugar. When I was a kid, mum used to sprinkle them on bread and butter. She called it fairy bread. They were left in my bag from when I had a sleepover with my friends in Ravenwood years ago. I hope they're not too old.'

'Hmm, sugar sprinkles. A tasty sound,' Gabe said approvingly. 'But what's a sleepover?'

Alex looked at Xavier blankly.

'Never mind, it's not important,' Xavier said as he realised how far removed his life in Ravenwood was from Griswold.

Alex grinned. 'We're all set then!'

'Did you find a birthday present?' Gabe asked Xavier.

Xavier opened the desk drawer and removed a worn sock that was concealing the box. He peeled the sock away and handed the box to Gabe.

'Where did you g-get that?' Alex said. 'It's amazing.'

Gabe examined the carvings.

'You're not going to believe this,' Xavier said and told them the story.

Alex shook his head. 'I don't get it. Why didn't Grub give you detention?'

'Maybe he's sentimental about birthdays.'

Gabe rattled the box. 'What's inside?'

'Have a look.'

He carefully slid the panel off the top of the box to reveal blue silk. 'Nice fabric,' he said as he uncovered the object, which looked very much like the whistle Craig had given Xavier in Karn Forest. He raised an eyebrow at Xavier, who grinned.

'It looks like a whistle g-gone wrong,' Alex said.

Gabe examined it closely. Three neat holes and a mouthpiece had been carved into a curved and gnarled piece of wood.

'Can I see?' Alex took the whistle and after turning it over a few times, raised it to his lips.

'Don't,' Gabe warned. 'We've no way of knowing whether it's a simple toy or something more complicated. Until we know its purpose, we can't use it, especially at Griswold. I think we'd better give Ethan the present before we go to the party, so we can warn him and keep it secret from the other boys.'

Xavier waited for Alex to question him, but he didn't. Obviously he had been at Griswold long enough to understand Gabe's warning.

The boys agreed and then hid the party goods under Howard's bunk.

'There's one problem we haven't considered,' Xavier said.

'I have,' Gabe said with a grin.

'You don't even know what I was going to say.'

'Yes I do, because it's logical. You were going to ask about how we were going to keep all of this from Howard.'

Xavier smiled.

Gabe took a tablet from his pocket and held it out.

'What is it?'

'*Drowsy Time* for when you really need your rest. That's what it said on the box. It sounds like a song,' Gabe said. 'It's extra strength.'

'Did Matron give it to you?' Xavier asked.

'Not exactly. Ethan gave me the key for the medicine cabinet. I told him I had a headache and needed a tablet but didn't want to ask in case Matron examined me.' Gabe turned to Alex. 'Did you get the bait?'

Alex fished in his pocket for a small parcel.

Gabe took it and opened it to reveal a chocolate.

'Not the teacher's stash?' Xavier said in a horrified tone as he remembered Gabe's punishment for stealing before they had escaped to Ravenwood.

'It's okay, they won't m-miss one,' Alex reassured him.

Gabe carefully pushed the tablet into the centre of the soft chocolate and then smoothed the surface to hide its contents. He left it on Howard's pillow and then licked his fingers.

'I'll see you just before m-midnight at the west wing entrance,' Alex said before leaving.

'Howard will be back from dinner at any moment,' Xavier warned.

Gabe threw himself on his bunk. 'Just follow my lead.'

* * *

'Where's Ethan?' Howard said as he entered the room.

Xavier looked over the top of his book. 'In the showers.'

'I didn't see you two at dinner.'

Gabe pretended to chew something. 'We ate early.'

'What are you eating now?' Howard asked in a suspicious tone.

'Chocolate,' Xavier said. 'We all got one.'

'Where's mine?'

'They left them on our pillows,' Gabe said.

'Who did?'

Xavier shrugged. 'One of the kids thought it was Crowley.'

'Who cares?' Gabe said.

'Mine was caramel. My favourite,' Xavier said. 'I didn't brush my teeth, so I can still taste it.'

Howard picked up the chocolate on his pillow. 'It looks a bit squashed.'

'I got orange,' Gabe said. 'If you don't want yours, can I have it, please?'

Howard threw the chocolate in his mouth and chewed but swallowed it quickly. 'Tastes odd.'

'Maybe it was marzipan,' Xavier said.

'Bad luck,' Gabe said.

Within half an hour, Howard was curled up and snoring under his blanket.

'Sweet dreams, precious,' Gabe said.

When Ethan finally returned from the showers, he glanced at Howard. 'What's wrong with him?'

Gabe kept a straight face. 'Probably overdoing his diary writing.'

Xavier opened the desk drawer, took out the sock-covered box and handed it to Ethan. 'Happy birthday!'

Ethan propped.

'Go on, take it.'

He looked surprised and emotional as he turned the present over and over in his hands.

'Are you going to open it?' Xavier asked.

'Or de-sock it?' Gabe said.

Trembling, Ethan slowly peeled the sock back as though he wanted to prolong the enjoyment.

While Xavier watched, it occurred to him that he had probably not opened a present since he was six years old. 'Take your time.'

Ethan dropped the threadbare sock and then took a deep breath as he examined the box. 'It's beautiful,' he whispered and ran his fingertip over the birds and clouds etched into its surface. 'Thank you.'

'You can slide the lid off,' Gabe said enthusiastically.

Ethan pressed on the lid and slid it off gently with an expression of wonderment and delight. 'A whistle. It reminds me of yours, Xavier.'

'I wouldn't blow it,' Xavier said.

'Why not?'

'Well not with the gargoyles and Ratti about. They might be able to hear it.'

* * *

Xavier shook Ethan awake a few hours later. 'Time to party.'

He mumbled and rolled over, so Xavier and Gabe pulled his blanket away and dragged him until he was sitting over the edge of the bed.

'Ready?' Xavier said.

Ethan blinked a few times and nodded. 'What about ...?' He tipped his head towards Howard.

Gabe grinned. 'Slipped him a sleeping tablet.'

'You don't trust him?'

'Can't be sure,' Xavier said.

Gabe dragged the pillow cases and their contents from under the bunk.

'What've you got there?' Ethan asked.

'Supplies.' Gabe picked them up and walked to the door. 'Let's get going.' He led them down the corridor to the west wing entrance to where Alex and two boys were crouching under the stairwell.

Alex unlocked the door and the boys filed out the doorway into the open air. After checking the front lawns of the school, they ran along the small path beside the row of lavender bushes. As it was nearly midnight, all the dormitory windows were in darkness. When they reached the other end of the building where months ago they had hidden from Beauty and Phineas, they stopped. Xavier was relieved to see Ratti's room was also unlit. Gabe stuck his head around the corner and raised his hand for the boys to follow his lead and sprint towards the chapel. When they reached the side entrance, Alex fumbled for a few moments before he displayed another key and unlocked the door. Ignoring the creaking door as it opened, he beckoned the others to follow him into the vestry. The boys pushed the swinging door open, which led them into the main part of the chapel. They stood for a few moments to survey the ceiling of arched wooden beams, the shadowy pews and the empty altar.

Seeing two thick black sheets hanging over the small front windows, Xavier knew there was no way light could penetrate them. Obviously, Alex had taken care of the windows at some stage through the day as he had promised. Like the other boys, Xavier hated the chapel. He loathed the lingering smell of incense, the chill of the holy water and the foreign chants and hymns he endured every Sunday with Father Augustine. Staring at the row of chairs usually reserved for Ratti, Phineas and Pittworthy, all he wanted to do was slash the padded velvet seats and toss them through the stained glass windows. The chapel was supposed to be about goodness, but it smelled evil. Celebrating a birthday gave them a chance to tip the balance and to reclaim the building, and with that thought, he was determined to make sure Ethan enjoyed it. 'Decoration time!' he called as loudly as he dared.

'G-give us a few minutes,' Alex said. 'We're going to change into our p-party gear.' He disappeared into the vestry with his roommates, Tim and Gregor.

'Go ahead,' Gabe said. 'We'll start. Keep it quiet though. Remember Ratti's room is close.'

'It's fine,' Alex said. 'As I said b-before, the walls are thick. With the doors c-closed you can't hear Sunday service or the teachers' meetings. Anyhow the witch left school with Phineas. We saw her p-pull out just after dinner. They must be staying in t-town.'

Xavier wondered at his choice of words. Did he call her witch because he knew her identity or because he despised her? He took a toilet roll and as he held the end of it, threw it at the ceiling, so it streamed into the air and over a beam.

Ethan and Gabe followed his lead.

A few minutes later, Alex and the other boys emerged.

'What do you think?' Alex said.

Alex was wearing one of Kennedy's navy nylon tracksuits and one of the other boys, Tim, had a Pittworthy-style jacket complete with an old fashioned button-up shirt.

The boys hooted with laughter.

Little Gregor stepped from behind the other two boys wearing a black skirt and buttoned shirt. 'What do you think you're doing, Mr Klee?' he croaked. 'Just because it's your birthday, doesn't give you the right to be a hooligan in my chapel!'

'Ratti! Having fun, thank you very much, you old bag.' Ethan laughed so hard that tears ran down his face.

'Although they d-don't know it, the laundry staff kindly lent us the outfits for the night,' Alex explained.

When the boys had finished hanging paper lanterns and chains from pews, light fixtures and the dark oil paintings of dead Griswolds, they turned their attention to the food. Xavier and Alex buttered the bread, arranged the pieces on a sheet of paper spread on the altar and poured the lollies into a bowl Gregor had borrowed. Gathering around, the boys watched solemnly while Xavier quietly hummed happy birthday and sprinkled the multicoloured sugar on the bread.

Xavier offered him a piece of fairy bread. 'You go first, Ethan. Try one.'

When the other west wing boys arrived after midnight, they filed in quietly at first, but once they had splashed juice into their cups and sampled the fairy bread and lollies, they chattered and laughed, and threw toilet paper at each other. While the boys devoured the bread, Gabe drew a pig complete with large hindquarters on a piece of paper and stuck it on the wall. The boys watched curiously as he took Ethan aside and blindfolded him with a long sock. He spun him around and handed him another sock with a pin through it. 'Pin the tail on the pig,' he instructed Ethan as he pushed him in the direction of the drawing.

Ethan swayed and giggled as he wandered towards the drawing then veered into the circle of boys, who laughed and pushed him towards the paper pig.

'Close! You're getting warmer,' Xavier called out.

Finally Ethan found the drawing and pushed the pin into the pig. As he removed the blindfold, there were squeals of laughter from the boys because he had stuck the tail in the pig's head.

'My turn, my turn!' The boys' voices tumbled over each other as they lined up. When they had finally exhausted the game, Gabe directed them to drag chairs before the altar, where they played musical chairs. No one seemed to mind that they had to wait their turn. As each group played the game, Gabe provided the music with some rather strange singing while the other boys laughed and teased the players from the side.

Exhilarated by the happiness Xavier could see in Ethan's face and elated by the boys' shared excitement, he felt a very unusual impulse to address the boys. In fact, he couldn't remember ever having volunteered to speak in public. He climbed onto a chair and called, 'Thank you ...' and then waited for the boys to listen. 'Thank you for helping to celebrate Ethan's birthday. Think of it as a shared celebration for all the birthdays you've missed at Griswold.'

The laughter and chatter dissipated and the boys stood silently.

'We'll do it again,' Xavier said in a tone of defiance. 'I know we have no cake, but we'll sing happy birthday anyway.'

After a few faltering starts, the boys began to sing softly to Ethan, who stood in the middle of the room. Despite it having been so long since any of the boys had celebrated a birthday, most of them remembered the song. Ethan was obviously overwhelmed as were the boys whose song sounded sad and mournful as it echoed under the high ceiling of the chapel.

Bringing the boys back to reality, Gabe said, 'Now we must clean up carefully. Pick up all the decorations. Take a share of the toilet paper and get rid of it how you would normally.' Within the next ten minutes the boys had picked up every scrap of food and paper and stuffed it in pockets and pillowcases. They dragged the chairs back to the vestry and turned the lights out until everything was just as they found it.

* * *

'That was the best birthday ever,' Ethan said when they had returned to their room.

'Pity Sleeping Beauty missed it,' Xavier said as Howard groaned and rolled over in his sleep.

'So you've been here seven years,' Gabe said. 'Alex told us many of the boys received an imprint when they arrived here. Did you get one too?'

'Yep,' Ethan said.

'Do you mind if I have a look at it?' Gabe asked.

Ethan shrugged and pushed his sleeve up.

'It looks a little different in design to Alex's.'

'He got here before me. Maybe it was done by someone different.'

'Who did yours?'

'I think he was a doctor. I remember how much it hurt and how frightened I was.'

Gabe yawned. 'It's been a big night. I'm going to bed now.'

When Ethan left a few minutes later to go to the bathroom, Xavier asked Gabe, 'What was that all about—the stamp I mean?'

'I didn't want to scare Ethan, but there's something strange about

Alex's stamp. According to it, he's been here for nearly fifty years,' Gabe said.

'How can that be? He's only fifteen,' Xavier said. 'What about Ethan's stamp?'

'It's normal.'

Xavier sat on the edge of his bed. 'Alex's stamp must be a mistake.'

'Maybe, but I think it may have something to do with why he couldn't come over the wall with us. Something's wrong and I'm beginning to wonder if any boy has ever graduated from Griswold.'

CHAPTER 15

* * *

Letters and battles

'My head's thumping,' Howard complained as the boys walked to class. 'I tossed and turned all night with bad dreams.'

'Maybe you need to see Matron,' Xavier said.

'Ask her for something to help you sleep better,' Ethan added.

Xavier dug Ethan in the ribs to stop him going too far. Since he wasn't entirely sure of his suspicions about Howard, it made him feel guilty about giving him the tablet and the headache.

The boys filed into the classroom and sat down. Phineas was standing at the window with his back to the class. They were starting geography and Xavier was genuinely interested in the subject and hoped he might learn more about the Southern Lands, in particular, the Ambrosian Forest. The only downside was that now they had two classes with Phineas every day.

'Mr Jones, would you distribute the texts on my desk.'

Instantly, Xavier regretted sitting at the front. So often he seemed to land the job of handing out books when he was in Phineas' class. He especially resented the way he ordered him around and never said please or thank you. When Xavier had handed out the last few books, he realised he didn't have one.

'I don't have a book, sir,' he said when he returned to Phineas' desk.

'You may borrow my copy, but you'll need to have your own this term for there will be considerable amounts of homework.' He threw his text on Xavier's desk. 'Come to the front office after lunch and I'll give you a book.'

Xavier tried to swallow as he remembered the last time he walked down the corridor that passed the front office to Ratti's lair. 'Actually sir, I could share with Gabe.'

'Did you hear me? I said to come and collect your text after lunch. Do you not understand Clanardian?'

'Yes, sir, I'll be there.'

Phineas turned to the class. 'Today we'll be exploring the eastern aspects of the Southern Lands.'

Xavier was disappointed to see once again, there was no colour in their textbook. It was dreary. If only he had some colouring pencils to fill the oceans with blue and hatch the land green.

'What's the largest town on the east coast of Clanarde?' Phineas asked.

Gabe raised his hand, but he ignored him.

Phineas searched the class. 'Anyone else?'

Xavier smiled. It was ironic that the only non-Clanardian knew the country better than those who had always lived there.

Phineas sneered at the boys and then turned to Gabe. 'Yes, Mr Shepherd?'

'Clearview, sir.'

'Correct, Clearview is located close to the border. It has good rainfall and a temperate climate. It's dairy farm country and produces most of the Southern Land's milk and cheese.'

'I think it's also quite famous for beekeeping, sir,' Gabe piped.

Phineas glanced at him strangely.

'There's a book about the region in the library, sir,' Gabe said as though reading Phineas' expression.

Xavier, who was sitting close to Phineas, noticed a ripple in the muscles around his jaw.

'Clearview is on the coastline and sits on the southern end of the Craggie Mountains, a rugged mountain range which extend to the

Ferntree River. Clearview is mainly flat with low hills on its westerly aspect that becomes more mountainous as you approach the range.' Phineas paused. 'I suggest you take notes as you'll be examined on this material.'

'Why is that, sir?' Gabe asked.

Xavier cringed.

Phineas stopped pacing and stared at him.

'I don't understand,' Gabe said.

'Which part of my description don't you follow?' Phineas spoke slowly.

'The exam part, sir. Why do we need to do them?'

The class was silent as if they were trying to predict whether Phineas would explode or explain.

Phineas' switch sat untouched on his desk and his neck veins were not throbbing. He had to be in a good mood, Xavier decided.

'Mr Shepherd, students sit examinations so we can measure whether you've understood and retained the information we give you in class. Do you understand?' He enunciated his words clearly and the last question was delivered in slow motion. Although it sounded ridiculous, no boy dared to laugh.

'Thank you, sir. What do you do with our results?'

'Ah, Mr Shepherd, with the results we measure your worth.' He sounded sarcastic now. 'That's how the outside world works.'

'When do we get to leave St Griswold, sir?'

Stillness fell upon the room as if the air had ebbed away.

Phineas' eyes narrowed. 'When you are sufficiently mature and educated,' he replied without missing a beat.

'What have some of your students done since leaving Griswold, sir?'

Phineas stood at the window and ran a finger along the sill.

'You must be proud of them, sir.'

Phineas inspected his finger for dust and then turned slowly. 'There are far too many to remember. My focus is here and now.' He eyed Gabe directly. 'Does anyone wish to have a career consultation with Ms Ratchet, who I know is well-qualified in this field? Anyone?'

No one replied.

'Turn to page fifty-seven.'

* * *

After lunch, Xavier made his way to the front foyer of the school. When he reached the east wing entrance, he could hear Phineas' voice echoing down the corridor. 'What do you idiots think you're doing?'

As Xavier approached the foyer he could see a boy from his year with a hand over his left eye and Phineas holding two boys by their ears. Xavier stood awkwardly to one side until Phineas noticed him.

'What do you want?' he barked.

'The book, sir, remember?'

'Go and wait in the office. I'll be there shortly. Don't touch anything.' Phineas turned his attention to the wriggling boys.

Anxious about navigating the teachers' corridor alone, Xavier was relieved to find it well lit. The patterned carpet was at rest and the bespectacled and bearded old men in the gloomy photographs seemed disinterested and aloof. Although the corridor appeared safe, he rushed along it to the office. When no one answered his knock, he let himself in. The door to the next room was ajar, so he peered around it. Inside it was warmer and the couch and furnishings more comfortable than he remembered when his parents had enrolled him here months ago. A large jar filled with a rainbow assortment of sweets sat on the table beside an ancient typewriter with stacks of blank envelopes and pale green writing paper arranged to the left. Heavier grey notepaper sat in another pile, and many small cardboard boxes filled with envelopes were scattered on the floor. From the trail of empty lolly wrappers littering the table and the sprinkling of sugar crystals, he knew this had to be

Phineas' desk. In the distance, Xavier could hear him launching into another attack.

'What were you thinking?' Phineas exclaimed.

Xavier couldn't hear the reply.

'Are you animals?'

Xavier crept to the table and picked up an envelope with a ridiculous crest depicting two vultures. The grey paper also bore the insignia and school motto, 'integrity and honour', which was a joke among the boys.

He could still hear Phineas' words faintly from the foyer. 'You're a disgrace to St Griswold College.'

Xavier checked the typewriter, which had a blank sheet of the grey paper wound onto it. Crouching on the floor, he pulled a box towards him and flicked through the envelopes. His breath quickened as he recognised many of the names and realised the envelopes were addressed to parents.

From the foyer, Phineas' voice was still distinct. 'You'll both have detention with Ms Ratchet.'

Xavier felt dizzy. His hands shook as he carefully flicked through the alphabetically arranged envelopes. Howard's was there, but there was no envelope for Alex or Ethan. He ran quickly through the box again … Crameri, Finn, Jackson … Jones. He plucked out the last letter and examined it closely. It was unsealed and had his parents' name on it and his Ravenwood address. He removed the letter inside the envelope and thrust it into his pocket. After folding a blank sheet of the grey paper and poking it in the empty envelope, he suddenly realised he could no longer hear Phineas. He replaced the envelope in the box and rushed to the waiting room where he threw himself on the couch moments before Phineas walked through the doorway.

Xavier sprang up and down on the couch. 'I like its springiness, sir.'

'Stop bouncing on the couch,' Phineas snapped. 'What are you here for?'

'You remember, sir, the geography book.'

Phineas glanced at the typing room door, still slightly ajar.

Xavier inspected his fingernails while he prayed Phineas could not see the outline of the envelope through his threadbare pocket.

Phineas strode into the other room. A full minute dragged by. He could hear him moving things around. Could he smell his presence in there or see a faint, grimy fingerprint? Had he altered the arrangement of the letters in the box he had disturbed?

'Here.' Phineas appeared in the doorway with the book.

Xavier jumped.

'Bit edgy, are we, Mr Jones?'

'Um no, sir. You just surprised me.'

Phineas held the book out and Xavier tried to take it, but the teacher didn't release it immediately.

Xavier's heart thumped.

'Well?'

'Thanks, sir.' Xavier held his breath as he took the book.

'What are you waiting for?'

'For you to say I can go, sir.'

'Go.'

Xavier walked as naturally as he could to the door, but once he reached the corridor, ran swiftly to the foyer and up the stairs, almost colliding with Chris Eaves, the school prefect.

'Don't run,' Chris warned.

'Sorry,' Xavier said, yet he still took two steps at a time all the way to the second floor. Only then did he pause and dare to look behind, as he half-expected Phineas to be in pursuit. He ran along the corridor to his room. Once safely inside, he locked the door, climbed into bed and drew the blanket over his head until his racing heart had slowed and his breathing eased. It was only then he had the courage to take the folded paper from under his jumper and to run a finger around its sides to confirm it was real. Gabe, Howard and Ethan would be heading to Crowley's class. The door was safely locked and the window closed. Slowly he peeled the blanket back and sat with his back against the wall. No stray vulture, horde of moths or even Grubner on an extension ladder would be able to witness his deed, but he was still afraid. With a deep breath, he unfolded the two pages of typing. He gasped and covered his mouth after reading the first line, '*Dear Mum and Dad*'. In an instant, he flicked to the second page and was stunned to read the final line, '*Love Xavier*'.

The last paragraph horrified him the most:

'*Please don't worry about me. I have good friends, great teachers and I'm being well looked after. The teachers have told me that it would be unsafe for you to visit me and I'm in the best place until the danger passes.*'

His hand shook as he resumed reading the letter from the first page. After reading it six times, he neatly folded the pages and rested the back of his head on the wall with his eyes closed and tears running down his face.

· * * *

'When you've finished warming down, hit the showers,' Kennedy barked. It was the final class before lunch and he was collecting sports equipment to return to the shed. Although the school spent little on food, heating and clothing, it seemed to always find money for sports gear. Ethan said it was to make sure they left all their energy to fight back or escape on the playing fields.

There were a few quiet groans as they were only ever allowed cold showers.

'You're quiet,' Gabe said to Xavier.

'It's 'cause our side smashed yours,' Ethan said, referring to the football game they had just played.

'Yep,' Xavier said half-heartedly. 'I'm going to do a jog warm down.' He ran half-way around the oval and then slowed to a walk. He could hear the others laughing and jeering, but he didn't care. He needed space and air.

Gabe jogged until he caught up with Xavier. 'I don't understand humans and your need to win at games.'

'I don't care about the game.'

'What is it then?'

Xavier leaned against a tree to stretch his calf. 'You can't help.'

'Come on, the suspense is … what's that human saying?'

'Killing you.'

'No, I don't think that's right.'

Xavier sighed. 'Remember how I had to collect the geography book from Phineas at the front office?'

'Yes.'

'Well, Phineas was distracted by some kids fighting in the foyer and told me to wait in the front office.' Xavier switched his stance to stretch the other calf while Gabe sprawled on the grass. 'I snuck into his office.'

'You did?' Gabe sounded surprised.

'What? You don't think I'm game enough to do things like that?'

'What happened?'

'There was a typewriter and all these letters addressed to our parents. I took mine.'

Gabe raised his eyebrows.

'I know it was probably stupid, but I couldn't help it.'

'Where is it?'

'I read it, tore it up and flushed it down the toilet. Not all at once though, in case it clogged the pipes.'

Gabe peered into the distance. 'Ugly has spotted us. We'd better start jogging back.'

'The letter was fake. It was typed and started with *'Dear Mum and Dad'* and finished with *'Love Xavier'*.'

Gabe let out a low whistle.

'It gets worse. It was full of rubbish about how wonderful the school was and how much I loved my classes and teachers. It told them how well I was going in the classes I was studying. It said I had many new friends and the food was great. There was also a photo of us.'

'What photo?' Gabe asked.

'Pittworthy snaps pictures at recess and during sport. He probably has photos of us all. I'm guessing all the letters are fakes. No wonder we don't hear from our parents.'

Gabe rubbed his forehead. 'Yes, that might satisfy parents during the school year, but what happens during the holidays?'

'The last paragraph of the letter said my parents shouldn't worry about me and should concentrate on sorting out their business until the danger passes.'

'So they've convinced parents their kids are in the safest place possible, and it would endanger them if they visited.'

'Would it stop your parents visiting?'

Xavier shrugged. 'I wouldn't have thought so. Maybe they can't get here because they've no money or they're in trouble. There's one good thing though. I don't think they can be in a Darklaw camp or they've become shells, because Phineas wouldn't be sending letters to them.'

'There are many possibilities. Perhaps they don't know where your parents are but keep sending letters to your home in Ravenwood assuming they'll visit if they can.'

Xavier nodded. 'I didn't think to check the letterbox when we were there. I don't remember it overflowing though.'

'I wonder if there's a letter for my parents,' Gabe said and grinned.

* * *

CHAPTER 16

Stinky Eye

Xavier checked the corridor behind him for the third time as Ethan unlocked the classroom door. It was close to midnight and the halls were silent. Were they going too far this time? Ethan had become obsessed with the new gargoyle ever since the newcomer had arrived. Although Xavier thought it was a stupid idea, he and Gabe had promised Ethan they would visit the gargoyle with him. Not telling Ethan about the plan they'd hatched with Artemis made Xavier feel uncomfortable. Visiting the gargoyle would ease his guilt.

'Where is it?' Gabe asked when they were safely in the classroom.

Xavier pointed to the window adjacent to the second last row of desks.

Ethan reached the window first, opened it and peered out. He scrambled onto the ledge and pulled out a jar from under his jumper. 'Stinky Eye's mine.' And before the boys could object, he had climbed onto the roof.

'Careful,' Xavier warned as the pitch of the roof was steep.

Ethan sat on the roof tiles and inched his way down the slope. When he reached the grey gargoyle, he opened the jar and poured most of its contents over its head. Bright yellow paint splashed over its face and stony scales and dripped onto the tiles.

Speechless, Xavier and Gabe watched as Ethan handed them the jar. 'Careful, don't let any of it get on you.'

Gabe took the jar but checked his fingers after placing it on the ledge.

As Ethan backed up towards the window, a tile came loose, clattered down the roof and shattered a few moments later on the concrete quad.

'Did you see that?' Xavier said in astonishment. 'Its eye glowed.'

'Hey! Stinky's vibrating.' Ethan hurriedly retreated to the window, just as the creature began to moan.

'It's waking up,' Gabe said.

Gabe and Xavier hauled Ethan through the window.

The sound from Stinky became louder with each passing second until it morphed into a growl.

'The other gargoyles are answering,' Xavier said.

'They were already awake,' Gabe said. 'Stinky's the only one that sleeps at night.'

The gargoyles' chorus of moaning and wailing became progressively louder. The window stuck as Gabe struggled to close it. 'We can't leave it open.'

The three boys tried to pull it down together. They persisted for another minute until it suddenly gave way and closed. Footsteps and voices rang out in the corridor outside and doors opened and slammed.

'Quick, under the teacher's desk,' Gabe urged.

Just as they scrambled under the desk, the door opened and light spilled from the corridor into the room.

'I'm sure it was coming from here,' Ratti said.

The boys heard footsteps of someone walking to the window while someone else flicked the light switch. A light bulb glowed for a few seconds before it failed, leaving only the light from the corridor and a moon.

'I'll check the window. You try the next room.' Ratti's voice was grating and urgent. 'Hurry up.'

Xavier was so afraid she would hear them that he held his breath until he felt faint. Ratti's skirt scratched and rustled across the floorboards to the window. Just then he remembered the paint jar on the ledge. He waited for her to explode when she saw it, but instead he was amazed to hear her heave the window open. How could someone so small and old manage such a feat? He gathered the courage to peer through a hole in the back of the desk close to where he was huddled. If he weren't so terrified, he would have laughed. After dragging a chair to the window, Ratti had gathered her skirt up to her waist, so she could climb out the window. He was stunned by the vision of her hairy legs and lacy bloomers, which he could just make out in the light spilling from the corridor. Unable to look away, he watched her scramble from the chair and climb over the window sill to the roof.

'She's on the roof,' Xavier whispered as Gabe and Ethan couldn't see through the hole. 'Let's go.'

Gabe shook his head and just then they heard more voices in the corridor.

'My poor dear, who did this?' Ratti said in a croaky tone. 'There, there, I'll make it better. They'll pay, I promise.'

A scratching, growling commotion erupted outside the window.

'No!' Ratti demanded. Tiles slid, clattered and smashed on the quad. She retreated to the window ledge.

Horrified, Xavier saw a large animal leap through the window onto the classroom floor.

'Stay!' Ratti yelled, but the creature, excited and snuffling, bounded across the floor towards the desk.

Xavier was unable to look away.

'Relensis!' Ratti called in a high-pitched tone.

The yellow paint-spattered creature froze, suspended in mid-leap and slowly sank to the ground.

Ratti circled it, waving her hands and muttering indecipherable words under her breath.

The creature lowered its head and trotted meekly to the window, where it jumped over the ledge and scrambled back onto the roof, dislodging a few more tiles with its action.

'Stasis,' Ratti said in a firm tone. She poked her head out the window. Minutes passed. She was singing to the gargoyle.

Gradually Stinky calmed and the other gargoyles' wailing faded.

When they heard another movement in the room, Xavier peered through the hole and almost yelled with fright. Ratti had climbed quietly back through the window and was now standing on the other side of the desk. She was close enough for him to poke her hip bone. Blood pulsed in his head as he silently signalled to the others she was there. Fearful, he shrank away from the hole in case she looked back. He heard her sniffing at the air and rifling through papers on the desk above their heads.

Xavier held his breath. Ethan had buried his face under his folded arms while Gabe stared emotionless at the floor.

Eventually Ratti left the room and closed the door behind her. The boys listened until her footsteps died away in the corridor and then tumbled from their hiding place. Ethan and Gabe were grinning with obvious relief. Xavier sat on a chair nearby waiting for his body to stop shaking.

'Are you okay?' Gabe said to Xavier. 'She's gone now. We're safe.'

Xavier couldn't hide his dismay. 'You didn't see it. I saw everything through the hole.'

'What are you talking about?' Gabe said.

'The gargoyle. It turned into a beast. It jumped through the window and ran towards the desk. I think it smelled us. Ratti stopped it with magic.'

'That's what that noise was,' Gabe said. 'I could hear a snuffling, scratching sound.'

'I'm certain it was that animal Beauty had in Lanoris—the thing that killed Harold Eastly.' Xavier's voice was still wobbly from shock. 'And the paint jar ....'

Ethan squirmed. 'I forgot about that.'

'It's gone,' Xavier said. 'Ratti probably took it with her.'

* * *

The boys sat around their room recovering from afternoon sport with Kennedy. Howard was still showering much to Gabe's amusement.

'Why he needs to shower after only carrying the clipboard for Ugly is a mystery.'

'What's Grubner doing on the west wall?' Ethan asked.

Xavier got up from his bed to join him at the window. Grubner was lugging something up a ladder. It was obviously heavy as he paused on each rung as though he was getting his breath and balance before attempting the next one.

Gabe looked over their shoulders. 'He's planting mini gargoyles on the wall. Ratti's getting her revenge.'

'We're surrounded,' Ethan said. 'Poor Grubner. I bet it was him called in to clean up Stinky Eye last night. There's not a drop of yellow paint to be seen.'

'Where did you get the paint?' Xavier asked.

'I visited the gardening shed last week and as soon as I saw the colour, I couldn't resist.'

As the afternoon wore on, Grubner hauled several more of the stony creatures onto the wall from a van that he drove to each strategic position. The cat-sized gargoyles were obviously intended to watch the students as they all faced towards the school ground with their wings outstretched.

Just then the chapel bell rang across the quadrangle. The boys lay on their beds and waited until the third chime.

'Assembly,' Howard said. After carefully inserting the paper he was writing on into his textbook, he stood up. 'Well? Are you coming?'

No one moved.

'Don't you remember Ms Ratchet said we had to assemble when the bell rang three times?' Howard leaned over the desk and peered out the window at the quad. 'Everyone else is lining up.'

Xavier sat up. 'We're coming, Howard. Go without us if you want.'

'It's fine,' Gabe said. 'We'll catch you down there.'

'You'll get into trouble if you're late.' Howard fidgeted for a few seconds and then as if the tension of waiting was too much, strode out the door.

Gabe jumped out of bed and retrieved the textbook Howard had slid under his mattress when he thought they weren't looking. 'Nothing here—just a letter to his father asking him when he'll be returning from his business in Hybath.'

'Do you think it's a fake?' Ethan asked. 'You know, to make us think his dad really is a politician.'

'How come he gets to write letters?' Xavier said. 'None of us do.' He hadn't yet told Ethan about the letters he had discovered in the front office.

'He probably doesn't realise there's nowhere to post it,' Ethan said.

The boys were the last to reach assembly. Ratti, who was standing on the platform, watched them carefully as they joined a row of boys.

After several minutes of silence, she said, 'We are concerned that the behaviour of students isn't up to the usual standard expected at St Griswold College. There have been acts of vandalism.' She paused. 'If I discover the perpetrators, I can assure you, they'll regret their actions. Remember this, you're privileged boys. Beyond the walls of this school are thousands of Clanardian boys who suffer hardship on a daily basis, boys who are hungry, homeless and alone. They'd give everything to have a fraction of the opportunity you've been given. You boys are not special or somehow deserving. You're just very, very fortunate.'

The rows of boys stood silently at attention in the cold wind, waiting for her to get to the point.

'To address this growing problem, today we'll be increasing disciplinary exercises.' She waved a skeletal hand at Pittworthy, who was standing by an old fashioned gramophone. At her command, he placed the needle on a record and the speakers squealed and then blared hideous ceremonial music. After a few bars, Ratti raised her hand again and Pittworthy stopped the music.

'You'll line up in four columns and then march to the front lawns of the school where you'll follow the chalked line around the perimeter. Mr Kennedy, Mr Phineas and Mr Pittworthy will be assessing your posture and marching style. Any boy not reaching the required standard will be given a warning today. If he doesn't reach our expectations, next time he'll attend early morning remedial marching classes with Mr Kennedy. Do you all understand?'

'Yes, Ms Ratchet,' they replied in unison.

'Please show the boys what we expect, Mr Kennedy.'

Kennedy puffed his chest out, obviously relishing the role. 'Chin in, head high, chest out, stomach in,' he bawled as he demonstrated. 'When you swing your arm forward it should align with your shoulder. Like this.'

After the boys had practised the action a few times, Ratti called, 'Very well, let the march commence.'

Pittworthy lowered the needle on the record again and the marching music blared from the speakers strategically placed around the school buildings. In the past they had marched once or twice around the quad to a mild, short-lived piece of music, but today it was formal and military with a thumping beat and a clanging excess of trumpets and cymbals. Ratti meant business.

Kennedy was in his element as he led the procession from the quad to the front of the school. Once they reached the sprawling front lawn, he stood to one side as though he was inspecting his troops. Occasionally he jabbed a boy in the stomach or between the shoulder blades. When he blew his whistle, the boys stopped and he instructed them to march on the spot.

Gabe hummed tunelessly to the music. 'This is fun.'

'You're kidding,' Xavier said.

'Fresh air, exercise. What's not to like? And you?'

'I feel ridiculous and embarrassed.'

'Interesting. Why embarrassment? We're all engaged in the same activity. Look, even Howard seems to be enjoying himself.'

Xavier glanced at the row behind them. 'Exactly, there's my proof.'

'Left, right, left, right,' Kennedy roared in Xavier's ear. 'No talking, boy.'

Once they had moved away from the teacher, they talked again.

Xavier was not familiar with this side of the building. Across the lawn, he noticed a circular structure overgrown with vines and purple flowers. 'What's that on the right?'

'It looks like an old well. Perhaps it's the school's water supply,' Gabe said. 'There are more watchers above on the front of the building.'

'Gargoyles?'

'Yep. I counted two on the west side and there must be six or so at the front. We won't be flying in the school grounds again unless we can figure out how to take care of them,' Gabe said.

The musical piece was replayed five times and just when Xavier thought he couldn't stand hearing it again, it ended. Everyone stopped marching and waited for their next order. Pittworthy twiddled with the gramophone and began playing a new record. Some of the boys stood still while others marched, causing collisions and disorder in the ranks.

'Stop!' Kennedy yelled. From his expression, it was obvious he suspected some of the boys had deliberately caused the collisions. 'On the count of three, begin marching again,' he commanded. 'One ... two ... three.'

Once again the procession resumed and Gabe hummed the tune again.

Xavier groaned. 'Spare me.'

'But I like the music.'

'What is the point of this?'

'Discipline.'

'What for?'

'To keep us under their thumbs,' Gabe said. 'The music has a military feel, doesn't it? It gets in your head and heart. Maybe they're preparing us.'

'For what?'

'Battle.'

Stinky Eye, the imprints, the letters, new gargoyles and military marches—the reasons to act were mounting up in his head. On top of that, the voices were relentless. Xavier was tempted to salute Ratti as they passed her where she was now inspecting the boys from the top step outside the school foyer. When they were out of her range of sight and hearing, he turned to Gabe. 'I think we need to begin what we planned.'

* * *

CHAPTER 17

Trust

Just after breakfast on Saturday morning, the boys were making their beds before heading to the study hall. Since the gargoyle night and Ratti's threat to find the vandal, Xavier was on edge and a sharp knock at the door made him flinch.

'Relax,' Gabe said.

The door opened and Xavier breathed again when Crowley ducked his head in. 'Howard, you're wanted in the foyer by Ms Ratchet.' He was one of the few adults at Griswold who used the boys' first names.

'When, sir?'

'Right now.' He looked over his glasses and smiled reassuringly. 'I don't think you're in trouble,' he added, probably because Howard had gone pale. Crowley looked tired with dark circles under his eyes and the shirt under his tweed jacket appeared rumpled as though he'd slept in it. 'Don't let them worry you.'

When Crowley left, Howard turned to Xavier. 'Would you come with me, please?'

If Ratti was going to be there, it was the last place Xavier wanted to go.

'Please?'

Xavier weakened. 'I'll come as far as the bottom of the stairs but not to see Ratti in the foyer.'

Howard nodded with a frightened expression.

'Crowley said there was nothing to worry about,' Xavier said.

'You'll be fine,' Ethan said.

'Easy for you to say,' Howard said with a grim expression.

If Howard was a spy, Xavier couldn't understand why he would be afraid of Ratti.

As they walked down the stairs, Howard said, 'Why do you suppose she wants to talk to me? I do my study. I've done nothing wrong.' He sounded panicky. 'Maybe she thinks I'm the vandal she talked about at assembly.'

'Maybe you have to fill out a form or something stupid like that. Lots of kids get called to the office. It'll be nothing,' Xavier said as they descended the last flight of stairs.

'I don't see her. Would you stay, please?'

'Maybe you need to check the teachers' corridor.'

'No way!' Howard sounded horrified. 'I've heard about the corridor; it's an evil place.'

Within the last few minutes, Xavier was realising he did not know Howard. Was he trying to trick him into believing he was just one of the boys? He felt awkward waiting in the foyer with him as other boys and the occasional staff member stared as they passed them.

'I'm scared,' Howard admitted.

'Don't be.'

'Wouldn't you be? Maybe Crowley got the message wrong. Maybe she doesn't want to see me,' Howard said with a tinge of hope in his voice. 'What do you suppose is in them?' He was pointing to a pile of large cardboard cartons on the landing outside the main doors.

Xavier stepped outside to inspect the boxes, which were addressed to the school and stamped with the name, Ambrosia and an insignia.

'They come from your town,' Xavier said as he stepped back into the foyer.

'Shh. Here she comes,' Howard said softly. 'Please stay with me.'

'Mr Linnaeus, I've good news.'

'Yes, miss.' Howard's tone and face reflected his relief.

Xavier relaxed too.

'Your father is expected to arrive in the next hour. He returned from his mission earlier than expected and contacted me. You're to return home today.'

Howard emitted a reflex squeak of joy.

Ratti ignored it. 'You'll need to gather any belongings you have and report here in half an hour in case he comes early. I understand he's an important man and I don't want him kept waiting. I trust you'll tell him about the wonderful time you've had here over the past few months?' Her request was more like an order.

'Yes, Ms Ratchet.'

'Would you help him pack, Mr Jones?'

Xavier had hoped not to be noticed by Ratti. 'Yes, miss.'

Initially Howard seemed to be in shock, but soon words expressing his joy and relief tumbled from his lips. 'I'm going home.' He sounded as though he needed to convince himself.

Xavier felt envious.

'Thank you for being my friend,' Howard said suddenly.

'Pardon?'

'You're one of the few who've been nice to me. It's been so hard and lonely.'

Xavier didn't know what to say.

'I'm sure it was the letter that did it. When I came here I found a stamp I'd forgotten in my pocket. I begged Matron to give me an envelope and I wrote a long letter telling my father how awful it was here. I told him how I thought the teachers were evil and how I was cold and hungry and wanted to die.'

'But how did you post it?'

'Alex told me to try Grubner. I visited him and begged him to post it. Initially he wouldn't help me, but he softened and said he'd try. He must have done it. Will you thank him?'

Xavier felt a rush of confusion and guilt as he remembered what they had done to him the night of the birthday party.

'I'm so glad to get out of here.'

'You have to help us,' Xavier pleaded. 'All the boys here need your help.'

'I know and I'll try. I'll tell my father. Like I said, he's important, so he might be able to do something.'

When they returned to the room it was empty. Gabe and Ethan had probably already gone to the study hall.

'Will you say goodbye to them for me?'

Xavier suddenly felt emotional.

'I think you'll need to be careful,' Howard said. 'I think there's something very wrong about Griswold College and it's not just the bad food, lack of heating or nasty teachers. There's something bad going on here.'

An hour later, Mr Linnaeus, a tall stately man in a grey suit, arrived and was greeted by Ratti in an uncharacteristic manner. Xavier stood quietly to one side after being introduced to Mr Linnaeus because he seemed to show no interest in him. When Howard was reunited with his father, the man didn't hug him or look him in the eye. Instead, he ruffled his hair and lectured him about how he too had found boarding school hard, but that he had stuck it out. Xavier's mind numbed as Mr Linnaeus explained to Howard, the importance of resilience and fortitude and his disappointment that he hadn't managed to persevere at Griswold, but Howard seemed oblivious to his lecture. Xavier knew all Howard cared about at that moment was leaving Griswold.

Ratti listened silently but nodded in agreement with Mr Linnaeus. When he was about to leave, she gushed over the man, seeming to know exactly the right thing to say to him.

'I apologise, Ms Ratchet as I realise it must be inconvenient having a student withdraw midway through the term. As a token of my gratitude for you being so tolerant and understanding, I organised the delivery of gifts for St Griswold. Much to my surprise, they arrived before me.' He waved at the boxes outside the door.

Ratti raised her eyebrows.

'Howard suggested that perhaps the students could do with some warmer clothing. In the boxes, you'll find new jumpers and socks. There should be enough to go around, but if not please ring me and I'll have more delivered.'

Xavier could see Ratti's lips tighten as she looked at Howard strangely. No doubt she was curious to know how Howard had communicated with his father, yet she wasn't going to ask in front of Mr Linnaeus.

'I'm sorry, Mr Linnaeus, I think Howard has exaggerated a little. All the students are well catered for in terms of clothing and other requirements. But we're grateful for your generosity and I'll make sure the gifts are distributed to the students as you've requested.'

'Yes, I know, Howard's prone to flights of fantasy at times.' He chuckled. 'However, I'm sure you can make use of the clothing. I'll also send you a cheque to cover the school fees for the rest of the year as I know it might be difficult to find a replacement at this time of year and especially in these rather grim times.'

Mr Linnaeus went outside and opened a carton. He returned to the foyer carrying a jumper and a pair of socks, which he handed to Xavier. 'Perhaps you can test these for me?'

The dark blue jumper was soft and woolly and smelled brand new. Xavier pulled it over the top of his thin cotton jumper. It felt wonderful.

'Very grand,' Mr Linnaeus declared.

'Thank you, Mr Linnaeus.' Xavier could sense Ratti silently watching him, but he did not dare look her way.

Later, Xavier stood alone on the front steps of Griswold and waved goodbye to Howard as he drove out the gates with his father. He fingered the two stamps in his pocket Howard had managed to scrounge from his father and had given him as a parting gift. He knew, however, there was little hope the stamps or Mr Linnaeus would be their saviour.

* * *

Gabe and Xavier were sitting on their bunks in the dorm. Gabe was absentmindedly whistling one of the marching tunes from the previous day.

'It feels strange without Howard. I feel bad we misjudged him,' Xavier said.

'Better to be careful than sorry.'

'How can we ever know who to trust?'

'We can't,' Gabe said and changed the subject. 'So, do you think you're ready for the plan?'

'I think so.' Xavier sighed. 'To be honest, I'm worried about what the potion might do to us.'

'Can you think of an alternative?'

'I trust Artemis, but I'm scared.'

'I don't blame you. He didn't actually reassure me,' Gabe said.

'Don't say that. You're supposed to be the fearless one.'

'Yes, I am, but I'm not stupid. I prefer plans to be solid and logical.' Gabe reached under the bunk to retrieve the hidden flask. 'Are you sure you're ready?'

Xavier wanted to say no but agreed.

Gabe held the flask of green-tinged liquid up to the light. He pulled the stopper and smelled it. After dipping his finger in, he licked it and then bravely took a large swig. 'Your turn.' He handed the bottle to Xavier.

Xavier sipped it. 'It tastes okay for the black death—like pears.'

'I'll take your word for it.'

'You don't know them?'

'No.'

'Fruit, usually yellow,' Xavier said.

'Mmm, I must revise fruits.'

'How long do you think it'll take to work? I feel fine so far.'

'I'm sure we'll be rewarded.'

Xavier grinned. 'Maybe it's a dud bottle?'

* * *

That night Xavier lay awake monitoring his body for signs of illness. Eventually he fell asleep but was woken an hour later with a pounding head and an urge to vomit. He crawled out of bed only to find Gabe sitting hunched over the edge of his bed.

'You too?' Xavier said.

Gabe groaned.

Xavier shook Ethan until he woke.

'What is it?'

'Get Crowley,' he managed to say. His head swam as he rushed along the corridor to the bathroom with Gabe following closely behind.

Crowley arrived soon after to find both boys curled up on the bathroom floor.

'What's happening?' he asked in an alarmed tone.

'Sick,' Xavier moaned.

'Stay here while I get Matron. You stay here too, Ethan and watch them.'

Ethan looked horrified. 'Stay here? What if I catch it, sir?'

Crowley covered his mouth with his hand. 'You're right. Stand guard outside the door. No one comes in or out. Tell the boys to use another bathroom. We don't want this spreading.'

When Crowley returned with Matron, she took one look at the boys from the relative safety of the doorway. 'We'll need a doctor,' she said and covered her mouth.

'We'd better wait for Ms Ratchet,' Crowley said in a concerned voice.

Feeling as though he was going to die, Xavier groaned and vomited. Gabe was lying face down and making strange noises. What had Artemis done to them? It was possible they might not survive while waiting for the doctor. He broke into a fit of coughing and then moaned loudly, 'I'm going to die!'

'Don't bother Ms Ratchet. I'll call the Rosegrove doctor,' Matron said from behind her hand as she turned and hurried away.

An hour later a pair of masked ambulance officers burst into the bathroom carrying a stretcher.

'Take him first,' Xavier said and waved weakly at Gabe, who was barely conscious. It seemed an eternity as he lay on the cool tiles and waited for their return. They lifted him carefully onto the stretcher and carried him out to the waiting ambulance. Each movement sent jags of pain into his aching limbs. Perhaps Artemis had miscalculated the strength of the potion.

The trip to Rosegrove was a blur. Men's voices merged with the roar of the engine, the clank of the gears and the hiss of the oxygen mask over Xavier's face. When the ambulance finally stopped, the men whisked Gabe away. Minutes later they returned for Xavier, placed him on a trolley and wheeled him down a long white corridor with lights flickering overhead.

'Xavier, Xavier,' a voice called to him.

He found it difficult to open his eyes.

'We've given you the antidote. It won't be long.'

Gradually the turmoil and pain eased and the faces above him started to make sense. Two people stood over him, one in a white coat.

'Are you alright?'

Xavier focused and grinned.

'You gave us a scare.' The voice belonged to Artemis.

'I gave you a scare?'

'I'm sorry,' Artemis said. 'The potion was obviously stronger than what I anticipated, but you'll be fine soon.'

'What about Gabe?'

'He's a little worse but recovering quickly.'

Xavier smiled weakly. 'For once I win.'

Artemis looked worriedly at the other man.

'Just a joke,' Xavier explained. 'Gabe likes to be the best.'

Gabe groaned. 'Rubbish, I obviously drank more of the potion.'

The man grinned at Xavier.

'I saw that.' Gabe sounded huffy.

'I must introduce you,' Artemis said. 'Angus, this is Gabe and Xavier.' He indicated each boy in turn.

'Thanks for helping us,' Xavier said to the doctor as he sat up.

'My pleasure, although I dare say it wasn't the most pleasant experience for you.'

'But necessary,' Artemis added.

'You're in the quarantine ward,' Angus said. 'The plan is that I'll keep the door locked to the ward and I'll be the only one permitted to visit. I don't imagine any staff members will be eager to come in here as they saw your state when you arrived and won't want to catch what they imagine is a virus. I'll get rid of the meals that are placed in the chute over there and put towels in the laundry hamper every day, so it looks as though you're here eating and showering. You can escape through a small locked door at the back of the ward.' He handed a key to Xavier.

'Thanks.'

'When do you plan to go?' Angus asked.

Gabe sat up 'Tonight.'

'Night? What of the demons?' Angus said with a look of horror. 'No one safely wanders the streets here at night or worse, the open country.'

Gabe shook his head. 'We're accustomed to the dangers. With two pairs of eyes, I'm sure we'll be fine.'

'Don't be too confident,' Artemis warned. 'There's another matter. I've contacted a friend. He's asked that I not give him your name or address, but rather he said he'll find you in Ambrosia.'

Xavier looked at him with an expression of disbelief. 'No name?'

'He's worried you might be captured and then spill his name to the Darklaw.'

Xavier was annoyed.

'I'm sorry,' Artemis said. 'I can't betray the trust of a friend. If you reach Ambrosia, he'll find you.'

'If we reach Ambrosia?' Xavier's look of dismay grew.

'You can return to Griswold if you fear this journey or it becomes to challenging,' Artemis said. 'No one will think any less of you.'

Xavier sighed. He knew they had no choice.

'I'll make sure you get an evening meal before you go,' Angus said. 'The hospital food will get you going.'

'High energy food is it?' Gabe asked.

Angus laughed. 'No, that was a joke. It's awful. Most patients can't wait to leave once they've had a few meals here.'

An hour or so after Angus left, there was a knock at the door.

'I thought no one was supposed to come in here,' Xavier said in alarm.

When the door swung open, a young nurse wearing a face mask stepped into the room carrying a tray. 'Your dinner,' she said and pulled the mask down to reveal her face.

'Beth!' Xavier said.

'Shh, not too loudly. Artemis helped me sneak in to see you. He told me you're leaving tonight. I wanted to wish you luck.'

Xavier wondered whether her visions told her they were going to need it. Surely though, if she thought something terrible was going to happen she would say.'

She looked at Xavier thoughtfully. 'No, I can't tell your future.'

'Cannot or will not?' Gabe asked.

'I thought if I came to see you I might get a vision, but there's still nothing.' She smiled wistfully. 'One thing I can help you with though is dinner.'

'I wish you were coming with us,' Xavier said.

'Please don't take any risks and try to get back here as soon as you can. I'll try and make it back here at the end of the week. While you're gone, I'm going to be helping Artemis and Sarah discover where the Darklaw are taking people.'

'Then you need to be careful too,' Xavier said.

'I will,' she said and smiled.

* * *

CHAPTER 18

Flight from Rosegrove

Xavier and Gabe pulled on the jumpers Artemis had left them. They were warm and lightweight with slits in the back for their wings. He'd also given them a torch, map, compass and a pair of swimming goggles each to protect their eyes from dust and insects while flying. Gabe had brought the special glasses Artemis had given them the first time they met. He had poked them in his pocket just before taking the potion. It was fortunate he hadn't broken them when he had fallen ill and ended up on the bathroom floor of Griswold College.

'I wouldn't mind staying here for a while. Great bed, hot showers, warm room and the food tastes great compared to Griswold's.' After pulling on the small back pack so it sat between his retracted wings, Xavier adjusted the straps.

The boys slipped out quietly into a small yard, which backed onto a lane. It was nearly midnight as Xavier opened the latch on the gate and a cat yowled and skittered through ahead of them. With effort, he took a few deep breaths to steady his nerves. A blustery wind sent leaves swirling ahead of them down the deserted lane. Clouds scudded across the face of the only visible moon, throwing the lane into darkness and making Xavier long to retreat to the hospital ward.

'We'll be fine,' Gabe said softly.

Xavier was surprised by his comment. Perhaps even he was scared and was trying to convince himself otherwise. Oddly it gave him courage. 'Sure, I know. Let's get moving.'

They started to run along the network of lanes that crisscrossed the town and towards the outskirts until eventually, they reached the surrounding farmlands where they stopped for Gabe to get his bearings with the compass. The wind howled across the paddocks, which were now only faintly lit by a moon showing through the cloud.

'Is this a good idea?' Xavier asked.

'We'll be okay. See that star?' Gabe pointed towards a large orange-tinged star blinking in the night sky and breathed a long sigh. 'Isn't it beautiful?'

'Yes, I suppose so.'

'Not only is it beautiful, but I can use its position to guide us.'

'Okay, which way do we go?'

'I've already calculated that.' He pointed at the dim outline of a hill in the distance.

The boys stretched their wings and pulled their goggles on.

'Ready?'

Xavier's heart thumped as he turned and faced the empty track beside the paddock. They ran quickly, picked up speed and then flapped and jumped until they were airborne. The air rushed across Xavier's face, through his fingers and across his back. Once again, he felt a surge of excitement. He would never take flying for granted. Effortlessly they skimmed over dark paddocks until they reached several gently undulating hills, where the wind died and the boys surfed pockets of warm and cold air. The clouds had cleared too, so both moons gave a ghostly light.

'If we fly parallel to the Northern Highway, we'll need to veer west about two thirds of the way to Shademoor,' Gabe said.

Xavier glanced at the old watch Artemis had given him, but its hands were still. 'How long do you think it'll take?'

'Just over two hours at this pace.'

Flying over farmland, Xavier noticed the occasional light from a lone homestead piercing the darkness. He wondered about the farming families living in fear of the demons prowling the night sky. No doubt they were too afraid to turn their lights off. 'I hope the moon stays visible, otherwise we'll need to go to ground and wait for daylight. Maybe we should use our torch.'

'We would only be inviting demons to dinner,' Gabe said.

Xavier noticed rows of dark regular shapes on the other side of the highway. 'What are they?'

'Land now,' Gabe ordered.

'Why?'

'Just do it,' Gabe said quietly as he surveyed the sky. 'It's a Darklaw camp.'

Both boys touched the earth and ran along the ground until they slowed to a walk.

'Do you think we were seen?'

'Hard to say,' Gabe said in a bare whisper. 'There's a rocky outcrop ahead.'

Both boys ran towards the deeper shadows and slipped behind a pair of large boulders just in time to see dark shapes swooping in from every direction. Two of the figures landed and from the cracking of leathery wings, Xavier knew at once they were demons.

'Nothing here,' hissed one of the creatures.

Xavier flattened himself against the rock and crouched as low as he could.

Another of the creatures sniffed at the air. 'Smell something,' it declared.

'Animal or stinking human?' asked another.

'Not sure,' it said and growled.

Xavier could hear their leathery wings creaking and claws scraping the sand as they circled them. He closed his eyes and covered his ears. Moments passed. Would they die here in the dark? Artemis wouldn't know their fate—and what about his parents? They would never know.

Something grabbed his arm. He wanted to scream but was too weak with fear. It was pulling him now, yet it felt strangely soft and warm.

He heard it call his name even though he had his hands over his ears. How did it know his name? Slowly he withdrew his hands from his ears.

'Xavier, open your eyes,' Gabe said. 'They've gone.'

'Where?'

'They just took off. Maybe they caught the scent of a rabbit or something. We'd better walk for a while.'

'I'm not sure I can. My legs are jelly.'

'You'll be fine once you get moving.'

'How come you're never afraid?'

Gabe shrugged. 'What's there to fear? If they'd caught us, it would have been only a few short moments. My job would be finished. If that's what's intended, I've no control over it.'

'So you don't care?'

'Care? I've never thought about it that way. I don't like pain, but if it's my fate—it is. All I can do is my best in the moment. The rest takes care of itself, for better or worse.'

Xavier looked at him intently. Gabe had no family or history, so there was no one for him to think about or remember. He felt sorry for him and as he thought about it, the more he suspected his fearlessness was probably nothing to do with bravery. It was just instinctive.

They walked for a few kilometres as close to the highway as they dared but kept in the darker shadows of the vegetation.

'We need to veer off here, towards the Eerie Lakes. We should encounter the road between Shademoor and Ambrosia if we do,' Gabe said.

'We could fly.' To Xavier, somehow the thought of moving more quickly seemed safer.

They took off again into the night air, thankful the wind had dropped and the sky was still clear.

'The road,' Gabe said and pointed ahead. 'We'll see the lakes in less than an hour.'

As they skimmed over the empty land, Xavier found the lack of farms or towns unnerving. 'What is this place? It doesn't feel right. Nothing's growing.'

'A signpost!' Gabe declared and as they approached it, he read aloud, 'Eerie Lakes 10k.'

Xavier wished for daylight. When at last he spotted a change in the dim landscape, he knew the lakes had to be close. 'I think we'd better slow down, just in case there are Darklaw or shape shifters camping by the water.'

When they spotted a lake, the boys crept between large rocks to the water's edge.

'Tastes okay,' Gabe said quietly after he'd sampled the water.

Both boys kneeled on the sand, cupped the water with their hands and drank. When they had finished they turned and retraced their steps but were startled to see a figure ahead in a white gown sitting on one of the rocks but looking away from the lake. She was brushing her hair.

'A girl,' Xavier whispered. She had pretty hair—long, blonde, beautiful and it was shining in the moonlight. He wondered if her hair matched her face. But what was she doing here?

Gabe grabbed his shoulder and whispered, 'Could be a shifter.'

The boys crept silently towards the passage between the rocks hoping not to disturb her, but she turned suddenly.

'Raphael!' Xavier exclaimed. 'I thought you were a ... I mean what are you doing here?'

'You thought I was what?'

'He thought you were a girl,' Gabe said bluntly.

Xavier wanted to elbow him.

Raphael flicked his hair back haughtily.

'I'm sorry but ... a gown, long hair and you had your back to us.

And my eyesight isn't great in dim light.' Xavier's voice trailed off with embarrassment. He introduced Gabe to Raphael and then asked, 'What are you doing out here?'

Raphael glared at them as though still simmering. 'Hmm well, I was expecting you, wasn't I?' He placed his hairbrush on the rock beside him.

'How did you know?' Xavier asked.

Raphael rolled his eyes. 'I'm not earthbound.'

'What's that?' Gabe asked looking at a glowing, pale-green pendant suspended on a loop of leather around his neck.

Raphael slipped it under his gown. 'Just a trinket.'

'Why were you looking for us?' Xavier said.

'You never stop asking questions, do you, Xavier?' Raphael brushed some dirt specks off his gown. 'Don't you remember our last encounter?'

'It's difficult to forget.'

'Is there going to be another battle?' Gabe said.

Raphael raised an eyebrow at him. 'Steady on. I'm only here to guide you through the Eerie Lakes and Affron Flats.'

'I've a compass,' Gabe said. 'We'll be fine.'

Raphael's eyes glazed over as though in a trance.

'And I'm a guardian angel,' Gabe said with a hint of indignation.

Xavier ignored Gabe and turned to Raphael, who was pulling his hair from his eyes. 'What is it? What do you see?'

'I doubt whether you'll have time to consult your compass. You could always throw it at them, I suppose.'

'Demons?' Gabe said.

Raphael shook his head.

Xavier was exasperated with his games. 'Just tell us, please.'

Raphael closed his eyes and swayed.

'What?' Xavier mouthed to Gabe, who tapped his foot impatiently.

Suddenly Raphael opened his eyes. 'A horde of shifters with wolves are headed this way—and they're hostile.' He picked up his hairbrush, poked it in a silver pouch on his belt and climbed down from the rock.

'Where should we hide?' Xavier asked anxiously.

'Yes, you've a dilemma. Hiding won't help as they have wolves. You can't fly away either as they'll morph into winged creatures and chase you. Water's your only hope.'

'Can't they shift into fish?' Xavier asked.

'No. They don't like water, so they won't venture far beyond the shallows,' Raphael said.

Xavier gazed across the black water at the delicate mist floating over its surface.

'The further you go in, the safer you'll be. But beware what lies in the lake,' Raphael said.

'What? What's in the lake?' Xavier asked frantically.

'Can't you just explain?' Gabe sounded angry.

'Well, ex—cuse me.' Raphael wandered behind a group of rocks.

'Where's he gone?' Xavier said.

Gabe shrugged.

'Did you hear that? It sounded like dogs,' Xavier said.

They raced back to the water and waded into the shallows. Immediately water filled Xavier's shoes, yet he was grateful for them as he felt things catching at his feet. Reeds draped and slimed his legs and as he pushed into the deeper water, soft jelly-like masses bumped and scraped him from all directions. Trembling, he tried to block out the sensations. He could hear the shifters shouting and squabbling in guttural tones as they moved closer. Through the reeds, he saw growling wolves on leashes snapping at the air. A fish disturbed by the boys' presence, broke the surface and then dived and swam away from them.

The shifters turned together in the direction of the splashing fish.

'Deeper,' Gabe whispered. 'Don't look at them. Your pale face will show in the moonlight.'

They waded silently into deeper waters until only their noses were above the waterline.

'Further,' Gabe whispered.

They paddled gently away from the shoreline. Suddenly a bird burst from the lake nearby and then flapped and squawked into the darkness. Instinctively, both boys slipped under the black water. It was too dark to see and all Xavier could hear were bubbles escaping to the surface. Terror of what lay underwater and of the shifters above paralysed him. Were they wading out to search for them now? How much did they fear the water? In the Ravenwood public pool, he was used to holding his breath underwater, but he wasn't used to dealing with bumping, slithery things. Soon the lake inhabitants were teeming, jostling and nipping at the boys. Xavier floated to the surface and poked his face above the waterline. Gabe had already done the same.

The cold seeping into his flesh and bones was unbearable. 'I can't stand it,' Xavier gasped.

'Wait,' Gabe said.

Xavier knew Gabe was right because he could still hear the shifters shouting and the wolves howling. Raphael had said as long as they stayed in the water, they'd be safe. The shifters would move on eventually. Xavier took a breath and sank again amid the churn of water creatures until suddenly something grabbed his arm. He screamed underwater and surfaced rapidly.

'It's okay, it was only me,' Gabe said. 'The shifters have gone.'

Shivering, they paddled cautiously towards the shore until they could feel the lake bed with their toes.

An enormous fish-like creature with rows of teeth and bulbous eyes reared from the deeper water they had come from. It dived and splashed water everywhere.

Yelling, the boys rushed to the shallows.

Seconds later and close to the boys, the fish burst from the water again with reeds draping and trailing its body. It gnashed its teeth and chopped at the air with its eyes fixed on them as it crashed to the water.

The boys tore through the shallows until they reached the dry sand.

Watching from the safety of the shoreline, Xavier shook violently as the lake creature flailed with fury at missing its prey. 'Wrong, wrong, wrong, Raphael's an idiot,' he said in a trembling voice. 'We could've died.'

'Not really,' Gabe said. 'I think he calculated the odds. He knew we wouldn't have stood a chance against the shifters and their hounds.'

'But, but, that,' Xavier said pointing a wobbly finger at where the crazed fish had disappeared.

'Raphael gambled and we won.'

Xavier sunk to his knees.

Gabe took his shirt off and wrung the foul lake water from it. 'I'm grateful to him.'

As Xavier slowly recovered, he knew Gabe was right but didn't admit it. He stretched out on the sand and stared at the sky. The stars had faded and to the east, the horizon was tinged with early morning light. 'How did he know we could fly?'

'He's one of us, of course,' Gabe said.

'Why couldn't he just tell us everything? Like where to go in Ambrosia and who to contact. I just don't get these heavenly messages or Celestial Power stuff. Everything has to be so complicated.'

'Don't ask me,' Gabe said. 'I trust there's logic or a higher scheme.'

'What do you suppose the shifters would've done to us if they'd caught us?'

'Enough questions. We've an hour or so of flying before we'll become obvious to those on the land. Our next landmark will be the Affron Flats.'

As the boys shook the water from their clothes and prepared to fly, Xavier said 'How will we recognise the Flats?'

Gabe looked at him as though he were slow.

'Oh, of course, the land will be flat,' Xavier said.

Once again they ran until they were able to take off. The soft light of dawn illuminated the circular lakes, which now appeared blue and friendly against the red soil. They skimmed over the shimmering water, sparse bushes and squat trees and beyond the gently sloping dunes. The shifters, wolves and water beings became a bad memory with the next uneventful stretch of the journey. They soared and dipped with the thermals, hearing only the whistle of wind in their ears. Gradually the land flattened and they realised they were crossing the Affron Flats. The earth was flat and unmarked by any landmark—no bush, tree or man-made structure—and free from observers.

* * *

CHAPTER 19

Reginald Gustavius

It was after midday when Xavier and Gabe spotted Ambrosia in the distance. Farmhouses now dotted the landscape, so the boys, fearing they might be seen, dropped to the main road and walked. Vegetables, green, leafy and plentiful, gorged on black, loamy soil either side of the road while the great Ferntree River roared nearby as it fed them water from irrigation pipes and sprinklers. Ambrosia was big and bustling, the largest city Xavier had ever seen. The roads from Lanoris and Shademoor converged just out of town and traders lined the short stretch of highway with carts bearing fruit, fabric, vegetables, wine and flowers.

The smell of sizzling bacon, brewing coffee and baking bread made Xavier giddy with hunger. He shelled out a few of the coins Artemis had given them to buy breakfast. 'So, where to now?'

Gabe contemplated his bread roll dripping with butter and stuffed with bacon. 'I think we should head to the centre of town and once we have our bearings, venture west towards the forest. If Artemis' friend finds us that will be useful, otherwise we're on our own.'

'Perhaps we could skirt around the city centre. Darklaw agents would probably hang around main streets.'

'Hmm, smart thinking,' Gabe said between chews.

Xavier tried to remember if this was the first time Gabe had given him credit for a good idea.

A steep road leading to the main street was crowded with shop owners promoting their wares and people sidling past each other carrying baskets of shopping. Some called to each other while others laughed and chattered on corners or ate and drank at tables in colourful eateries. They wore a range of attire from exotic gowns, vivid scarves and sashes, tunics or formal robes to the plain garb of workers and farmers. Here in Ambrosia, it was as though someone had plucked people from every status and culture, time and place and shaken and scattered them to the wind. Xavier liked the fact that no one seemed to notice or mind. But as he thought about it, he realised how hard it would be to tell anyone's true nature in this chaotic jumble. As they wandered along the pavement, he ogled at the shops brimming with chocolates, perfumes, art, toys, herbs and books—from the mundane to the bizarre. He had never seen anything like them. 'Ambrosians must be very wealthy.' He wished he could take basketfuls of food back to Griswold College.

'Darklaw,' Gabe said suddenly under his breath. 'Don't look. By the fountain.'

Three men in dark grey suits turned into the main street from an alley.

'There's a lane ahead,' Gabe said.

The boys slipped down the small side street and ran until it crossed another lane, which they turned into. After another turn, they had come full circle back to the main road. As they entered it cautiously, they could see the Darklaw marching in the opposite direction.

'That was close. Do you suppose they'd recognise us as strangers?' Xavier said.

Gabe shook his head. 'I don't know, but I didn't want to wait around to find out.'

'Where do we go now?'

'If we found a library, we could check maps of the area.'

'Great idea,' Xavier said. 'I don't understand; Artemis said his friend would know when we'd arrived here.'

'We've just got here. Be patient.'

A boy close to their age and dressed in a long shirt and leather pants and boots strode by carrying a basket of vegetables.

'Hi,' Xavier called to him.

'Me?'

'Do you know where the library is?'

He stopped and put the basket down.

'We're visiting here for the first time,' Gabe added.

'Where from?'

'Lanoris,' Gabe said. 'Our parents are visiting friends and we decided to look around.'

'And you want to go to a library?' He wrinkled his nose and looked at them suspiciously. 'Brothers, eh? You don't look much alike.'

'We have different fathers,' Gabe said. 'And we both love reading.'

The boy raised his eyebrows. 'You're going to have to be more careful with your stories around here.' He pointed to a side street on the other side of the fountain. 'Follow that road. You can't miss it.' He bent over and picked up the basket. 'Like I said, be careful.'

After walking several blocks they reached a park, and Xavier began to worry. 'How do we know if the boy was telling the truth? I think we need to ask directions again.'

A slight, dark-haired woman, who was rocking a pram while watching two children play on the swings, glanced at them several times. After Gabe took the glasses from his backpack and checked her aura, he nodded at Xavier.

Xavier approached the woman. 'Are you a local?'

Startled, she stepped back without replying and pulled her pram away from him.

'Sorry, I just wanted directions to the library.'

The woman relaxed slightly. 'Head down this street to the left about four blocks. It's the large building next to the fire station.'

Xavier thanked her and both boys took off in the direction of the library.

'Is it open?' Gabe asked when they reached a three-storey sandstone building beside the fire station.

They climbed a flight of steps leading to a double door entrance. Xavier pushed on one of the heavy wooden doors, which creaked as it slowly swung open. A typical airless smell of books and floor polish met the boys in the foyer, but unlike the Ravenwood Library, no cheery posters, bulletin board or pot plants greeted them. Another set of glass doors led them to a hunched, old woman sitting at a desk as though guarding the book collection behind her. Black eyebrows and a severe expression dominated her face, making her grey dress, cloud of white hair and ball of pale knitting wool fade into a soft fuzziness.

'Hello,' Xavier said.

She continued to knit and read from an old book that was propped on a wooden frame.

Although disconcerted by the echo, he repeated his greeting in a stronger voice. As they stood to one side, Xavier could see the book's yellow pages. He was impressed by her ability to knit and read at the same time, but wondered what the strange text was about. The small bell on her desk tinkled as he picked it up. 'Excuse me, miss.'

She jerked and glared at him through her bushy eyebrows while quickly slipping a bookmark in her text and closing it. 'Can I help you?'

Her voice wasn't familiar although the colour and intensity of her eyes disturbed Xavier. Every instinct screamed at him to be careful. He noticed Gabe had forgotten to put the glasses on, but he didn't need them to confirm it this time.

'Are you a librarian?' Xavier asked. She grunted, which he assumed meant yes. 'Do you have any geography books?'

'We're doing a school project,' Gabe added with an endearing smile.

'Indeed, what topic have you chosen?' Her voice was deeper and stronger than Xavier expected.

'I'm not sure,' Xavier said. 'What do you think, Tyson?'

Gabe shrugged. 'The Ambrosian Forest?'

'There's nothing remarkable about the forest. Every Ambrosian schoolboy knows it's just a wild wasteland. You'll not find anything of use in the library to help you. I can assure you.'

Gabe sighed. 'We know that, but a friend suggested it might be interesting.'

The librarian's eyes narrowed.

'She said it was once a place of wonder, so we're a little curious.'

'The Ambrosian Forest?' She snorted. 'Pray tell, what's your friend's name?'

'Annabelle Axley,' Gabe said with an innocent expression.

'And what school do you attend?'

'Ambrosia High,' Gabe said.

The woman rose to her feet and disappeared down an aisle. She returned a minute later with a large book and handed it to Gabe. 'Have a look at this and you'll be equipped to describe the jungle wasteland to your friend. If she isn't convinced, tell her to come and see me and I'll show her the book,' she said with a watery smile.

Gabe and Xavier wandered down the aisles until they found a few lounge chairs. Only a handful of people were in the library. They sunk into the chairs and enjoyed their softness. If the silence of the library hadn't been broken by coughing and the clatter of a dropped book, Xavier knew he would have fallen asleep within moments.

Gabe opened the volume in his lap. 'She's right. There are no roads or towns. From this map, it's just unexplored jungle. Look at the coastline to the far west of the forest. It's called the Wilderwreck Coast. Wilderwreck—I like that word.' He looked at the map again. 'There are shipwrecks everywhere, all the way to the bottom of Clanarde, especially where the Lonevale and Blackwater Rivers empty into the Deadly Strait.'

'Yes, I studied a map and memorised it last week at school.' Xavier felt a rush of excitement. 'Do you think one day we might see it all?'

'Maybe,' Gabe said.

'Sss'

'What was that?'

Gabe looked up from the book and frowned. 'What?'

'You didn't hear it? Sounded like an air leak.'

'Sst'

Both boys heard it this time.

A tall man with grey hair flowing over his shoulders and wearing grey robes stood nearby in the shadows of a column that stretched to the ceiling. With a stooped gait, he sidled to a chair where he sat and pretended to read a book. He kept his head down and whispered, 'Don't look at me.'

Xavier tried to ignore him by chatting softly to Gabe about a picture in his book of a shipwreck on the Wilderwreck Coast.

'Why did you ask about the forest?' the man said.

Xavier glanced at him.

'Don't look,' he repeated. 'You're not from around here, are you?'

'Why do you want to know?'

'I can help you. That's if you need my help.'

'How do we know who you are?' Gabe asked quietly.

'Artemis,' he said and then closed his book and stood. 'Come outside in ten minutes. Follow me but not too closely.' Not waiting for their reply, he turned and strode towards the front doors.

The weather had changed by the time the boys left the library and entered the street. The wind blustered and the air chilled as the sun disappeared behind murky clouds. On the corner of the next block, the man was standing at a bus stop. When he spotted them, he set off in the direction of the park. They followed, but when they got to the park, he had vanished.

Xavier plonked on one of the seats. 'Now what?'

'Sss'

'Did you hear that?'

'It's me, behind the tree. Don't look up.'

Xavier couldn't help himself and when he turned his head, caught a movement behind the trunk of an oak tree nearby.

'There are shifters everywhere—the librarian, the man in the uniform outside the library. You didn't notice him, did you?'

'How do you know?' Xavier said.

'I make it my business.'

'What about you?' Gabe asked. 'How do we know you're not one of them?'

'You don't, but I'm not, and you need to trust someone. I know Artemis.'

'So?' Gabe said.

'He contacted me last week and said you might need help. I tracked you to the library.'

Although he seemed trustworthy, the boys were wary from habit.

'Come with me to my house. I can give you food and lodgings for the night and tell you about the Ambrosian Forest.'

Xavier glanced at Gabe questioningly.

'I'm guessing the book you were looking at in the library wasn't particularly helpful? Others have sought the same information.'

'What were they looking for?' Xavier asked.

'The Farseers—to know their future or seek refuge with them. What's your reason?' The man suddenly retreated into the shadows. 'Quick! We must go. Darklaw are coming. The librarian must have alerted them.'

The boys followed him through an alley between two houses that backed onto the park. Within a few minutes, they had reached a small cottage at the end of the lane.

Although Xavier didn't sense any particular danger, he still felt the urge to run away. This was reinforced when he noticed Gabe discreetly checking the man with his glasses.

'What's your name?' Gabe asked.

'Reginald Gustavius at your service.' He unlocked his front door and welcomed the boys inside. When the boys had introduced themselves, he said, 'Yes, I've been expecting the leader and guardian for many days now.'

Xavier flinched as he was surprised and unsettled knowing Artemis must have revealed some of their story to him.

They followed him into a surprisingly bare room devoid of character or decoration that served both as a kitchen and lounge. Gustavius hummed and snapped his fingers at the fireplace. A flurry of iridescent particles swirled from his fingers through the air, settled on kindling in the fireplace and then burst into flames. 'Now do you trust me?'

Intrigued by the magic, Xavier said, 'You're a wizard, aren't you?'

Gustavius nodded. 'Just like Artemis.' He took a pot from the fridge and poured its contents into a saucepan. 'Sit and warm yourselves.'

Apart from a mantle over the fireplace with a few framed photos, there were few signs of colour or comfort. Xavier sat before the fire on a brown, threadbare couch, which was parked on a matching rug. To one side, he noticed a small cupboard with drawers while at the kitchen end of the room there were only a few chairs and an old wooden table.

Gabe surveyed the empty room. 'No, I wouldn't say you're just like him.'

Gustavius stirred the saucepan. 'You'll join me for dinner?'

'Yes, thank you,' Xavier said.

'If I had more time, I would've prepared a special meal. I hope you don't mind leftovers?'

'Why don't you cook with magic?' Gabe asked curiously.

'I do most things manually. Cooking is a small pleasure. I especially enjoy taking ordinary vegetables like potatoes or leeks and seeing how creative I can be.'

'Artemis is like that,' Xavier said.

'He enjoys cooking?' Gustavius said. 'He never used to.'

'No, he enjoys repairing and making things with his hands.'

'It's a wizard thing,' Gustavius said.

Xavier salivated at the smell of the soup as he noticed the delicately carved carrot slices like little flowers and the spirals of leek bobbing to the surface. It puzzled him that a wizard who enjoyed creating food would live in such a dismal home.

Gustavius took a loaf of crusty bread from under a cloth and then cut and buttered slices to accompany the soup. 'I made the bread this morning, so it's fresh. Help yourselves.'

'What work do you do?' Gabe asked as he examined his soup.

'As you can see, I teach.'

The boys regarded him with puzzled expressions.

'All instructors in Ambrosia wear grey teaching robes.'

'What do you teach?' Gabe asked.

'Cooking at the Ambrosian Culinary Institute.'

'That's why this soup's so delicious,' Xavier said with a grin.

'How did you find us?' Gabe asked. Although he had checked the wizard's aura with his glasses, he still seemed wary.

'Easy. The locals notice every stranger and word passes quickly between us. We've had to develop a network to counter the Darklaw and Artemis said you'd be coming. We also have a mutual friend, I believe.'

Gabe and Xavier looked at each other.

'Raphael.'

'You know Raphael?' Xavier said in surprise.

'Yes, I met him last year. He just appeared at my front gate like a long-lost friend.'

'Why did he visit you?'

'It's not every day you're interrupted while hosing the garden by a man in a white dress with long golden hair. I thought he'd escaped from a hospital.' He chuckled. 'I hadn't seen him for ages, but last week he popped up again. I'm not sure why he singled me out, but he warned me of the growing Darklaw threat.'

Xavier smiled at the mental picture of Raphael although he thought it odd that Gustavius found his appearance strange when he himself was wearing a robe with a sash at his waist and long silver-grey hair beyond his shoulders.

'Raphael's a strange one—a bit unpredictable.' Gustavius looked at each boy in turn. 'So now you want to travel to the Ambrosian Forest?'

'We just need directions and a contact name,' Gabe said in a business-like tone.

'You don't trust me, do you?'

Gabe searched his face. 'It's not personal. I don't trust anyone, not lately anyway.'

'It's also because we don't want to put those who help us in danger,' Xavier said quickly as he didn't want to offend the wizard.

'I'll be back in a minute,' Gustavius said as he walked into another room.

Xavier picked up his glass of water and wandered over to the fireplace. As he enjoyed the warmth of the flickering flames, he caught his reflection in the large mirror hanging over the hearth. He had grown taller and his face looked different; his eyes were too wide open as though they had forgotten how to relax.

Gustavius returned with a photo album and handed it to Gabe, who leafed through the pages as Xavier peered over his shoulder.

'That's Griswold College,' Xavier said. 'And there's Artemis. I'd recognise his face anywhere, but he's so young.'

'The boy with the blonde hair on his left is me,' Gustavius said.

Surprised, the boys peered at the photo closely. Although the two boys looked close in age in the photo, Gustavius now seemed older than Artemis with his face more lined and shadowy and body, gaunt and angular.

'Griswold was a good place to be in the early years. Artemis and I were orphans and were brought up there.'

'So you're the child in the photo on the mantle?' Gabe said pointing at a framed photograph of a couple and a child.

Gustavius nodded.

'And they're your parents? What happened to them?'

Xavier felt embarrassed by Gabe's directness.

'I was never told,' Gustavius said with a sad expression. 'I was about five or six in my first year of school here in Ambrosia. One day someone came in a car to pick me up after school. He said my parents had been killed and drove me to Griswold. I never saw the driver again and no one at Griswold knew what had happened to my parents.'

Xavier imagined the horror of being so young and facing this tragedy alone. He could see the remembered pain in Gustavius' expression and attempted to change the subject. 'Did they teach you to be wizards at Griswold in the old days?'

'I was born with magic,' he said proudly, 'just like you and Gabe are angels. But I received further wizard tutoring at Griswold College.'

Xavier's glass slipped through his fingers, smashed on the floor and spilled water on the threadbare rug. 'I'm sorry,' he mouthed as his voice failed him.

Gustavius reached into a sleeve and pulled out a wand. He waved it slowly over the mess while humming a peculiar tune and in a flash the glass was restored. 'As for your identity, you can trust me, just as I trust you not to divulge my true nature.'

Xavier stared in astonishment at the slender wooden wand which was tapered and dark. It appeared old and well-used with scratches and divots covering its surface.

'You've not seen one before?' Gustavius said.

Xavier shook his head.

'Before my parents died, my father gave me my first wand. This is it, the original. I've never wanted to upgrade or do away with it. It's all I have to remind me of them, other than this house and my photos.'

'I haven't seen Artemis use a wand,' Xavier said.

'I like the old ways. Some see them as ostentatious and unnecessary, and I suppose these days there's a risk of being caught with one. When Artemis and I were brought to Griswold, we were assigned a tutor with a number of other young wizards. She refined our magic by teaching us how to use our wands and the spells—but things changed. Since leaving the school, I've always been careful, and I'd never leave my wand here.' He returned to the table. 'Shall we continue our dinner?' He removed the lid from a pot on the table to reveal a pie, which he sliced into large portions. 'Would you like cream with your blueberry pie?'

'Yes please,' Xavier said.

Gustavius flicked his wand at a silver canister on the table and conjured a swirl of cream on each pie slice. 'I apologise for not making it from scratch.'

'I wish I could do that,' Xavier said.

'It's not really an angel thing, but I'm sure you'll discover many talents that will compensate for not being able to conjure whipped cream,' Gustavius said.

'What music are you humming when you wave your wand?' Gabe asked.

'Spell songs. My father taught me some of them when I was very young and the Griswold tutor also instructed us.'

'I like them very much,' Gabe said. 'What I don't understand is why you and Artemis don't simply wave your wands and sing the Darklaw and demons away. You could march up the drive of Griswold College and flick and flatten teachers like Ratti and Ugly.'

'Magic isn't logical or free,' Gustavius said as he replaced his wand up his sleeve. 'It's a complex creature that usually exacts repayment in some form. Unfortunately it also attracts the attention of evil.'

'What did the cream cost?' Gabe said.

'For trifling magic, it looks the other way, but if you overuse it, the beast is less generous. Unless you bank energy before you dabble in more powerful magic, it drains you. Overly ambitious wizards have died conjuring powerful magic.'

'So when you use your wand, creatures like the demons know?' Xavier said.

'Not here within my home. The rooms are lined with cherry wood, which shields my magic from curious beings.'

Xavier frowned as he couldn't see any walls made from wood of any kind.

'Under the wallpaper you'll find plaster and under that is cherry wood,' Gustavius said. 'No demons or Darklaw can sense the magic I conjure here.' He rose from the table and carried his plate to the sink. 'I want to show you something.'

Xavier cleared the plates and cutlery from the table while Gustavius went to the large drawer in the lounge and took out a long cardboard tube. He took a cap off one end and carefully teased out a parchment and then unrolled it, spread it on the table and fixed its corners with paperweights shaped as little metal cats.

'It's Clanarde,' Xavier said.

After Gustavius hummed and tapped the parchment with his wand, the coloured ink on the map ran in different directions and reformed. 'I've learnt to be careful because if the Darklaw caught me with this map, there would be consequences.'

The boys didn't need to ask what the map depicted. To one side was a small black dot representing the town of Ambrosia while the rest of the expanse was filled with the Ambrosian Forest. The old map was covered in curly handwriting and beautiful symbols of waterfalls, tracks, rivers, trees, mountains and in the middle there appeared to be a town, but it was the only sign of civilisation in the entire forest.

'What is this place?' Xavier asked.

Gustavius shook his head. 'It's a secret place not many outside the forest know. Ariel is home to the Farseers and if you can get there, they may be able to help you.'

'If?' Gabe said.

'It isn't the Darklaw, shifters or demons that will worry you in the forest but rather, its elements.'

'I don't understand,' Xavier said.

'The trees, animals and weather are invested with old magic. They will try to prevent you reaching Ariel. It's said only those with good intentions will ever find Ariel.'

'We have to go there,' Xavier said firmly.

Gustavius regarded him with a thoughtful expression. 'Tomorrow morning I've a graduation ceremony to attend at my college, but before I go, I'll drive you to the entrance of the Ambrosian Forest. Right now however, you need to rest.' He led them to a spare room, which was like the rest of the house, unadorned and empty, apart from two beds. 'Where are my manners?' He hummed and waved his wand. Instantly, red quilts and plump pillows appeared on the beds, a plush rug covered the floor and two bedside lamps cast a golden glow over the room.

Once Gustavius had left, the two boys crawled into bed and quickly fell asleep.

* * *

CHAPTER 20

Tricky layers

Gustavius stood with the boys in a car park near a trail leading into the Ambrosian Forest. Unlike yesterday, he was wearing navy robes with a brilliant embroidered stole draped around his neck in readiness for the graduation ceremony he was attending later that morning.

With Gustavius' hair braided into multiple plaits, Xavier thought he looked odd, like an old grey octopus, but it was obviously an accepted custom in Ambrosia so he pretended not to notice. He felt nervous knowing that soon he and Gabe would be leaving him and heading into the forest.

'Before the arrival of the Darklaw, the tourists would arrive here in droves.' Gustavius' expression changed to one of sadness. 'Now only a few turn up and only in full daylight. The tourists would pour from the buses with their children and set up picnics on the lawn. While they feasted on chicken wings and bread rolls, guides told them about the magical creatures and folklore of the Ambrosian Forest and peddlers manned stands selling toy wands, magic tricks and glass globes with miniature scenes inside.'

'Do you mean snow globes?' Xavier said.

'Yes, that's right, but when you shook them you saw falling stars instead of snowflakes.'

'I'd very much like one,' Gabe said with a faraway look.

'So what do we need to know about the forest?' Xavier asked.

'Simple. Just stay on the path.'

'That's it?'

'That will be enough; however it won't be easy. Not many people venture into the forest and of those who do, few return. Seeking Ariel is fraught with danger.'

Xavier peered down the path bordered by overarching trees, but all he could see at the far end was darkness. 'Have you tried?'

Gustavius shook his head. 'Not everyone wants to know the future. Dealing with the past is often enough.'

Xavier noticed how Gustavius seemed to force a smile.

'Of course, it may be that those who ventured into the forest loved Ariel so much they decided to stay. I wish you luck, boys. Hopefully the Farseers can help you.'

The boys waved him goodbye as they ambled down the path in the sunlight.

Xavier felt a curious mix of excitement and fear as they set off. According to the map, it would take them half a day to reach Ariel if they stayed on the path. Knowing that the Darklaw and demons didn't venture into the forest made him feel relaxed and free for a change. He could sense Gabe felt the same because he was whistling marching tunes and swinging his arms to their beat.

As they wandered further into the forest, the trees and bushes grew closer together until the light began to dim. Eventually the blur of leaves, vines and branches became so crowded and entangled that he began to worry. What if the trees and plants encroached on the path? Birds screeched and insects scratched around them and overhead until their noise engulfed the boys.

After a couple of hours of steady walking, the vegetation thinned and daylight shone through, relaxing Xavier and convincing him Gustavius' warning about staying on the path had been exaggerated. The forest either side of the path now opened onto soft grassy verges like manicured lawns. He felt an overwhelming urge to lie and roll on the grass in the sun, but it was their third day away from the hospital, so he knew they had to keep moving.

Xavier pointed. 'What's that?'

A creature hopped ahead of them as though playing a game. It stopped, glanced at them and when it was close enough to pat, dashed from the path and scampered across the grass.

'That's an odd looking rabbit,' Xavier said. 'Where did it go?'

They slowed to examine the grass where it had disappeared.

Xavier gasped. A pile of clean bones and bloodstained white fur lay in a hollow. 'What happened to it?'

'I don't know,' Gabe said quietly. 'Maybe a fox or dog got to it.'

'I didn't see one.' Even after their encounter with wraiths and the First Strike battle, Xavier was left shocked. 'I don't like the look of this place. I want to go back.'

'We can't. If Gustavius' map is correct, I think we should have another hour of walking before we reach Ariel. If we turn back, we won't get out of here before nightfall. I know Gustavius said demons don't come here, but what if he's wrong?'

Unsettled, Xavier said, 'I think you need to check the compass.'

'Why?'

'I swear we're going in the opposite direction to what we were. Look at the sun.'

Gabe flicked his compass open and examined it. 'That's strange. You're right. Maybe we've taken a few turns.'

Xavier rubbed one of his aching legs.

'I think we need to jog,' Gabe said.

As they ran, each step jolted Xavier's legs causing him to moan. After a few kilometres he slowed to a walk. 'Can we rest for a while?'

'Okay, okay, we'll stop to eat, but only for a short time.'

The boys sat in silence after they had eaten their sandwiches.

'Listen,' Xavier said. 'That's weird. The wind—it sounds like someone's breathing. It's as though the bush is alive.'

Gabe's eyes were half-closed and he didn't reply.

'Wake up.'

'I'm so sleepy,' Gabe said. 'I just want to stretch out here for a few minutes and snooze.'

Xavier stood. 'Get up. It isn't safe. I can feel it.'

'It's fine.'

Forgetting his aching legs, Xavier grabbed and dragged on Gabe's arm. 'Remember what happened to us in Mourn Forest? We have to keep going.'

'Ouch!' Gabe rubbed his shoulder before turning onto his hands and knees and slowly standing up. He swayed, but Xavier pushed him firmly in the back.

'Move!'

Startled, Gabe opened his eyes wide.

'We could fly just above the path, so that we're still on it.' Although Xavier was afraid to fly because he feared that if they weren't strictly on the path they might be breaking a rule of the forest, he was now more fearful of walking slowly. 'Ready?'

They ran until they lifted off the path and then skimmed close to it. As they negotiated the curves of the path, Xavier relaxed slightly. His legs no longer hurt and they were rapidly gaining ground.

When the sun dropped lower in the sky and the trees and plants had lost their colour, and there was still no sign of Ariel, the boys decided to walk again.

Exhausted, Xavier wondered how much further he could go without resting. Suddenly the boys were both brought to a halt as the ground shook and rumbled and they battled to stay on their feet. As the motion and noise faded, an eerie silence pervaded the bush for a minute or so.

'What was that?' Xavier whispered.

'Thunder or a quake, I'm not sure. The light's almost gone. We can't go on.'

Reluctantly they agreed to stop for the night. They sat back to back on the path and stared into the growing darkness while listening to the creaking and scratching sounds surrounding them. Once again, the ground rumbled and shook, sending tremors through the boys' bodies. Soon the light faded until all they could see was the odd luminescent insect. A few more quakes rippled from underground.

Xavier gasped and pulled his knees up under his chin after something brushed his ankle. Were they fingernails? From the darkness, something seized his ankles and dragged him from the path. 'Help!' he screamed, not caring who or what heard him. But Gabe was yelling too and moving away from him. The hands—were they hands—yanked him harder causing his head to flick back and bang the ground. Dazed from the knock, Xavier's mind swam in mud. His eyes closed as he lost consciousness and when he opened them again, the bush had vanished. He was lying on his back in grass gazing up at a dazzling blue sky. Shocked he lay there gasping like a goldfish thrown from its bowl.

'Hello!'

As Xavier's head stopped spinning, his focus returned and he saw the speaker was a white-haired, young girl dressed in a wispy robe that looked as though it had been stitched from a pale rainbow. A wicker basket was strapped on her back. He watched as she leant forward and snapped a flower from its stem and threw it in the basket.

He closed his eyes for a few moments fearing he was seeing things, but she was still there when he opened them again.

'Are you alright?' the girl asked.

'I'm not sure.' He propped on his elbows. 'I was in the forest. It was early evening. Something dragged me here. Where am I?'

'Where were you before?'

Xavier sat up. 'My friend and I were in the Ambrosian Forest ...'

She leant forward to pluck another flower. 'You're in Ariel—well, almost. It's early morning. You'd better get up or you'll get wet with the dew.'

Xavier looked around the field and was relieved when he spotted Gabe striding through the grass towards them.

'Do you live in Ariel?' Xavier asked her.

'No, I'm from the Boundary Land, but I often visit to collect these.'

If she was from the Boundary world, Xavier knew he could trust her. 'We know your world. Is Ariel part of it?'

'No, but it's protected by us and the Ambrosian Forest.'

Xavier turned to Gabe as he joined them. 'Are you okay?'

Gabe nodded and greeted the girl.

'This is Gabe and my name's Xavier.'

'I'm Evie, I'm the flower collector.'

'What just happened to us?' Gabe asked her.

'The Ambrosian Forest's a strange place. Some are allowed passage to Ariel. You're lucky.'

Gabe picked one of the flowers. 'They're ayras, aren't they? They grow in Mourn Forest too. I read a book about flowers and I'm sure it said they were good for keeping moths out of cupboards.'

Xavier shook his head. How did he remember such things?

'We use ayras to keep demons and wraiths out of our portals.'

Xavier wondered why they needed flowers to do this. He thought they were safe. 'We met the Boundary Keeper in Mourn Forest,' Xavier said. 'Do you know her?'

The girl seemed surprised. 'You've actually met her?' There was a tone of reverence in her voice.

'She saved us from wraiths,' Gabe said.

'Actually we're in need of help again,' Xavier said to Evie. 'Can you help us?'

'Depends on what you need.'

'We're seeking a Farseer in Ariel. She might live in the hills. We were told she might be able to help us,' Xavier said.

'I'd seek the Ambrosian Princess. She lived as an outsider for a while. Although it may be difficult to find her. She'll decide if she wants to see you.' The girl adjusted the basket on her back. 'See the town in the valley behind you?'

The boys turned.

Confused, Xavier rubbed his eyes. 'Where did that come from?'

'She lives on the only hill in the town. Go there, but be warned, Ariel's like an onion with layers.'

Shading his eyes from the sun, Xavier noticed a building at the top of the hill. 'Does she live in the white-domed building?' When the girl didn't reply, he turned to see she had vanished. 'Where did she go?'

Gabe shook his head. 'I wonder if the princess is the woman on the hill who Beth saw in her vision.'

They both ran across the field, gathering speed to lift off the ground, yet as soon as they were airborne, the turbulent air tumbled and spun them back to the grassy field. After a few more attempts the boys decided to walk, but eventually both realised they were getting nowhere. To make matters worse, the gusts of buffeting wind were growing stronger.

Watching a butterfly, Xavier wondered how it seemed to have no difficulty flying towards the city. It flew in irregular spurts and rested at short intervals in the grass. Once it got caught in a gust and was flung backwards, but for the most part it made progress. 'It's like a game of snakes and ladders,' he said suddenly.

Gabe looked at him blankly.

'It's a human game,' Xavier explained. 'When the wind blows, we must stop or we'll get blown backwards, but when it drops we need to run towards the city. Watch the birds and butterflies; they get it. Perhaps it's a wind enchantment—the first layer of the onion.'

Gabe studied a tiny blue wren flitting in the direction of the city.

When the wind blew, it dropped to the earth to shelter in the grass. 'I think you're right. Shall we try it?'

They waited until the wind died and then sprinted towards the town. When it gusted again, the boys dropped to the ground. After a few efforts, they found themselves free of the field and on a dirt road they could trace all the way to Ariel.

'That wasn't so difficult,' Gabe said as they rounded a bend. 'And now the wind has dropped, it will be simple.'

'Or not.' Xavier had noticed to one side of the road ahead, an old wooden building with many windows that looked like a school or hall. A figure descended the steps at the front and was now almost running towards them. 'What's that?'

'Not human,' Gabe murmured.

A strange creature wearing a uniform, hat and gloves trotted towards the boys. When it was close enough to be heard, it stopped, pointed a white-gloved finger at them and in an officious tone said, 'Visitors, come here.'

As the boys neared, Xavier realised the official appeared to be a fully-clothed, male goat. He felt a giggle surfacing, but obeyed the creature.

The goat glanced at a clipboard of notes it carried and then asked in a wobbly voice, 'What is your business in Ariel?'

Xavier's lip twitched with the urge to laugh, yet Gabe seemed to think it perfectly normal being interviewed by a goat.

'We're here on a private matter,' Gabe said.

'And what would that be?' The goat bit the top off his pencil and crunched on the lead as he waited.

Gabe talked over the top of a gurgling noise Xavier made. 'We can't safely say.'

'Then you must follow me.' He led them to the building and like a traffic conductor, directed them with a solemn expression and a wave of his glove. 'Up the steps. That's the way. Don't dilly dally.'

Deciding it was safer to comply, the boys climbed the stairs and walked into a hall which housed a circle of desks manned by more goats. An oppressive stench of musk and humidity hung in the air. Xavier wondered if he had hit his head harder than he imagined and it was just a dream.

The first goat looked up from a pile of notes she was stamping and regarded them with pale eyes and a vacant expression. 'Fill out Form A and bring it back to the desk to my right,' she bleated and handed them a wad of papers and a pencil each.

The boys took the papers and wandered to one of the numerous booths lining the walls that were occupied by others obviously completing forms. Holding his nose to block the noxious smells, Xavier listened to a pair of dog-like beings squabbling in the booth next to them on their right.

'I've had enough,' one growled. 'These are the same questions on Forms A and B.'

'Shh, darling,' the other said. 'Don't complain; they'll hear you. It must be the procedure. They're testing our worthiness.'

In the booth to the left of the boys was a woman with a fish-like head wearing a blue and white summer dress and high heels, who was weeping quietly. Her tears were spilling onto her form, pooling and causing the ink to run and bleed across the page.

Shocked by her appearance, Xavier tried not to show it outwardly. 'Are you alright?'

'It's no use.'

'Just get another form. I'm sure they won't mind,' Xavier said.

She gulped and surveyed them with her closest eye. 'No, no, I can't do this anymore.'

'Take a break, you'll be fine.' Xavier smiled to cheer her up.

She looked as though she was going to burst into tears again. 'I've been here for days. I keep making mistakes and they keep giving me more forms.'

A goat hovered nearby and offered them sandwiches from a tray. 'You'd better take them. You'll need your strength for this.'

Xavier took a sandwich and after the goat had gone, he bit into it but gagged moments later.

'They're all goat cheese and cucumber, I'm afraid,' the fish woman said as she dabbed her nose with a spotted handkerchief. 'They're ghastly. I've heard they make the cheese out the back themselves.'

'Very interesting,' Gabe said. 'The goats' desks are in a circle, so you can never reach the end. What form do you have?' he asked her.

She flapped the puddle of tears from the page. 'Form AABM.'

'So it's a loop that never ends. I think we've seen enough. Come on,' Gabe said.

The woman's gills flapped agitatedly and she shook her head. 'If you want to go to Ariel, you must do it the right way. They have rules.'

Xavier followed Gabe out the door past the seated goats, who raised their heads and watched with surprised expressions. When they reached the bottom of the steps, Gabe confronted the gloved goat. 'Everything's in order. We have special permission to go on to Ariel. The Ambrosian Princess has requested our presence,' he announced boldly.

The gloved goat blinked and chewed. 'This is irregular. It's not the usual protocol. Please wait while I confer with my superior.' He trotted up the steps and glanced around several times obviously to check they were still there.

Once he had stepped inside the hall, Gabe turned to Xavier. 'We have to go.'

'But what if ...'

It was too late as Gabe had already begun to run down the road towards Ariel. Not wanting to be left when the goat returned, Xavier sprinted after him and launched into the air. Soon both boys were soaring high above the road while the dumbfounded goats emerged from the hall and stood in a huddle, watching them escape. And when they realised the boys were not coming back, the goats soon broke into a scuffle, arguing, bleating and head-butting each other.

'Do you think we're safe now?' Xavier asked when they finally reached the town.

'Since we've got this far, perhaps we'll be accepted.'

They passed under an archway where the road changed from dirt to cobbled stone and soon divided into three smaller paths. The boys chose the middle one which seemed to be heading in the direction of the hill. Either side of the path and as far as Xavier could see, white, low-set dwellings filled the landscape. They were built on curved lines with painted doors and shutters in various shades of brilliant aqua, gold and purple surrounded by gardens brimming with roses and jasmine.

Eventually the boys reached a lawn-covered clearing with several long cloth-covered tables set end to end. A rainbow chaos of flags and balloons strung overhead fluttered and bounced in the breeze. People laughed, chatted and sang as they sat at the tables enjoying a feast. Children ran around the lawn dodging men and women who were dancing on the lawn to music played by a small band.

'What are you celebrating?' Gabe asked a young woman carrying a bowl of salad to the table.

She laughed. 'Do we need a reason? Are you going to join us?' She pointed to two empty chairs.

Xavier smile politely. 'We're not guests. We're just visitors passing by.'

'I see you practise etiquette,' Gabe said as he inspected the blue and red napkins and cutlery arranged on the tables. He turned to Xavier. 'I'd very much like to practise and I'm rather hungry.'

The woman handed them plates and napkins. 'Have some chicken wings. Once you taste them you won't want to go!'

A tick of fear pulsed in Xavier's mind. Gustavius had said once they reached Ariel they might never want to leave. He glanced compulsively at this watch and noticed the second-hand moving slowly. 'Thanks, but we must keep going.' Xavier steered a complaining Gabe away from the table. 'We can't waste any time or become trapped, no matter how appealing this place is.'

Another woman pushed a plate of bread under their noses while a man jumped from his chair and offered it to Xavier. Children tugged at their hands and pleaded with them to dance and play. The boys declined their pleas and kept steering towards the path, but more people pushed towards them offering food and begging them to stay.

Trying to control his panic, Xavier said, 'Gabe, we have to go.'

'I know.'

People in the crowd became more insistent. Hands reached for the boys as they backed up.

'Stay with us,' voices clamoured.

'No, we can't,' Xavier said in a panicky voice.

'Don't go!' a child pleaded.

'Run!' Gabe yelled.

The boys turned and sprinted towards the cobbled path with some of the people in pursuit. It wasn't until they reached the path and had run for a few hundred metres that they heard the footsteps behind them die away.

'No more detours,' Xavier said in a shaky voice when they finally stopped to catch their breath.

As they neared the city centre and twilight fell, overhead lanterns inset with red and gold glass lit the pathway. They followed the path over an arched footbridge to steps set into the hill which led to the white-domed structure at its peak. Dusky pink petals that had dropped from vines overhead lay on the steps like a welcoming carpet. When the boys finally reached the top of the path, they walked onto a neat lawn that looked out over a glittering web of lanterns strung across the city. The lantern light illuminated more white buildings and in the centre of town, a circle of houses around a lake. In the distance, in every direction, dense forest surrounded Ariel and in the west, they could see the sun setting on the horizon of a black ocean.

Gabe appeared puzzled.

'What is it?'

'If Gustavius' map was correct, I would've thought we were hours from the coastline.'

The boys sprawled on a well-lit lawn to rest.

'What are you doing here?' a high-pitched voice demanded.

'Oh no,' Xavier said.

'This is private property.' A tall, middle-aged woman wearing sky-blue robes was restraining a powerful looking Great Dane while advancing towards them. 'Who are you?'

'We've come to see the Ambrosian Princess,' Gabe said as he and Xavier stood.

'I am the princess, but who are you?' She was a striking-looking woman with strongly arched eyebrows, brilliant blue eyes and high cheekbones, but she appeared strained with deep furrows between her brows and hollowed cheeks.

Xavier introduced himself and Gabe. 'We've travelled a long way to see you, Princess um.' He wondered how he should address her.

'Where from and why?' Her tone was cool as though she didn't trust them.

'Our school in Mourn Forest,' Xavier said and noticed her face blanch.

'St Griswold College,' Gabe said.

'That isn't possible,' she muttered.

'Please, we need your help,' Xavier said. 'Our friend had visions about you, an angel called Nisroc said we needed to see you and Gustavius helped us ...'

'Slow down.' She seemed to relax slightly. 'You may call me Merewyn.'

'And you're a Farseer?' Gabe said.

She nodded. 'Come.' With her head held high and a seemingly effortless gait, she guided them through a doorway and up a flight of stone steps that led to the main entrance of the domed building. However, she didn't relax her white-knuckled hold on the dog's leash, keeping the animal close by her side even while she stopped at a gate to unlock it.

'I promise we won't harm you,' Gabe said and patted the dog's head as if to reassure her. He pulled the glasses from his pocket and after checking Merewyn with them, handed them to her. 'You can test us.'

She obviously recognised their purpose and after inspecting her own hand, checked the boys' auras. Immediately her demeanour changed.

'Even in Ariel, I'm wary these days. Come with me.' She guided them down a walkway lined with white columns and statues.

'This place is beautiful,' Xavier said.

'The style is from ancient Greece.'

Xavier and Gabe looked at each other with puzzled expressions.

'You haven't studied history?' she said in surprise and then explained, 'The building is designed in the style that belonged to an ancient Earth civilisation, the Greeks.'

'Our knowledge of history before the Atomic War is very basic,' Xavier said. 'We were taught to look ahead.'

'This place reminds me of the Boundary Keeper's home in Mourn Forest,' Gabe said.

Merewyn glanced at Gabe and appeared as though she was going to comment, but instead invited the boys into a large room with a sunken lounge adorned with many bright coloured cushions. 'Please sit and relax.' She rang a small crystal bell and then released the dog, which padded over the carpet and lay in front of the boys.

A man emerged from an adjoining room.

'May we have refreshments, please?' Merewyn asked.

He bowed and returned in the direction he had come.

'This place doesn't really belong to Clanarde or the Boundary Land, but rather, sits on the cusp. Ariel is guarded by those from the Boundary world and the natural elements of the Ambrosian Forest. It has long been a place of refuge for Farseers from those who might exploit them, but the world's changing and even we are no longer so sure of our safety.'

'The Boundary Keeper said we couldn't stay in her world,' Xavier said.

Merewyn paced as she spoke. 'The Keeper knew it wasn't right for you to stay in the Boundary Land. She has great wisdom.'

'People stay here though, don't they? That's what Gustavius said.' Xavier noticed her eyes widen.

'Yes, you could stay in Ariel and you'd be welcome. In fact, I'd recommend it as it isn't safe at all for you to return to St Griswold College.'

'Do you know Gustavius?' Xavier asked and watched her reaction more closely. This time she didn't flinch, or was she working very hard to control her response? Xavier couldn't tell.

'His name rings a bell,' she said as she sat on the couch. 'Now tell me your story and why you've come to see me.'

Xavier curled up amongst the cushions and gazed at the blue and white mosaic on the wall as Gabe told their story. He was so exhausted that he found himself drifting off and didn't stir until he was woken by the sound of clinking glass. A breeze wafted through the archway ruffling the red and gold tapestries framing the entrance to the room. The servant returned with a tray of sandwiches and glasses filled with clear liquid and decorated with lime slices. Xavier took one of the drinks gratefully. Things had changed since he had left Ravenwood. He couldn't even have a simple thought about heaven without stirring giddy thoughts about the Celestial Force, shifters, wars, angels and demons. He wished he could turn his mind off and go back in time two or more years when he was safe with his family. At least here though, he was warm and comfortable, had a roof over his head and food, he thought as he bit into his sandwich and relished the taste of lamb, mint and tomato. He listened as Gabe told him about their journey to Ambrosia and Ariel.

'What exactly do you want from me as a Farseer?' Merewyn asked. 'My visions like your friend Beth's are often incomplete. I can give you the pieces I know about your past and perhaps glean future glimpses. I'll do my best.'

'Would you tell us what you think is important to us,' Gabe said.

'First there was the birth of the universe nearly fourteen billion years ago. Earth began around 4.5 billion years ago, but man arrived recently in comparison. A thousand years ago, brave explorers set out from Earth. Some who were born in space also died on the journey. Those who reached new planets like Kepler settled and multiplied.'

Xavier stifled a yawn as he felt as though he was listening to a Crowley history lesson back at Griswold.

'Can you tell me more about how the evil came to be?' Gabe asked.

The light faded in the room. Merewyn stood and held out her hand to reveal a golden sphere, which floated from it into the air where it spun like a planet suspended in space.

Fascinated by the hint of magic, Xavier sat upright.

Merewyn pointed at the sphere. 'Kepler before the war.' She waved her hand and several more spheres of varying colour appeared in the air as did pinpricks of white light. 'Our moon, stars and surrounding planets.' In the far corner of the room, a fiery red orb materialised and floated to the centre of the room. 'Our sun.' The coloured orbs revolved around it. 'This was our universe, but then there was war. Generations have fought and died in many wars on Earth and Kepler, but it was the Atomic War that proved the most devastating. I know you would've learnt about it at school, yet there's much you wouldn't know.'

The boys listened intently.

'The Atomic War tore the fabric of Kepler. Every school child knows the planet's spin was altered by the bombs and everyone was told it was harmless. But the war caused other ripples within an unseen dimension in our universe.' She pointed to one corner of the room and a ribbon of glowing green slipped across the room, and wove in and out between the planets until it touched lightly against Kepler a few times. 'The green ribbon is the Boundary Land. New portal connections formed between Kepler and parallel places like the Boundary world. This association proved harmless because the Boundary people had no desire to meddle with the lives of humans.'

She flung her arm dramatically and from the other side of the room, a black ribbon and shiny dark orbs slipped and spun towards Kepler. The ribbon snaked and lashed at Kepler and then arched and rippled until it rebounded away from the planet drawn to something else in another dark corner of the room with the dark orbs following. 'But other links, though temporary, were forged between dark worlds and Kepler. Demons, shape shifters and other foul creatures crossed over and remained here when their links vanished. It did not take these beings much time to establish their evil ways. Some humans sided with them and so the Darklaw and darkness began.'

'What does Griswold College have to do with this darkness?' Gabe asked.

Merewyn lowered her hands and the glowing orbs and pinprick stars faded. Soft lights now lit the room with reassuring warmth. 'I do not see the school in my visions,' she said in a distant tone.

'Have you ever seen it?' Gabe asked.

Xavier noticed her eyes were glassy and unfocused and wondered if the magic she had just woven drained her or whether she was avoiding the question.

'Have you ever travelled outside Ariel?' Xavier asked.

'When I finished my schooling, I grew restless, so my parents allowed me to go to university in Laurendale. Once I finished there, I didn't last long in the outside world.'

'What about our part in all of this? They said I was meant to lead, but I've no idea what that means,' Xavier said.

'Look how far the quiet schoolboy has come. You've already begun. My visions tell me you risked your life to help others in the First Strike and again coming here.'

'Would you be able to help us?' Gabe said to her.

'We wouldn't expect it of you, but there's no one else. We must bring the six to Griswold.' Xavier said. 'The angel Nisroc said so.'

She startled.

'If we need you to come to St Griswold, would you please?' Xavier persisted.

'I've not been entirely truthful,' she said.

The boys looked at her expectantly.

'I actually know St Griswold well, yet it is the last place I want to return to.'

'How do you know it?' Xavier asked.

'In my first year at university, I met an older student, who I befriended. After finishing my studies, he invited me to Griswold where he was already teaching. They gave me a job. At first it was wonderful, but after two years I returned to Ariel. I don't want to go back.'

'Who was the student?' Xavier asked.

'Artemis.'

Xavier was stunned. 'Artemis? You know him? He's our friend and helped us get here.'

'I knew so many from Griswold, but it's been so long. Are Patricia, Ernie and Stephen still there?'

Xavier remembered Ratti's name was Patricia because he had heard Phineas call her that. 'Do you mean Patricia Ratchet?'

'Yes, and that dear little boy she doted on.'

The boys looked at her blankly.

'He'd be grown up now. His name was Eric—Eric Phineas. What a terrible time he had with the death of his brother. It should've been different.' She sighed. 'I'll only come to St Griswold if you can convince the other six.'

'Six? Don't you mean the other five?' Gabe said.

'My visions show seven including me. Try Mortimer from Green Isle next. If you can convince him and the others, I give you my word, I'll come,' she said in a resigned tone.

Xavier knew she didn't think it likely they would succeed. It was an easy and hollow promise, but once she had spoken it, he relaxed. 'Who are the others?'

'If you make it to Green Isle, Mortimer will tell you. That way it's less of a risk if you're caught, which I fear is likely.'

Xavier's eyes grew wide. 'Do you see our capture in your visions?'

She shook her head. 'Not yet.'

As the evening wore on, Xavier was so tired that he struggled to follow the conversation. Merewyn frequently spoke in riddles, or was it just his fatigue making it difficult for him to concentrate? Eventually he surrendered to sleep. When he woke, curled up on the couch under a cotton blanket, he felt disoriented for a moment.

Gabe looked up from a book he was reading. 'Nice nap?'

'Where's Merewyn?'

'She was called away to the city about an hour ago, but she'll be back.'

Xavier yawned and stretched. 'What do you think of her?'

'I don't know.'

'That's it?'

'I couldn't understand her logic. There were bits and pieces, but they did not make sense as a whole or perhaps I was tired. At one stage she started talking about golden hawks. She said she would send them to Griswold.'

'Why?'

'Presumably to assist us.'

'Do they speak Clanardian?' Xavier said in an irritable tone. They had risked their lives for a bunch of birds and lamb sandwiches. And just when he needed to find out more information, he had been too exhausted to stay awake. He felt cheated and annoyed with himself.

'We could attach messages to their legs like pigeons.'

'If we can catch them,' Xavier said and sighed. 'And what if the hawks are intercepted? Demons would just treat them like flying fortune cookies—eat the bird and read the note.'

Gabe shrugged. 'I'm puzzled she was able to conjure magic with the balls.'

'You're right. Beth never mentioned Farseers having other abilities.'

'We'll need to ask Beth or Artemis,' Gabe said.

'What have you been reading?'

'Ancient writings from Earth.'

Xavier glanced over his shoulder.

'*The Definitive Guide to Home Decorating*,' Gabe said and shut the book with a snap. 'It had an interesting chapter about revitalising your living area with carefully selected cushions and a lick of paint. I found it informative.'

Xavier grinned.

'What?'

'No, it's good. You obviously learnt something. The trip hasn't been a complete waste of time.'

'Shall we go?' Gabe said.

Xavier knew Merewyn would not be coming back. 'I think so.'

They grabbed the leftover sandwiches, wrapped them in napkins and stuffed them in their pockets. It was best to be resourceful, although Xavier felt rude taking them without asking. But life was different now and the threat of going hungry had changed the way he thought.

CHAPTER 21

* * *

The Wilderwreck Coast

The boys stood in the grassy field where they had last seen Evie, the white-haired Boundary girl as they tried to work out how to return to the Ambrosian Forest. The wind had dropped and there had been no sign of the crazy goats when they passed the wooden hall on the dirt road.

'Going so soon?' Evie was plucking flowers nearby.

'Where did you come from?' Xavier asked.

'I've been here all morning. Did you find the princess?'

'Yes,' Xavier said.

'Are you happy with what you learned?'

'Not altogether.'

She adjusted the strap on her shoulder. 'Perhaps the pieces will find each other eventually. The princess would be mindful to only tell you what you need to know.'

'Well she told us ...,' Xavier said.

'Please, no more. I don't dabble in the lives of those external to my world because I don't want to hold secrets I might be unable to keep.'

'Surely we're safe here?' Gabe said.

'You never know who or what listens, even here.'

A chill brushed across Xavier's shoulders. If the flower girl was worried about holding secrets in Ariel, what hope did two teenage angels have outside? He reached forward and grabbed several flowers and stuffed them in his pocket alongside his sandwich.

'Would it be possible for us to travel through your world from this boundary to Mourn Forest?' Gabe asked.

The girl shook her head. 'It has not been done. It would go against the will of my world. I can, however, take you quickly to the border of the forest. Like those from my world, I've the power to fold and shape the elements of the forest. That's how we keep Ariel safe from outsiders. Here we can bend and compress space and to some degree, time.'

Xavier nodded although he didn't really understand.

'So that's why we could see the ocean on the horizon, yet Gustavius' map showed it to be kilometres away,' Gabe said.

'The maps you see were created long ago by Farseers when Ariel was at rest.'

'How many have wandered in here and got lost?' Gabe asked.

'Usually we just bend space and cause them to wander out again. Those who are truly evil we leave to their own devices. Many become lost and perish.'

'You kill them?' Xavier said.

'No, just ignore them and the forest takes care of them naturally.'

Xavier shuddered. 'Could you bend space in other places?'

'No, we only have power within the forests. It's an old magic like that found in the portals.'

'What portals?' Gabe asked.

She didn't answer. She lifted her arms causing the bush around them to wobble and shimmer. When it settled, the boys could see the path leading out of the forest where they had begun their journey. 'See, it's morning again, so you're safe from the demons until nightfall.'

Xavier turned to thank her, but she had vanished.

As they walked in silence along the forest path, Xavier felt disappointment. He didn't know what he had expected and suddenly felt tired again. Why did they have to shoulder all the responsibility of trying to find six or was it now seven people linked to the Lithos stone?

Soon they saw the open sky again. When they emerged from the forest into the empty tourist park, it was breakfast time.

'So what now?' Xavier asked as he sprawled on the lawn, took out a sandwich he had stuffed into his pocket and chewed it.

Gabe remained standing. 'I would rather keep going. We should skirt around Ambrosia and try to get back to Rosegrove Hospital as soon as we can. If we head south and then east, we could probably risk flying in short bursts as it's not populated in that region.'

Finding the sandwich dry, Xavier walked to a tap on the lawn, turned it on and drank. He wiped his mouth. 'Alright, let's go.' Every instinct told him not to return to Griswold, but it had become a duty, a nagging voice he could not ignore.

The winds buffeted them as they took off in a southerly direction, following a river that skirted the boundary of the Ambrosian Forest.

When they had been flying for an hour, Gabe pointed to the west. 'What's going on there?'

Xavier turned to see what looked like brown scars reaching into the green of the Ambrosian Forest and puffs of smoke billowing from machinery riding up and down denuded land.

'We need to change direction, now,' Gabe said urgently. 'I see tents.'

Without speaking both boys instantly shifted to a south-easterly direction.

'They were Darklaw tents, weren't they?' Xavier said after they had flown far enough to no longer be seen.

'I think so.'

'Why would they be cutting trees down in such a remote area?'

'Why do you think?'

'To get to Ariel?' Xavier said gloomily.

'I would imagine so.'

They battled crosswinds as they flew further south.

'I've never visited this part of the world, but I think we're not too far from the Wilderwreck Coast. It curls around the south and western end of Clanarde.' Xavier heard Gabe whispering Wilderwreck under his breath a few times. 'Some say it's haunted by those shipwrecked in the waters of the Deadly Strait between the mainland and Green Isle.'

'According to the princess, Mortimer comes from Green Isle,' Gabe said.

'It's where Ethan came from too.' Xavier felt excited at the prospect of seeing a place he had only ever imagined. 'We could fly as far as the coast to the ocean and then go east.'

Gabe nodded approvingly. 'That would be interesting as I've never seen an ocean, other than that glimpse from Ariel. What's that ahead? Water, a river, it's massive.'

Pleased with himself for having remembered, Xavier said, 'That'd be the Blackwater River.' Ever since they had entertained the idea of going to Ambrosia, he had tried to memorise the landscape of the region in geography classes. 'If we follow it, we'll reach the coast.'

The river, a deep black wound in the desolate landscape widened and devoured land as it neared the coastline. On either side of the river, jagged rocks and the odd gnarled tree dotted the empty windswept fields. They saw no farms or humans. And the further south they ventured, the colder it grew as clouds massed, heavy and grey overhead.

'There it is,' Xavier exclaimed. As the great river rushed ahead of them at a wild pace to meet the steely ocean, the boys veered left of the river towards the beaches. 'Come on!' he called and dipped towards the sand and then skimmed just above the line of waves breaking in the shallow waters. Apart from the odd lone seagull, the beaches were deserted. He slowed his flight to a run and waited for Gabe to join him. They took their shoes off and walked for a while along the sand, occasionally stopping to wade in the shallows. After a spell they sat on the sand and watched waves crashing and foaming and gulls wheeling and arcing above.

'I like this place,' Gabe said.

Xavier scooped sand and moulded a shape.

'What are you doing?'

'Building a sand castle.'

'For what purpose?'

'Fun.'

Gabe looked at him doubtfully.

'We used to spend our holidays at a beach near Ravenwood called Fay. It's warm and sunny there. My sister and I would build massive castles with turrets and spires from wet sand because that's always best for building. We'd spend hours digging and decorating castles with sticks, shells and seaweed. The only problem was you had to do it close to the water for the sand to be wet enough, so sometimes a big wave would just swamp and flatten it.'

'What did you do with them once they were complete?'

Xavier shrugged. 'Not much. Look at them. If my parents were there, they might take a photo. Eventually the tide would come in and the waves would wash them away.'

'I don't understand. You'd spent hours building a structure you knew would be washed away. Why?'

'It's called play. Kids and even some adults like to do it.'

'Play—hmm.'

'Actually it's probably why you like drawing and marching to music. You may not do it for any purpose, yet it makes you feel good.'

Gabe regarded him with a thoughtful expression and then scooped and piled some sand into a mound. 'When I came to Griswold, I arrived with much information, but I can see there are many gaps in my learning. Perhaps when all is done, I could have more fun.'

Xavier stood up and brushed the sand from his legs. 'Are you ready to go again?'

Gabe seemed disappointed.

Although Xavier knew Gabe was enjoying the experience of the ocean and was reluctant to leave, he pulled on his hand. 'Come on.'

They put their shoes on, stood and stretched and then ran along the beach until they had gathered sufficient speed to take to the air again.

'See there,' Xavier yelled above the wind and waves. 'On the horizon. The small grey peak?' He pointed. 'That's Mount Eroba, the only peak on Green Isle.'

'Shall we head towards Rosegrove now?' Gabe said.

The wind direction had changed and was now a cold and salty blast that lashed and stung one side of their faces as they flew. Eventually they veered up the cliff face and when they reached the top, both boys landed.

'What time is it?' Xavier said.

Gabe reached into his pocket and checked his watch. 'Four o'clock.'

Xavier felt a pang of fright. 'How did we take so long?'

Gabe shrugged. 'Distracted, I suppose. We'll need to seek shelter as there's no chance of us reaching Rosegrove before nightfall.'

Xavier looked behind them but saw nothing, just miles of low windswept grassland. 'We could risk it.'

'Travelling by night? No,' Gabe said. 'Have you already forgotten the night life we met on the Affron Flats and Eerie Lakes? We've no way of knowing how the demons detect their victims. Just because this land looks deserted, doesn't mean it's safe.'

Xavier sighed. 'So I suppose we need to look for a cave or some form of shelter.' The truth was he was just as fearful of sleeping in a dark cave as he was of flying into the night.

The boys dropped off the cliff and flew slowly along the beach in silence until the light faded, the winds dropped and the ocean was almost still.

'It's so quiet,' Xavier said.

'I know. I don't like it. Let's hurry.'

'What's that?' Xavier pointed at a smudge high on the cliffs ahead. As they approached it, he saw an opening in the cliff face leading to what appeared to be a cave. 'What if it's a demon's lair?'

'Or an angel's haven?' Gabe said and grinned. 'Only one way to find out. It's safer than sitting in the open.'

'I suppose.' The growing stillness and encroaching darkness unnerved Xavier. Movements and shadows, real or imagined, were appearing in his outer vision. Landing on the ledge, he took a couple of steps into the cave. It seemed safer with a ceiling overhead. Yet as he glanced deeper into the cave, it became shadowy and then merged into blackness. He decided to stay close to the entrance and once he sat, his wings curled around him like a blanket. Sometimes he felt they wanted to protect and comfort him. He pulled them closer.

Gabe sat with his back facing one side of the entrance. He didn't seem to trust the cave either. 'Shall we take turns to keep watch?'

'You sleep first. I'm not tired.'

Gabe didn't argue. Instead he lay on the smooth sandstone and closed his eyes. Immediately, Xavier felt uneasy and alone. As he reached into his pocket to take out what remained of his sandwich, he discovered the flowers he had plucked near Ariel. He sprinkled a few at Gabe's feet and kept the remainder. Chewing the sandwich, he waited for one of the moons to rise. An hour later he ventured to the ledge and listened to the easy slop of slight waves on the sand. At last he relaxed, but no sooner did he drop his shoulders when he noticed a green shimmering play of lights across the water. He stood to see where the lights were coming from. Eventually they came close enough to make out the source. A great white boat with sails and rigging was floating down the strait, close to the beach. He could hear men's voices. He strained to see the sailors, but the boat appeared deserted.

'Gabe,' he said softly and bent to wake him. 'You have to see this.'

Gabe rubbed his eyes and propped on his elbows before struggling to stand. 'Why are they sailing at night?'

'Quiet.'

As they listened, the cries of men and the creaking and flapping of sails carried across the water. There was no wind, yet the ship's sails billowed as it glided by the beach.

'A ghost ship,' Gabe said in an awed tone.

Soon the ship was joined by others in an ethereal dance across the strait. Some were manned with faint white figures while the older vessels appeared empty.

'Mesmerized by the amazing scene, both boys sat and watched the gliding boats sail past them.

'How is it possible?' Xavier said.

'Ask Lily.' Gabe chuckled. 'After seeing demons, angels, wraiths and magical wizards nothing should surprise us any more.'

'I wonder why they're here,' Xavier said.

'No idea. You need to get some sleep. I'll keep watch.'

When the last ship had vanished, Xavier settled on the ground and after giving the dark recesses of the cave another glance, closed his eyes. Within minutes, he had sunk into sleep, yet a few hours later, he was woken by a noise. He opened his eyes, but was disoriented by the darkness. Panic seized him until he remembered where he was and why the ground was so hard.

'Gabe,' he whispered.

There was no reply.

Outside the cave, Xavier could see a dim night sky, a moon partially covered by cloud and the dark strip of ocean. He approached Gabe, who was curled up on the ground snoring softly. So much for the guardian angel, he thought. He rearranged the flowers from Ariel in a circle around them. Hearing a rustling sound deep in the cave, he dropped to his haunches and stared into the darkness until his eyes watered and he had to blink. For a few moments he wondered if he should blow the wooden whistle Craig had given him. But if it were a wild dog, it would only alert it to their presence and no whistle would deter it. He resisted the urge to wake Gabe because if he muttered or groaned on wakening, it might be enough to lure the creature from the shadows. Holding his breath to listen, he decided if the creature ventured towards the front of the cave, he would immediately wake Gabe so they could escape from the entrance. Even if it were a demon or wraith, he reasoned they would probably have a better chance outside.

For the next couple of hours, Xavier kept watch. As the temperature dived, he shivered and hugged his knees to his chest while Gabe slept blissfully at his feet. A few growls and grunts emanated from the depths of the cave, but Xavier tried not to listen, although he couldn't ignore the cracking and crunching that followed. Pushing his fingers into his ears to block the sounds, he wished he were asleep like Gabe. Silence eventually fell upon the cave. When the first gold hint of dawn edged over the horizon, Xavier shook Gabe. He didn't want to wait a moment longer in case the creature discovered it had been sharing its home with uninvited guests.

Gabe mumbled as he stirred.

'Shh,' Xavier said softly. He put a finger to his lips, as he was still wary.

Gabe frowned.

Pointing to the back of the cave, Xavier imitated the actions of a monster.

Gabe raised his eyebrows, quietly rose to his feet, and then instead of preparing to leave, tip-toed further into the cave.

'No!' Xavier whispered as he dragged on his sleeve, but Gabe ignored him and pulled away.

The morning light grew, revealing the cave's smooth orange sandstone walls.

Gabe wandered to the back of the cave, which now they both could see was clearly empty. 'Whatever was here has gone.' He peered at the ceiling. 'I wonder if it escaped through this opening.'

As Xavier approached Gabe, he passed a narrow opening, which led to a dark passage. 'Or maybe through here,' he whispered as he feared the creature might be lurking in the dark. 'What's that?'

Gabe crouched and peered at debris on the cave floor and then raked it with his foot. 'Bones, skin, teeth and fur.'

'Enough.' Xavier swung around towards the entrance. 'Let's go.'

* * *

CHAPTER 22

Into the vipers' nest

By mid-morning, Xavier was relieved they had reached the foothills of the Uraki Ranges and were only an hour from Rosegrove. He was looking forward to seeing Artemis, Beth, Hayley and Ethan again, even if it meant returning to Griswold. They had become like his second family. As they skimmed over the landscape, his mind drifted and he allowed himself to focus on an image of his mother and father but only for a few precious seconds.

Suddenly something hard and scraping knocked him from overhead making him spin in a circle and nearly tumble from the sky. Gabe was flailing in the air as if he had been hit too.

Xavier gasped and struggled for balance. 'What was that?'

Gabe pointed towards the sun. 'Demon,' he said as though winded.

A leathery tail flicked in the glare.

'Dive! Trees,' Gabe grunted.

Without asking for an explanation, Xavier pumped his wings and rushed after Gabe.

'Where did it go?' Gabe said.

When they reached a grove of trees, Xavier said, 'It's daylight. It can't be a demon.'

'I'm surprised it didn't attack again,' Gabe said. 'Maybe it's tracking us.'

The boys kept snatching glances behind them as they jogged along the ground.

Xavier knew even with two of them, they had no chance of fighting a demon. Maybe they could outsmart it though.

Gabe checked his compass and pointed. They searched the undergrowth for signs of life. 'We need to head east here, over the lower slopes of the range. I think we'll be able to spot Rosegrove when we hit the peak of one of these hills.'

The ground became rocky and uneven as they climbed the slopes, and without a path, their journey was slow. With their heads down, they resorted to hands and knees to negotiate some of the steeper parts.

'I'd have flown, myself,' said a voice with an unnatural vibration.

Both boys froze.

'Maybe they need the exercise,' another voice said, deeper than the first but with the same unearthly tone.

And yet another higher-pitched voice chuckled in a mechanical, buzzing tone and piped, 'That's what you get for living too long with human trash.'

Perched on a rock in front of the boys were three red demons. The oldest was leaning back on his elbows as though sunbathing or relaxing. 'So what are you angel boys up to?' he asked as he scratched nonchalantly at one of the horns on his head.

Xavier opened his mouth to speak, but nothing came out.

The oldest demon looked at Gabe. 'What about you? Cat got your tongue?' He stood up and stretched with his tail swinging and twitching.

The demon with the deep voice followed his lead and rose onto his large and muscular haunches as though ready to spring. 'I say we finish them off now. I'm filthy hungry.'

'Patience, the angelings will attract more fodder like worms on fishhooks. In the meantime, let's get to know each other,' the senior one said and then grinned to reveal a row of sharp fangs.

'What for?' The muscular one sounded disgusted.

The senior one examined a talon. 'Food appreciation.'

'Food wot?' said the third one with the high-pitched voice, who was obviously quite young.

'Food appreciation, you clot,' the muscular one said.

'It's a joke,' the senior one explained. 'A year or so ago, I kept a human captive for a few weeks. I learnt a little about their strange sayings and customs.'

'Ohh,' the young demon said. 'What happened to him?'

The senior one chuckled.

Hissing and curling his lip, the muscular demon stared at a gap in the rock. With a deft movement it leaned forward and plucked a snake from the space and held it briefly in the air before opening its mouth and devouring it whole.

The dim-witted youngster wailed.

The muscular one turned and stared at the youngster.

'I'm hungry too.'

'And?'

'Shut up!' the senior one snapped. 'There will be plenty of food for all soon.' It smiled at Xavier. 'Let's be sociable. My name's Oranta and these are my associates, Garunge and the little fellow is Snifter. We've recently moved into the neighbourhood, so we're making an effort to get to know the locals. Now, what are you angelings doing here?'

'Exploring,' Gabe said. 'We're citizens of Rosegrove.'

'Angels from Rosegrove?' Oranta's leathery red brow puckered. 'Hmm, not likely. Where are your kin?'

Neither boy answered him.

Oranta turned to Garunge. 'Show our guests to their quarters.'

Garunge sprang from the rock and grabbed each boy by the scruff of the neck. Xavier was terrified and repulsed by the power of his grip and the sensation of his scales and talons squeezing and scraping his skin.

'Escort them to their accommodation,' Oranta said.

Garunge dragged the boys effortlessly up the slope they had struggled to scale earlier. Oranta and Snifter followed them. When they reached the peak, Xavier could see Rosegrove. His heart sank. Would he and Gabe die here? Would their friends and his family never know their fate? Instead of feeling panicked, he felt detached and sad. Perhaps his family was already dead. Oddly, the thought comforted him because if it were true, they would never learn what happened to him.

Garunge yanked on their collars and tightened his grip. 'Move,' he growled. 'Hurry up.'

'We recently moved from Anthica,' Oranta said as the boys laboured up another hill. 'Do you know it? It's a godforsaken place halfway between the frozen wastes of the Castrel Islands and here.'

'Godforsaken,' Garunge repeated and chuckled.

'We didn't fancy the cold climate. Clanarde's more to our liking although I must say we're interested in venturing further north—out of the fog zone. Hunting's tricky in fog, isn't it Snifter, old chap?'

The young demon laughed at Oranta's banter. 'When are we going north, Oranta?'

'When we've settled business here.'

Both boys scrambled and skidded down the slope until they reached a thick grove of trees in a level area. Under the dense canopy was a camp site where a few demons ambled around in the dense shade while others appeared to be sleeping on the ground. Xavier wondered why the demons they had encountered seemed unfazed by the light.

Garunge hauled them past a cluster of sleeping demons to the far side of the grove, where they emerged into the daylight again. On a stretch of flat ground was a giant cage that looked and smelled like it had once housed zoo animals or cattle. Xavier couldn't imagine how it got there.

'And don't think you'll escape from the cage. It held greater apes before you.' Garunge tipped his head and gazed wistfully into the distance for a moment. 'And what tasty morsels they were—far better than humans. No putrid aftertaste.' He unlocked the cage, shoved them in and then locked the padlock on the door.

'What are you going to do with us?' Gabe demanded although his voice trembled.

'Patience, my dears,' Garunge said in a growling tone. 'Wait and see. Hopefully your kin will visit soon.'

Xavier slumped to the floor of the cage, oblivious to the dried animal droppings and flies. He closed his eyes and hoped it would be over soon.

Garunge returned to the shadowy grove while Gabe paced the floor of the cage. He stopped several times to rattle the padlock and pull on the bars as though he hoped they were defective.

'We're not going to walk out of here,' Xavier said softly.

'How do you know? What's wrong with you? Get up and help me find a way out of here.'

Xavier shrugged without opening his eyes. As he lay there a thought entered his mind. What about the Celestial Power? Perhaps they were close enough now to Griswold for them to hear him. He cleared his mind and focused. We need your help, he begged mentally and pictured the cage and demon grove. But there was no answer. After trying a few more times he gave up.

Xavier opened his eyes to see Gabe fiddling with the lock again. When his attempts failed, Gabe sat on the cage floor and ran his fingers through his hair. They sat in silence for an hour or more.

'Do you suppose we'll be dinner?'

Gabe shook his head. 'No, Oranta said we were bait, and Garunge hoped our kin would visit. My guess is that they think angels are going to try and save us, but they'll be waiting and ready for them.'

Xavier felt the blood drain from his face. 'A trap?'

'I think so.'

'I've been calling to the Celestial Power in my head,' Xavier said softly. 'They didn't answer, but what if they heard and are coming? I don't want to be responsible for their deaths.'

'There must be a way out,' Xavier said with a new sense of determination as he stood. 'If the angels come in the daytime, they'll be fine because the demons hate light.'

Gabe raised his eyebrows. 'Three of them were in full sunlight today. You saw them. They must have used a spell or something.'

'I have to warn them. Can you please try too?' Xavier pictured the cage in his mind and the grove full of demons. Be careful, he repeated in his mind, but the voices were silent.

'Any luck?'

Gabe shook his head.

Xavier tugged on the metal bars in an effort to bend them.

'You'd need supernatural strength to bend these bars.'

'Well Gustavius said I'd discover talents I never knew I had, so who knows.' Xavier pulled until he was red in the face and puffing, and then felt the bar. 'It isn't even warm.'

'How about the floor? What's it made of?' Gabe said.

'Metal. Any other ideas? Come on, think.'

'No escape,' said a small demon with an ugly scar over one of his eyes, who approached them carrying a battered tin bucket. 'Food. Get back, or I get Garunge.' This demon seemed young and his speech was primitive. Keeping one eye on them, he quickly unlocked the cage door.

Xavier gagged and looked away from the small pile of animal entrails the demon emptied on the cage floor.

'What's your name?' Gabe said.

The creature grunted as he locked the cage again.

'Name?' Xavier said as he turned while keeping his line of sight above their dinner.

The demon's eyes narrowed. 'Don't talk to humans.'

'Then what are you doing now?' Gabe said brightly. 'Why are you worried? How are we going to hurt you, locked away like this?'

'What's your name?' Xavier asked, focusing on him.

'Alster. I feed animals,' he said proudly.

'That's an important job, Alster. Why can some demons go out in the daylight?' he asked in a gentle monotone.

The creature looked at him suspiciously and rubbed the scar over his eye.

Xavier focused harder.

'Daybrew,' Alster said.

'Where did you get it?'

Gabe watched silently, as though fearful of breaking the hypnotic spell.

'Witch Queen,' Alster said.

'Where do you keep the daybrew?' Xavier said.

'Can't tell.'

'Why not?'

'We need it.'

'It's alright, you can trust us,' Xavier said in a soothing voice.

Alster paused.

Xavier concentrated.

'In cooking pot. Precious. Keep it warm ...'

'How much do you have?' Gabe asked but then covered his mouth, obviously realising the creature might hear the difference in their voices.

Alster shook his head as though gaining awareness.

What could he do? Reach out and strangle the creature? Not much chance of that with its thick scaly neck. Xavier glanced at Gabe for inspiration.

The demon turned.

'Relax, listen to me,' Xavier said aloud while continuing to stare.

After a few moments of talking to him with monotonous suggestions, the demon's mouth hung open, as it took a wobbly step backwards and dropped the key. It seemed dazed and confused and frowned at Xavier, whose concentration was faltering.

Regaining his composure, Xavier repeated, 'Listen to me.'

'Wot?' the creature mumbled. 'Wotta you doing?' The demon seemed ruffled and hurriedly picked up the empty bucket and rushed back towards the grove.

'I had him, but I stuffed it up,' Xavier said in frustration. 'I could've got the key, but it's so hard to keep my concentration going. It felt like his mind was fighting back.'

'Don't worry, it's okay because he dropped the key. We just have to figure out how to reach it.' Gabe poked his arm between the bars but discovered it was still about a metre away from his fingertips, so he searched for a stick.

Xavier slumped to the floor of the cage, despondent he had failed. As he tried to think, he threw some of the scraps from the cage at a hungry-looking bird, which pecked aggressively at a hunk of raw meat. He watched the bird eat, repulsed by its eagerness. It stopped, turned and regarded him for a few moments, but then resumed pecking at the fleshy prize. A sudden realisation crept over Xavier. 'I wonder,' he said aloud and refocused on the bird. This time he talked softly to it and concentrated hard. Again the bird stopped and looked at him. Xavier pictured the bird walking towards him as he focused on it and was shocked when soon after, the bird took a few steps as though obeying his mental suggestions.

By now Gabe was standing to one side watching with fascination. 'What are ...'

'Shh, the key,' Xavier whispered. He turned his attention to the bird and pictured it walking towards the key. The bird obeyed and then eyed him again as though in a trance. Pick up the key, he urged the bird mentally. The bird pecked at the key and tried to grasp it with its beak, but it slipped and fell. Xavier watched as it fumbled with it a few more times. The bird stopped trying and stood with its head cocked to one side looking at Xavier.

'Make it push the key,' suggested Gabe quietly.

Once again Xavier focused. The bird's mind was simpler than Alster's. It didn't fight him although it took more to effort to keep the idea in its head as though it was quickly forgetting. This time he pictured the bird nudging the key closer. The bird eyed the key again and flicked at it several times until it was only a couple of arm lengths away. Suddenly a gust of wind sent dirt and leaves swirling. Disturbed, the bird, took off into the air away from the cage.

Gabe threw himself onto the floor and reached out as far as he could towards the key. 'You try,' he said after straining unsuccessfully for several minutes.

Xavier lay on the bottom of the cage and pushed his shoulder between the bars and although his lanky arm reached further, he was unable to reach it. 'How stupid am I,' he suddenly exclaimed. He stood up, pulled his jumper off and extended his wings. They were bent over under the confines of the cage, but when he pushed one wing out between the bars he was able to manoeuvre until his wing tip touched the key. He dragged the key towards them until Gabe reached out and grabbed it.

'We're free,' Gabe said after unlocking the cage. 'We have to get out of here.'

'No, first we have to find the daybrew and destroy it,' Xavier said as he shook dirt from his wing and then pulled his jumper on.

Gabe looked at him with a stunned expression. 'No, it's too dangerous.'

'We have to, after dark though. When the demons go hunting.'

'But they don't need to wait for night when they have the daybrew,' Gabe said.

'Well why are they still sheltering and sleeping in the shade?' Xavier said. 'Do you think it's just habit?'

'If the brew takes a long time to make, maybe they're trying to preserve it. They might not have a lot of it.'

It was late-afternoon as the boys left the cage to hide further up the hill behind a few trees.

Xavier squinted at the grove downhill to see if any demons were stirring. 'I hope they leave to go hunting without checking the cage.'

'It would only take us ten minutes to reach Rosegrove from here,' Gabe said. 'We could just fly away.'

'I know but the daybrew … '

Gabe sighed. 'Things might not end well.'

'Yes, but think how many innocent people could die if we don't get rid of it. The demons might even attack Griswold College.'

As the sun slipped from the horizon and the light faded, the boys watched the grove until they saw dark smudges rising over the trees. Only the flapping and creaking of their leathery wings gave their identities away. The demons flew in different directions, yet none of them passed by the cage.

The boys set off towards the grove with a small torch their only guide. When they reached the demon camp, Gabe pointed and whispered, 'A fire.' He grabbed Xavier's arm. 'Shh, something's moving over there.'

They crouched for a few minutes and then continued towards a large cauldron suspended over the fire.

'Step away or die,' a voice vibrated behind them.

The boys turned slowly with their hands raised.

'Who are you?' a demon asked.

Xavier's heart raced. It obviously wasn't one of their original captors. He took a deep breath. It was worth a try. With all the focus he could muster, he stared at the demon and concentrated.

'Who are you?' she repeated in a more aggressive tone as she stepped forward into the firelight with her teeth bared and eyes crazed.

Despite her expression, Xavier smelled fear. She was a young demon with small, half-formed wings and he could tell she was nervous.

'You know who we are,' Xavier said.

'What?'

He repeated the sentence in a calm, low tone and focused hard on the demon.

She baulked. Moments passed. 'Ohh,' she said softly as though she had a quiet revelation.

'That's right. We're your friends.'

'Good,' the creature said, as though in a trance.

'We need you to help us.'

'Yes?'

Xavier was delighted. He could feel this young demon's mind unlike the previous one, was soft and malleable. 'We want you to empty the cauldron.' Xavier glanced at Gabe, who grinned. 'Tip the daybrew, I mean soup in the fire.'

'But we need soup for day eyes,' the demon said in a faraway voice.

'The soup has gone off. It's very nasty,' Xavier said in a firm voice. 'We need to get rid of it, otherwise it will poison everyone.'

'Ohh, yes, very nasty,' the creature said as she turned and almost flicked Xavier in the face with her tail. She wandered in a wobbly line towards the fire and grabbed at the cauldron but then let out a terrible wail. 'It bites me,' she cried.

'Your hands are fine,' Xavier lied as he felt her mind slip away from him.

The creature whimpered. 'Fine,' she repeated in an uncertain tone.

'Use this stick to tip the pot over,' Xavier said.

The demon took the stick and after a few attempts with her burnt hands managed to tip the contents into the fire.

'Now sleep,' Xavier suggested and added, 'Your hands feel fine.'

Obediently, the demon wandered to the base of a tree, dropped to her knees and then to the ground, where she curled up and within a minute was snoring loudly.

Feeling exhausted, Xavier rubbed his temple. 'I hope there are no more minds to bend.'

They hurried to the edge of the grove and had just got their bearings, when suddenly something large, leathery and familiar dropped from the sky.

Garunge stood with his hands on his hips and wings outstretched in an intimidating stance. 'Ahh, dinner has arrived. Good, I'm famished.'

Oranta and Snifter dropped from the air and stood either side of Garunge.

'Yes, we're peckish too,' Oranta said. 'Hunting was disappointing tonight. Well, until now.' He chuckled and turned to Garunge. 'Why don't you do the honours? A thigh would be nice—or perhaps a wing. Kill them, Garunge.'

The young one started to whine.

'Patience, Snifter. Your turn will come.'

Snifter scowled.

In a desperate bid, Xavier focused on Garunge and tried to overpower his mind.

Within a few moments, the demon's eyes were glassy and his jaw slack.

Xavier quickly turned to Oranta only to hear Garunge cough and burst into buzzing laughter. 'You think your pitiful angeling mind could overwhelm mine?'

The other two demons joined in his laughter. Just as Garunge stepped forward and raised his arm ready to slash at Xavier with his talons, a rippling flash of light erupted behind the boys.

The demons covered their eyes and moaned in pain.

Xavier gasped. 'What was that?'

After two larger flashes exploded around them, Gabe grabbed Xavier and pulled him away. The demons were covering their eyes and screeching.

'Run,' Gabe said.

The two boys set off into the bush using the flashes to navigate their way.

'Are they fireworks?' Xavier said as he turned towards the display, which was lighting up the valley below. He crouched behind a bush while checking to see if any demons were pursuing them.

'We should go further up the hill. They'll expect us to head to Rosegrove, not deeper into their territory,' Gabe said as he hid with him.

A massive volley of booming sounds accompanied by a brilliant shower of flashes erupted over the fields between Rosegrove and their vantage. A cloud of pinpoint lights burst and showered over the grove. The boys could hear the demons scurrying and screeching under the trees into the open. The boys flattened their bodies on the ground and prayed that the demons would not see their outlines from below.

'Agh, it burns!' a demon cried.

Xavier could smell smoke and burning meat. 'The lights—they're embers. We need to find cover.'

Through the chaos an angry voice called, 'The brew's gone!'

Many voices clamoured at this news. Some were furious while others seemed panicked.

'Shut up,' another screamed. 'We can get more.'

'How, Oranta?'

'Focus on the enemy. Find the angelings. Kill the vermin.'

The lights in the sky intensified and fell like fiery rain. As the trees in the grove burst into flames, the demons howled at the intense light.

'Bad luck. Obviously didn't get enough daybrew,' Gabe said.

Soon the light was accompanied by a sound that at first, Xavier didn't recognise. When he finally did, he turned to Gabe, who was grinning.

'Angel song?'

Gabe was humming with them.

They heard howls of anger and cursing from the demons.

Xavier crouched on his hands and knees. 'Careful, they might see you.'

'Listen to them. They're squabbling while the grove burns. No daybrew, so they'll have to move on for shelter.'

'Wow! Look at them.' Xavier slowly rose to his feet and stared at the sky in wonder. 'I've never seen anything so beautiful.'

A formation of dazzling angels skimmed over the grove with swords drawn. They were so close, Xavier could see their faces. They weren't angry or aggressive—just dreamlike. It was as though they were accepting a higher order. He could hear the power of their massive wings beating in unison and their singing. He could also see the glint of their light golden armour over white gowns; the leather strapping on their wrists and legs and their hair flowing in the wind. Xavier wanted to reach out and touch them. 'Don't go,' he said in a hoarse voice.

The angels soared high above them.

'They're not going. Just regrouping,' Gabe said.

'How do you know?'

Gabe shrugged without looking at him. 'I can feel them. It's thrilling.'

Another volley of brilliant flares lit the sky and rained over the hillside.

Xavier heard more cursing, howling and screeching.

'The demons aren't worried about us now. Let's go,' Gabe said.

The boys scrambled up the slope away from the furious demons. From the higher ground, they could see a massive formation of angels circling above the grove.

Gabe pointed to a dark mass in the western sky. 'We're not out of danger yet.'

'Yep, looks like demons. Lots of them,' Xavier said.

'Hmm, I dare say you're correct,' said a voice from the shadows.

The boys startled.

'It's only me.' The flares lit Raphael's face as he stepped from the darkness.

For a moment Xavier forgot the demons downhill.

Raphael stood with his hands on his hips and surveyed the scene below. 'It looks nasty.'

'What should we do?' Xavier asked him.

'Well—you could just leave. But perhaps you might want to see what happens next. I know I want to as it should be a good show.' Raphael perched on a rock and drew his knees to his chest. 'Bit chilly, isn't it?' He looked around and waved his hand at a bush close to the rock. It erupted into flame. 'That's better. Maybe not overly warm but definitely more cheery.'

'I hope the demons don't see your fire,' Xavier said.

'Hardly.' He chuckled. 'Too busy with the fuss down there.' Raphael gazed at another formation of angels arcing through the sky towards the grove, which was now just a flaming bonfire. 'Freeons, they're pretty, aren't they, although a little on the showy side for my liking.'

'Freeons—you mean the angels?' Xavier said.

'Yes—a lithe, showy lot with immaculate hair and impeccable fighting skills.'

Raphael was a strange angel, Xavier thought. He tried again by repeating his question. 'So what should we do?'

'Hmm,' Raphael said. 'Are we talking practically or ethically? Short term? Long term?'

'What?' He was getting on Xavier's nerves. 'I just want you to tell us what to do. You're an adult—you should know.'

'Three hundred Kepler years old, so technically I suppose I qualify.'

'You're part of the Celestial Power, you should know,' Gabe said.

Raphael looked at each boy. 'I was, but ... well, we did have a slight falling out.'

Xavier groaned.

'They're so—hmm—particular.'

Downhill, a few demons burst from the fiery grove into the atmosphere and lunged at a line of freeons.

Xavier gasped.

'It's alright.' Raphael reached out to Xavier and patted him on the shoulder. A demon had caught one of the freeons and as they tumbled from the sky, more demons descended and in a frenzy, tore at the beautiful creature.

'Oh no,' Xavier cried. 'We must help him.'

'Too late,' Raphael said. 'Just don't look.'

Xavier covered his mouth and looked away as the angel's mournful cries rang out across the night sky.

'Or listen,' Raphael added.

'Where do they go?' Gabe said quietly.

'Dead angels do you mean?' Raphael said.

'Nisroc told us they can only return to the Celestial Power as spirits but never again in physical form,' Gabe said.

'We return to the universe—we're reabsorbed,' Raphael said.

Xavier looked at him with a horrified expression.

Raphael shrugged. 'Recycling, it's the way of the universe, but there's a memory of us like a—smudge.'

'They're risking eternity for us. I don't want ....' Overcome by emotion and guilt, Xavier shook his head.

'They can't help themselves. Freeons—what can I say? Give, give, give. They're programmed to be protective. Bit of a death wish, if you ask me. They really need to think for themselves.' Raphael stood and surveyed the scene below.

Instead of worrying about how they would return to Rosegrove, Xavier fixated on the unfolding battle. The demon horde grew in number as more and more dark shapes flew into the area and dropped from the sky to join those battling on the ground.

'We need to help the freeons,' Xavier whispered.

'You can't,' Raphael said in a calm tone.

'Don't you care?'

Raphael continued to watch the battle. 'It wouldn't matter if I did.'

Xavier looked at him in disgust.

'I'm just the messenger.' He chuckled. 'Don't shoot the messenger. That's what humans say, don't they?' He pulled at his hair again. 'Anyway how could I help the freeons now? They've got themselves into a fine mess. Just typical.'

Amongst the din of howling demons and the chorus of freeons, Xavier's head spun as though the universe was churning and circling him. He was the pinpoint, the centre of the hatred and pain. He squeezed his eyes shut and put his fingers in his ears. Gradually his erratic breathing eased and slowed until he opened his eyes and stood still. Gabe and Raphael were still watching the battle.

'Don't you care how many of our kind will die down there?' Xavier struggled to control his voice.

'Our kind? I'm not a freeon and I'm not a part of their cosy world. Whether I care or not is of no consequence. For all I know they may not want to live forever. Imagine having to fight battles over and over, century after century. To go out in a blaze of glory, perhaps that's preferable? It can be so tiresome.' Raphael sighed. 'Anyway they're not dying for you. They're predestined to fight evil. You however, must survive. In the bigger scheme, that's the only thing that matters. You and Gabe need to return to Rosegrove and more importantly, Griswold

College. It's there you and Gabe will fulfil your destiny—our destiny.' He stretched and yawned. 'I've seen enough. The show's just about over.'

'The fireworks seem to be dying down,' Gabe agreed.

'It's the demons. They've summoned something nasty,' Raphael said. 'You need to go now while they're distracted.'

A dark cloud was slowly engulfing the light and as it did, the angels' singing became distorted by a buzzing sound.

'Demon song,' Raphael said. 'The freeons are outnumbered now. They're brave, but their strategy is abysmal. Go now,' he repeated. 'Once they're finished with the freeons, they'll look for you. You should be okay if you hurry and fly in the darkness.'

'Well?' Gabe looked at Xavier searchingly.

'I'm off. Good luck.' Raphael stepped into the shadows and vanished before they had a chance to reply.

Xavier took one last look at the battle scene. Sickened with guilt, he couldn't help believing the freeons had heard him and Gabe call and come to their rescue. No matter how responsible he felt though, he knew Raphael was right. They had a duty now and a destiny.

He followed Gabe down the hillside away from the battle using only the small torch to guide them. As he scrambled over the rocky ground, Xavier struggled to block out the vibrating hum of the demons, the dying angel chorus and the occasional forlorn cry of an angel as it met its end.

Gabe pushed Xavier ahead of him and prodded him occasionally to keep him focused. When they had reached the edge of the field at the base of the foothills, it was silent and quite dark, with only a half moon to guide them.

'See the glow of Rosegrove over there?' Gabe said as he pointed.

'Barely.'

'We have to fly towards the light, no matter what we see or hear.'

'Perhaps we should go wide towards Mourn Forest and fly close to the perimeter.'

'No, we should go directly—the shortest route.'

Although terrified, Xavier stood squarely and waited for Gabe's signal.

'Keep your fingers crossed. Let's go.'

Xavier ran alongside Gabe and as they took off, he kept his gaze on the soft yellow light in the distance.

When they came around the base of the hill, they could hear and see the battle directly. The fire raged in the grove and black acrid smoke drifted towards them. Shrieks and howls echoed from the rocky hill across the fields. The angels singing had ceased and now all they could hear were their terrible cries as the demons attacked them.

Xavier pointed at what appeared to be a freeon curled up on the ground ahead. 'We could help.'

'Careful,' Gabe warned. 'You don't know that. It could be a trap—a shape shifter.'

'He's injured. I must stop.' The beautiful creature was writhing in pain. He lifted an arm towards him as though begging for help. His white gown was soaked in silver blood and one wing was half-torn from his back.

'No.' Gabe grabbed Xavier's arm and pulled, so they arced away from the angel, who moaned and then vanished.

'He died. I saw the moment. I even felt it. What if it was my fault he was here?'

'We couldn't have helped him,' Gabe said. 'We must hurry.'

The angels' song was replaced by the ugly vibration of demon voices chanting in the darkness.

'Faster,' Gabe urged. 'The town's only about half a kilometre away. Don't look back.'

Both boys panted with fear and the effort of driving their wings.

In his mind Xavier could hear the creaking of leather wings. Was it real? He dug in and flapped harder. 'Come on!'

They gasped raggedly with the creak of leather almost on them. It had to be a demon. They were nearly there.

'Head for the light posts,' Gabe screamed.

Tipping their wings, the boys soared full pelt towards a bank of lights on the highway at the edge of town. They both grazed the light posts and then as they hit the ground tumbled over each other.

'Ouch!' Xavier grunted as he slid on the gravel and skinned an elbow.

Overhead a whirl of leathery wings and scales skimmed and then sailed away from the lights, disappearing into the darkness.

'Forgot your daybrew?' Gabe screamed after it.

'Shut up! There are houses over there. The Darklaw might be about.' Xavier rubbed his shoulder. No doubt it was bruised, but at least they were both alive. He stood and brushed the dirt and gravel from his clothes. 'Time to hide our wings and get to the hospital. We'd better get rid of these jumpers because someone might notice the slits in the back.'

They had left their backpacks in the demons' cage, so they searched for a clothesline laden with washing until they found one. Gabe slipped down the drive and plucked a couple of jumpers from the line. He returned with them and threw one to Xavier. Although they were damp, the boys pulled them on, and then ripped the old jumpers to pieces and stuffed them in a garbage bin sitting in the front garden of a house. They then jogged to the lane outside the hospital where they had left a week ago.

A wave of exhaustion hit Xavier as he pushed the side gate open. 'I wonder whether we should've gone to Artemis first?'

Gabe fiddled in his pocket for the key. 'Here it is.' He quietly pushed it in the keyhole. 'We might see him before we return.' Gabe slowly pushed the door open and peered into the ward.

Suddenly the door opened fully and someone reached out and grabbed each boy firmly and dragged them into the room.

'Well, well, well, what has Mr Kennedy dragged in?'

The boys looked up in horror at Ugly and then turned to see Ratti and a nurse in a tight white uniform sipping tea at the main desk in the quarantine ward. The nurse was familiar to Xavier. Then he knew—she was Beauty.

'Imagine my surprise when I arrived this morning and Nurse Oakshof informed me you boys were missing. It's been such a frightful shock for us. We've been positively sick with worry.'

The boys stood frozen.

As Ratti stirred her tea, the clink of teaspoon on china was the only sound in the room.

'Where's Dr Magin?' Xavier asked in a tight voice.

'He was called away last night,' Beauty said.

'Well yesterday he told Gabe and me, we had to get up and go for a walk this morning to get our strength back because he said we were to return to Griswold College tomorrow.'

'I see,' Ratti said. 'You left rather early—before dawn obviously.'

'It felt good to have fresh air. Griswold College is wonderful, but the freedom of wandering around alone was pretty exciting,' Xavier said.

'Interesting,' Ratti said.

'Nurse Oakshof arrived here late yesterday afternoon and found you boys were missing. Imagine her concern. Dr Magin couldn't shed any light on the mystery, so she had staff searching high and low for you boys.'

Think fast, think fast, Xavier thought. He sighed. 'We're sorry, the truth is we went walking yesterday afternoon but got tired of walking around, so we went to a friend's old house. She's at Griswold College now. I just wanted to get a few things for her. She was so sad when her father disappeared and had to come to college.'

Ratti stood and paced a few steps as she eyed the boys. 'Show me what you brought back.'

'That's just it. We found her old home, but it was empty. We ended up sleeping on the floor and were too afraid to come back to the hospital in the dark. You know what it's like with all the night creatures.' Gabe gazed innocently at Ratti, but she just stared at him.

'Where did you get the jumpers you're wearing?' Ratti asked.

Gabe spoke before Xavier could even think of an answer. 'Dr Magin got them from a lost property bin.' He pointed to a cupboard by the beds. 'Our school jumpers are over there.'

There was a knock at the door and Ratti went to answer it.

Beauty stepped in front of Gabe and lifted his chin with her fingertip. 'You look familiar.'

Xavier began to tremble as his heart pounded.

'You remember me,' Gabe said to Beauty.

She frowned.

Xavier could hear Ratti questioning a girl standing in the doorway with a mop and bucket.

'I was at the opening of the new school building. I spoke to you after the assembly,' Gabe said to Beauty in a relaxed voice.

With Ugly behind him and Ratti distracted, Xavier focused on Beauty as hard as he could and tried to plant the image of her speaking to Gabe and Ethan at the assembly.

'I want you to come back in an hour when the patients have left,' Ratti said in an abrupt tone.

Beauty paused and looked at Gabe with a confused expression. 'Y-yes, I vaguely remember.'

Xavier focused harder.

'Yes, I do remember. You were with that thin, pinched-face boy.' She sounded slightly dazed.

'That's right, Ethan you mean,' Gabe said with a big smile. 'You were very kind to us.'

As Ratti returned to them, Xavier didn't dare try any more mind games with the witch focused on him.

'Strangely, no other student caught the virus you and Gabe were stricken with,' Ratti said. 'Your young roommate made a rather startling discovery.'

Xavier gazed at Ratti, unblinking.

'Mr Klee brought a bottle to me that he discovered in your room.' Ratti peered over her glasses. 'He was concerned.'

His name sent a shock wave through Xavier's body.

'We brought it here to be analysed.'

Xavier held his breath.

'It contained a poison. Where did you get the bottle?' Ratti demanded in a steely voice.

'Umm, it was in the kitchen. I know we shouldn't have, but we were hungry and thought there might be something good in it,' Xavier said.

Ratti pursed her lips. 'You stole it from the kitchen?' Her facial muscles twitched. 'Are you sure?'

'Definitely.' Gabe gave her an innocent look. 'It didn't taste like there was anything wrong with it. It was delicious.'

'Stealing, sneaking out of hospital and staying out all night. I simply don't like what I'm hearing. After leading us on a merry chase to Ravenwood a few months ago, I can see now you boys are trouble. You're to return to school for your punishment. You obviously need special guidance.' She gave a dry, mirthless laugh. 'I'm so disappointed, particularly as you're both in the chosen class.'

'But what about Dr Magin? Won't he need to see us before we leave?' Xavier asked.

Ugly snorted. 'If you can wander the streets, you can't be too ill.'

Beauty looked at Xavier and said, 'In any case, I'm afraid Dr Magin isn't returning to Rosegrove Hospital. He's been headhunted, you might say. Such a talent. We'll be sad to see him go. Such is life.' Beauty adjusted one of her patterned stockings with a pair of long red fingernails and then gave the boys a sickly sweet smile.

'Where did he go?' Gabe said.

'Never you mind.' Ratti picked up her cup from the desk and sipped her tea.

Xavier was horrified. What had happened to Angus? He felt a familiar sinking feeling. Everyone who came in contact with him either disappeared or died. His mind drifted back to the cries of the dying freeons. 'Where did he go?' he asked determinedly.

'As I just said to Mr Shepherd, it isn't your concern.' Ratti's voice had hardened.

The ward door swung open as a girl carrying a breakfast tray backed into the room.

Xavier almost smiled when he realised she was Beth.

'The boys will only need a piece of toast each as their stomachs are unsettled this morning and they're leaving now.'

'Yes, miss. I'll wrap them in napkins and put them with their belongings, so they can eat when they're hungry.' Beth swiftly gathered the boys' clothes in a plastic bag.

Clever Beth, thought Xavier as he saw her discreetly slip two boiled eggs into the bag.

Ratti nodded at Ugly. 'We'll go now.'

As she turned and walked from the room, Xavier shuddered as he heard the familiar rustle of her skirt.

CHAPTER 23

* * *

Home again

Eventually Xavier caught sight of the grey stone buildings of Griswold College looming from the shadowy Mourn Forest as he and Gabe sat in the back of the car being driven by Kennedy. Once again, his heart sank as the car pulled into the school's driveway. He listened for the familiar grinding of gravel and saw a handful of small pale faces watching from the windows.

What had he and Gabe achieved? Had they helped anyone? Certainly not Dr Magin or the freeons who had died in battle in the Uraki Ranges. He tried to fight the depressing thoughts. They had made new contacts, Gustavius and Merewyn, but for what? If what Raphael had told them was true, their destiny lay here at Griswold College. Xavier sighed as Ugly opened the car door and ordered them out. While they stood for a moment by the car, a cheer erupted from a room above. Xavier and Gabe couldn't help grinning.

'Think that's funny?' Ugly snarled. He grabbed them each by the collar and hauled them up the steps away from the watching boys' view. 'You won't be so pleased with yourselves after the week Ms Ratchet has planned for you.'

The boys expected Kennedy to trot them before Ratti again, but instead he took them downstairs from the main entrance to an area out of bounds to the boys. He opened a heavy wooden door with a key and pushed the boys along a sparsely lit, stone-floored corridor where the air was cold and the air damp.

'You're privileged, you know. Not too many boys have had the opportunity to visit the basement. Rumour has it, there are more levels below. Although I don't believe anyone's visited them in recent times. They'd have to be game.' Ugly's chuckle sounded like insects scratching.

Kennedy stopped outside a narrow door and unlocked it. 'Mr Shepherd, these will be your lodgings for the next week.' He opened the door and flicked the light switch to reveal a small windowless cell. There was a bunk with a grey blanket and a rickety table on one side and on the other, a toilet and washbasin shielded by a screen decorated with a dark pattern Xavier thought familiar. Ugly shoved Gabe into the cell and closed the door. He then pushed Xavier further down the corridor to another door. 'Mr Jones, I do hope you'll be happy with your accommodation.' He opened the door and turned the light on. 'Please let us know if there's anything we can do to make your stay more comfortable.' He thrust him forward and slammed the door shut.

Xavier was left standing under the only light source, a bare bulb suspended from the ceiling. A cockroach scuttled across the floor and disappeared into the shadows under the bed. He sat on the edge of the bed and examined the screen. Where had he seen it before? He gazed at the dark red and black patterns. It was moving. Suddenly he knew. He rushed to the screen and kicked it over, ripped the fabric from the frame and tore it to shreds. It was the same pattern he had seen in the hallway leading to Ratti's room. He gathered the pile of fabric and forced it out of the room through a chute at the base of the door.

He lay on the bunk and closed his eyes. Even though he was fatigued from lack of sleep and his ordeal over the past week, he found it difficult to sleep. It was weird to think of the school functioning as usual above him. Without windows, the cell could be anywhere. He was woken later when he heard scratching and hissing from the far wall. After struggling to his feet, he searched for the source of the sound.

'Hss, Xavier.'

'Xavier!' The voice was coming from a small vent in the corner.

He crouched on his hands and knees and peered at it.

'It's me, Gabe!'

Xavier laughed with relief. He picked the cover off the vent and could see Gabe's eyes and nose at the other end of the outlet.

'What's it like in there?'

'Same as yours—double bed, television, wall-to-wall carpet,' Xavier said.

Gabe laughed. 'At least now we'll have each other to talk to.'

'Maybe it's just a bluff and they'll let us out soon,' Xavier said when he heard footsteps in the corridor outside. A sense of hope flickered yet was extinguished after someone pushed a plate of food and a bottle of water through the flap on the bottom of the door. Xavier yelled at the person who had delivered the food, but all he heard was the sound of footsteps retreating.

'Don't waste your breath. It was probably just one of the shells from the kitchen,' Gabe said.

Xavier discovered a note under the plate. It said: When you're finished, wash your dish and push it back under the door if you want breakfast tomorrow. He stared at the brown slop in the bowl. Was it soup or stew? He picked up the spoon and forced the cold mess down his throat. Whatever it was, it tasted as though it was starting to go off, but he was hungry after missing lunch. Before he pushed the washed spoon through the chute, he scratched a short groove in the door with it to signify their first meal in the cell. This way he would be able to keep count. That's of course if they continued to feed them.

'Did you get mushroom sauce with your steak?' Xavier called to Gabe through the vent.

'I think mine could have done with an extra minute in the pan. How about yours?'

'Perfect,' Xavier said, 'although the serve was far too generous.'

'Yes, I'll need some exercise to walk it off. I might take an evening stroll under the stars before I retire for the night.'

Both boys started to laugh.

'I'm going to try to sleep now. The feather quilt and plump pillows are calling,' Xavier said.

Just before he sank into sleep, Xavier thought he heard a low moaning below the floor. Probably water pipes, he thought. Before he could consider any other possibility, he drifted into a deep sleep and didn't stir until he was woken by the sounds of breakfast being shoved through the door slot.

He rolled over and opened one eye. Was it worth getting out of bed? He scratched at his legs and arms. Bed bugs no doubt. He was probably the first decent meal that the creatures had enjoyed in a while. He forced himself to rise and inspect the dark puddle of porridge, which looked burnt. He took it and sat by the vent. 'Hey, Gabe. Still there?'

'Yeah.'

Xavier took a mouthful of the porridge. It was definitely burnt. 'Did you those odd noises below the cells last night?'

'No.'

'It was probably the water pipes.'

'I don't think so. The school water's heated in the boiler by the side of the chapel. Why would the pipes go under here?'

After Xavier washed his dish and spoon, he notched the door. Nineteen to go. This time he pushed the dish halfway under the flap, and then sat by the door and waited. It seemed like an age, but eventually he heard footsteps coming down the hallway. When they stopped outside his door, he grabbed one side of the dish. As the hand reached to take the dish from the other side, Xavier resisted and waited. The person tried again, but Xavier kept resisting and lay on the floor to stare into the chute. Eventually two eyes met his from the other side.

'Hello,' Xavier called and focused all his mental powers on the pair of eyes.

The other person flinched but met his gaze.

'I'm Xavier. Who are you?' He fixed him with his unblinking gaze.

The person cleared his throat. 'Jack.'

'That's a nice name,' Xavier said in a slow hypnotic voice. His mind seemed easy to penetrate and control, even easier than the young demons from the Uraki Ranges. Jack had to be a shell and no doubt the poor man's mind was broken. Xavier felt relieved and guilty at the same time.

'Yes.'

'Jack, do you think you could get us some decent food?' Xavier knew from watching the kitchen staff that they were able to follow directions and remember directions but didn't seem able to think independently.

'Yes.'

'The same food the teachers eat.'

'Yes.'

'But you must not let anyone see you bringing it. Cover the tray with a cloth.'

'Yes.'

'If someone asks why you are bringing the food, tell them Mr Kennedy ordered it.'

'Mr Kennedy.'

'Yes, that's right, Mr Kennedy. Thank you, Jack.'

As Xavier walked over to the vent, he wondered who Jack had been before the Darklaw had meddled with his mind. He took a deep breath as he tried to block the thought of his own family. Another cockroach scuttled across the floor and disappeared under the bed. How did they survive in the cell without food or water?

'Psst.'

'Yeah?'

'Have you got roaches in your room?' Xavier asked.

'Too many.'

'How are they getting in and what are they eating?'

'No idea.'

Xavier looked around the cell, but there were no windows or cracks in the wall. He peered under the bed, but it was too dim to see anything, so he grabbed one end of the bunk with both hands and hauled it from the wall. There was nothing but dust and dirt. He rubbed some of it away with his foot to reveal what appeared to be a trapdoor. The roaches were obviously able to squeeze through the crack where the trapdoor edges met the stone floor.

'Hey, Gabe, I've got a trapdoor,' he yelled into the vent. 'See if you have one.'

After searching his room, Gabe called back, 'No, I can't find one.'

'Rats.'

'Rats? No, I haven't noticed any.'

'Sorry, it's just an expression.'

'Can you open the trapdoor?'

'I haven't tried, but I think so.'

* * *

When lunch appeared through the chute a few hours later, Xavier was waiting and knew immediately he had been successful. The smell was glorious. He lifted the cloth to reveal roast chicken and vegetables. Obviously, teachers at Griswold enjoyed better pickings than the students. He rushed to the vent to tell Gabe, but he could hear from the clank of utensils on his plate that he had already discovered the good news. Steam rose from the crisp chicken. Apart from a swirl of green peas, gold surrounded the chicken; golden potatoes, orange pumpkin and brown gravy. He wolfed it down until midway, he slowed deliberately and forced himself to chew and appreciate what remained. How had he forgotten that food could taste so good? His mind wandered back to

Ravenwood to Sunday lunches with his family, but this time he wasn't going to let those memories weaken and sadden him.

After rinsing the dish, knife and fork, he lay in wait for Jack. He decided to keep the knife and hid it under his pillow. After a short time he heard the now familiar sound of doors opening and footsteps in the passageway outside his cell.

'Jack?' he called as he focused on the dark space in the chute.

No response.

While he waited, he held on to the dish firmly.

The hand on the other side grabbed the dish but when the person couldn't budge the dish, bent down and looked into the chute at Xavier.

'Hello,' Xavier said awkwardly to the girl looking at him.

'I want your dish,' she said in a monotone.

Another shell, Xavier thought sadly. 'Hello,' he repeated. 'I'm Xavier. What's your name?'

'Alice.'

'That's a pretty name.' He blushed in embarrassment at making such a stupid comment, although what did it matter? She wouldn't notice. He concentrated and focused his mental energies on her.

She was silent.

'I need your help, Alice.'

'Okay.'

'Can you bring the same meal the teachers are having this evening to me and the boy in the next cell?' Keep concentrating on her, he told himself as she gazed back at him. 'I also need a torch. Can you get one?'

'Yes.'

'Please make sure no one sees you bringing the food or torch. Cover the tray with a cloth.'

'Yes.'

The shells were so easy to influence. As Alice left, Xavier wondered if there would be any way to retrieve the minds of the poor people the

Darklaw had damaged. He hoped so. As he slumped to the floor near the vent, he heard fluttering and thumping from the next cell. 'What are you doing?'

'Perfecting my hover. If you pump your wings with very short flaps and keep your body vertical, you can get off the ground without running into the wall. You should try it.'

'Maybe later. I'm going to take a nap.' In truth, Xavier wanted to focus on the trapdoor, to gather his courage to open it. Once they were released from the dungeons, he knew they would need to start planning how they were to get to Green Isle. Since the arrival of Stinky Eye and with the increased numbers of gargoyles about the school, Xavier knew they had to find another way out of the school grounds. The trapdoor and the passage it led to might be their answer. If only the thought didn't terrify him.

* * *

Xavier was already awake when heard the clank of the main door opening to the passage. He jumped from his bed and jigged up and down as he waited for the footsteps to reach his cell. When a large bowl of soup and a hunk of hot buttered bread were pushed through the chute, he dropped to the floor and pulled the flap up.

'Hello?' He had to be careful.

'Yes?'

It was definitely Alice. He could see her dark lashes. 'Did you bring the torch?'

She slid it through the chute.

'Thank you, Alice.' He gazed into her eyes. 'Can you please bring us the same breakfast the teachers are having tomorrow?'

'Teachers, tomorrow, yes.'

'Remember, don't tell anyone and keep the tray covered with a cloth.'

'Yes.'

There was no spoon, so he picked up the bowl of soup, tipped it and drank. When he had mopped the last residue of soup with the bread, he popped it in his mouth. After months of poor food and hunger, he couldn't bear to waste anything. He quickly rinsed the bowl and pushed it through the chute.

Now for the trapdoor he thought. He hooked his fingers under the latch and pulled, but his first attempts at opening the door were unsuccessful. It had probably been a while since anyone had used it. After a few more efforts, the door lifted a few centimetres. He jumped up and paced around the cell nervously.

'What are you doing?' Gabe asked.

'I just lifted the trapdoor a little.'

Gabe was silent for a spell. 'Careful.'

On Xavier's next attempt, the trapdoor opened suddenly and easily, almost as though someone had pushed it open from underneath. As he peered into the dark hole, he felt uneasy.

'It's open,' he called to Gabe as he stood up and stretched. Cold air filled the room. Did he really want to explore the hole? He wished the trapdoor had been in Gabe's cell. He knew however, that the hole might lead to a passage and that could lead under and out of the school. It might go all the way to the Shay's tunnels in Mourn Forest. The more he could find out where the hole went, the better—but only he could do it. But the hole was so dark.

'What can you see?' Gabe yelled.

'Nothing yet, but I haven't tried the torch the shell brought.'

'Are you going to?'

'Yes.' His voice sounded angry with fear.

'You're not thinking of going down there are you?'

He wondered if Gabe had heard the anxiety in his voice. 'I'm just going to finish my dinner first.' He sat and stared down the black hole.

All he wanted to do was slam the trapdoor down and pull the bed over it. Twenty minutes passed.

'I really don't think it's a good idea to go down there.'

Xavier sighed. 'I have to.'

'Rubbish.'

'If I don't, we'll have no way of getting out of the school with the gargoyles around. I have to see if there are tunnels we could use. We may not get another chance.' Xavier wasn't just nervous; he was terrified. 'I'm going, but I'm just thinking first.' He was thinking of the creatures lurking below. Perhaps it was a bottomless pit. What if he got lost down there and couldn't find his way back? Or what if it were a maze built with the purpose of confusing prisoners who tried to escape. There were too many possibilities, but he had to be brave.

'I think I might wait until morning.'

'That's a good plan.'

Xavier pulled the trapdoor shut and jumped into bed. It would be better to explore the hole during daylight hours, he thought, not that this was logical, as it would be dark in the hole regardless of the time.

He didn't sleep well. His dreams were dark and menacing and even though the cell was chilly, he woke several times in a sweat. When he heard breakfast arriving, he bounded out of bed and lifted the flap. It was Jack and breakfast was the usual miserable slop. Although it wasn't burnt, several maggots floated on the surface. With precision he scooped and flicked the worms from the bowl. He carefully reordered lunch, so that if he managed to return from the hole, he would have something to anticipate.

'Are you going today?' Gabe said.

'Yes.' He didn't feel chatty.

'Here, this might help.' Something rattled through the vent between the cells. 'I'd aim to go west if you can.'

Xavier picked up Gabe's compass and put it in his pocket. 'Thanks.'

After finishing his gruel, he pried open the trapdoor and braced himself for the rush of cold air. He flicked the torch on and examined the entrance. It was lined with stonework, so it had to be man-made. A ladder attached to one side of the wall led to the ground about a body length below. It couldn't be a bottomless pit, so that was positive, he reassured himself. With a deep breath, he put one foot on the first rung and the other foot on the next rung. As he lowered himself further into the hole, he dropped the torch and it clattered to the stone floor. He held his breath. The torch was still working, but he had probably alerted every demon or ghoul lurking in the hole that he was entering their lair. He dropped quietly from the last rung to the ground and picked up the torch. As he waved the torch ahead, he felt he was being watched.

A dank and putrid smell emanated from the seeping stonework lining the passageway. The dripping sounded like whispering voices. Xavier took a step. Despite the dampness, the sound of his step echoed crisply, and was it his imagination, or did the sound become louder before dying away? 'Toughen up,' he said aloud and then regretted it because his voice seemed to magnify in the echo and then split into many softer voices.

He examined the wall and was surprised to see what appeared to be handwriting, yet he couldn't decipher the language. He reached out to trace the letters with a finger, but pulled back in shock at the first contact. Someone or something was talking to him through the stone. The voice was telling him to go back. Shaking, he held his finger out again and touched the stone.

Young, old, high and low voices repeated the message in his head. 'Go back or die,' they said.

Xavier crouched on the floor as he tried to think what he should do and which direction he should go. The voices were definitely not those of the Celestial Force, whose voices always felt right. These sounded like an automatic message left on a phone. He took a deep breath and stood, deciding he would venture to the end of the passage. What if he got lost?

He placed the knife on the ground under the ladder and pointed it in the direction he planned to go. After pacing around 50 metres, he felt a rush of cold air, far colder than before. The echo of his watery steps was gaining in volume and he could hear the voices aloud.

'Go back angeling,' they whispered audibly.

Now it was personal. They knew what he was and he was unwelcome.

'Why are you here? Go back,' the voices hissed.

As the chorus grew, Xavier's torch flickered a few times. His hand shook. If the torch failed, he would end up in total darkness. The further he walked, the stronger the musty smell became and the colder the air. He was terrified. Although a school filled with children and teachers was only a couple of levels above him, he felt so alone, as if there was no one left in the universe. The air grew colder. He shivered.

The torch flickered and failed. He gasped and the echo of his voice surrounded him and grew in the dark. The voices gasped too. They were mocking him. Seconds passed. Rigid with fear, Xavier waited until the light came back on. As he breathed again, he heard the voices imitating him.

When he had retreated halfway down the passage, the light failed again. In those few moments of darkness, he felt fingers touching and poking him.

He began to run. The sound of his footsteps thundered around him. He tried to protect his ears but only had one hand free as his other was grimly grasping the torch. Finally, he found the knife. He bent over and snatched it from the ground. When he caught sight of the lowest rung of the ladder, he almost wept with relief.

At that moment his instinct was to scramble up the ladder to relative safety, but if he did that he would never know where the tunnel led. Xavier reasoned that at this point, the voices hadn't attacked him. He had only felt the grasping fingers when the torch failed. Although there was no guarantee the torch would continue to work, he knew he had to try again.

In one hand he carried the torch and in the other, the knife, although he imagined whatever belonged to the voices belonged to bodies that could not be slashed or stabbed.

With a deep breath, he took a few steps forward. He could do this. He had to.

'Stay,' the voices whispered.

Horrified, Xavier realised they had changed their minds and now wanted him. He had to follow the passage and pray there was another opening. There had to be. Otherwise what was the point of building tunnels and passages? They were there to connect places. Boldly, he strode along the passage, ignoring the hiss and cackle of voices. In his mind there was no choice.

He tried to picture where he was in relation to the school above. Suddenly he remembered the compass Gabe had given him. He took it from his pocket and waited for the needle to stop spinning. The passage was heading towards the chapel. He shuddered at the thought of Ratti's lair above. When he reached the end of the passage, it branched. He decided to choose the passage which would lead to the west wing. The voices were obviously upset with this choice.

The torch flickered again. Xavier called out in horror as fingers grabbed at him. He lashed out with his knife but only encountered air. The voices mocked and threatened.

'Do you know what we're going to do to you, angeling?'

Xavier ignored them as best he could.

Suddenly a moaning voice vibrated the passage. Unlike the others, it was deeper and seemed to be coming from below. The other voices were silent for a spell, but resumed when the moaning died away. What else lurked in the tunnels, Xavier worried. The voices seemed to be respectful or perhaps afraid of the moaning.

'Keep going,' the moaner said.

'Who are you?'

There was silence.

Xavier hurried along the passage to a fork. He chose the left one which he hoped would take him closer to the western wall. He waved the torch ahead of him and felt a sinking feeling as he realised the passage led to a dead end. He was about to turn around when the moaning voice started again.

'Don't turn.'

Xavier slumped to the floor. It was obvious that the moaner had led him into another trap. The other voices chuckled and cackled, louder and louder.

'Shut up,' Xavier screamed at them.

'Look,' the moaner called.

Xavier slowly trained the torch around him.

'What am I supposed to be looking at?'

There was silence.

He climbed to his feet and peered at the surface of the walls closely. There was no ladder, but there were divots, deep enough to allow him to get a foothold. He shone the torch above and noticed a manhole, although its entrance was protected by a closed trapdoor. Carefully he climbed. The trapdoor was at least two body lengths above. When he got close to the door, he reached up with one hand and pressed. Was it stuck? Please, not another dead end. As he pushed on the trapdoor, his heart thumped. It wouldn't budge. Several more times he tried. His breath was ragged with the effort.

He noticed a sliding bolt was holding the door closed. He wiggled it and pulled until it gave way. Focus, he told himself angrily. With all his might he heaved at the door and this time it opened a fraction and rewarded him with a flash of brilliant light—daylight. He rested for a few moments before climbing as high as he could so his shoulder and back were wedged under the trapdoor. As he straightened, he pushed up against the door which finally caused it to flip open. He climbed out of the hole, pulled it shut and collapsed onto the ground with fatigue and relief. Whatever lurked below, he wanted to make sure it didn't follow him.

Blinded by the light after having been underground for so long, he covered his eyes. When they adjusted, he realised he was just outside the school's perimeter wall. He had found a way out. For a few moments, he revelled in the warmth of the sun on his skin and the sounds of birds and wind in the trees. Feeling proud and strong, he let the tears of relief and joy spill from his eyes.

With renewed purpose he pulled the trapdoor open and climbed down, pulling the door shut and securing the bolt after him. Once he'd reached the floor of the passage he ran along it at top speed. The voices howled at him, but he knew they wouldn't catch him now.

When he reached the ladder below his cell, he scrambled up the ladder and nearly burst through the trapdoor. He slammed the door shut and pulled the bed over it and then went straight to the vent to tell Gabe about the passage dwellers and his discovery

* * *

CHAPTER 24

Freedom

When the week of confinement in the dungeons was finally over, Kennedy came to release Gabe and Xavier.

'Ahh, how is our delicate mushroom faring?' he asked as he unlocked Xavier's door. 'A little peakish, I see. Nothing a little fresh air and exercise won't cure.'

The boys were silent as they were marched by Kennedy along the passage and upstairs to the foyer.

'I hope you've both learned about the error of your ways?' He sniggered and held his hand to his ear. 'Pardon?'

'Yes, sir,' they mumbled.

Kennedy grinned. 'Much better. Be very careful in future. Next time we won't be so accommodating. We've many ways of escalating punishments as you might imagine. While you think a week in the dungeons was unpleasant, next time you may experience it without food or light. A subtle change can quickly magnify the horror.'

After being dismissed, Xavier and Gabe felt strange as they walked along the west wing corridor towards their room. They both agreed not to talk of their adventures outside of the Rosegrove Hospital.

Ethan was sitting at the desk doing homework. He swung around. 'You're back!' he said in a delighted voice.

'Did you miss us?' Gabe asked as he launched himself onto his bed.

'I was going crazy,' Ethan said. 'You're both famous now.'

Xavier sat on his bed without commenting. He watched Ethan as he chatted for a sign that might hint at his innocence or guilt, not that he knew what he was looking for.

'What was Rosegrove Hospital like?'

Xavier answered quickly. 'Fine! Good food, good pillows and warm.'

Ethan looked searchingly at Xavier and then Gabe. 'So, what happened?'

'We tried to stay there as long as possible,' Gabe said. 'Who wouldn't?'

'No, I mean why were you sent to the dungeons? There were all these rumours getting around the school.'

'Yeah?' Gabe said.

'There's something you're not telling me. Why? Kids are saying you faked the sickness to get out of here.'

'Who told you that?' Xavier asked.

Ethan shrugged. 'Kids.'

'You were here. You saw how sick we were.'

'Did anything happen here while we were away?' Gabe asked.

'Dunno. We're getting a new roommate this week. Oh, and Matron's gone. She came to me two days ago and told me to tell you we had to be careful not to trust people. I didn't understand what she meant and she wouldn't explain. She seemed scared.'

Xavier felt his throat constrict.

'She disappeared yesterday. Kids are saying her mother's sick and she left to be with her ...,' he shook his head, 'but I don't know.'

'When's she coming back?' Xavier asked.

'Everyone said she resigned. Her mother lives in the Northern Lands.'

Xavier felt ill. After the disappearance of the kitchen staff and Dr Magin, he knew Matron could be in danger. He was also no closer to knowing if Ethan was to be trusted.

* * *

Later that evening, Xavier borrowed Gabe's glasses from his hiding place in the cupboard. He waited until Gabe and Ethan were asleep. He felt nervous as he quietly sat up and put the glasses on. In the moonlight shafting through the window, he focused first on Gabe, who was facing him. His aura was unchanged, strong and purple-white. The last time he had viewed Ethan's, it was mottled blue. This time Xavier couldn't see him clearly enough to tell as he was curled up facing away from him. He pulled his blanket back, climbed out of bed and padded across the room.

Ethan suddenly rolled over. 'What are you doing?'

Xavier snatched the glasses from his face and hid them behind his back.

'What are you hiding?'

'Nothing.'

'Show me.'

Gabe mumbled and stirred in his sleep.

'Shh,' Xavier whispered.

'You're different,' Ethan accused. 'Ever since you went to Rosegrove, you've both changed.'

'No we haven't.'

'Prove it then. Show me.'

Xavier shook his head.

'When Howard was here, he told me not to trust anyone, but I didn't imagine he meant you and Gabe. I thought he meant the teachers.' He spoke quickly, clearly upset.

Xavier stood with his eyes unblinking.

Ethan put his hand out. 'Show me! I saw you. I saw them.' He was angry now. 'Why are you hiding the glasses? Are you trying to hide your true nature from me?'

Awake now, Gabe rolled over and listened.

Xavier held out the glasses. 'Here, look for yourself.'

Ethan took them and slowly perched them on the bridge of his nose.

'Well?'

After taking a long look at Xavier and Gabe, he grinned. 'You don't know how worried I was. Howard had me believing him and I couldn't find the glasses to check when you came back. I thought you'd hidden them. Matron's warning had me imagining all sorts of terrible things.'

'We took them with us.'

When Ethan handed the glasses back, Xavier put them on and scanned him.

He appeared surprised. 'You're checking me?'

Xavier nodded.

'Well?'

He smiled. 'Your aura's lighter than last time. You must be doing something right.' Xavier felt guilty lying to him because it remained the same murky blue.

Ethan looked at him with a puzzled expression.

Trust

Startled by the voice in his head, Xavier decided to tell him about the potion and how they had left the bottle under the bed. Despite what Ratti had said, in his heart he felt Ethan hadn't ratted on them.

'Why did you want to go to Rosegrove so badly you'd risk getting sick?'

'I wanted to see Artemis again. It was stupid, I know. The potion made us a lot sicker than we expected.'

'Ratti told us you'd found the empty bottle and that it was ours.'

Ethan stared at him with an expression of disbelief and shock. 'No, I didn't. Why would she say that?' He looked close to tears. 'Do you believe her?'

Xavier shook his head.

'You trust me, don't you?'

'Of course,' Xavier said.

'And you got a week in the dungeons for that?'

'Ratti said she had to set an example,' Xavier explained.

'But where did you get the potion?'

'Artemis.'

Gabe propped up on one elbow. 'Now it's settled that you didn't tell Ratti, who do you suppose did?'

Xavier was happy Gabe seemed to have changed his mind about Ethan's guilt.

'That's easy. While you were away, the teachers started doing room checks. We had two. They must've discovered the bottle,' Ethan said.

'That's possible,' Gabe said.

'There's more, isn't there?' Ethan looked at them both with a hurt expression.

Trust

Xavier exhaled sharply and without looking at Gabe, said. 'We travelled to Ambrosia.'

'Go on.'

Although still harbouring some doubt, Xavier launched into a full account of their journey to see Merewyn and what they had learned.

For the first time in many weeks Ethan seemed to relax. As Xavier told him about Raphael, the demons and the battle, he stopped tapping his fingers and just listened. 'I wish I could've come with you,' he said finally.

Xavier nodded. 'Next time.'

'What were the dungeons like?'

Xavier told him of the voices in the tunnel and the trapdoor.

'I'm not surprised. I've heard some weird stories from the old kids,' Ethan said.

'You must keep everything Xavier's told you a secret,' Gabe said.

'Of course,' Ethan said.

'Only the three of us must know—apart from those outside like Beth, Sarah and Artemis.'

'Oh and Merewyn, Hayley, the Boundary Keeper and Raphael.' Xavier began to laugh. 'Have I forgotten anyone?'

* * *

Xavier listened to the squeaking trolley Tomkins wheeled across the classroom. Possibly apricot, he thought as he tried to identify the pastry on the blue plate between the steaming pot of coffee and the bowl of cream with a silver spoon by its side. While Tomkins arranged morning tea on the desk, Phineas stood beside the window. The ritual was unchanged. Once Tomkins wheeled the trolley out the door, Phineas would take four steps to the desk, lift the lid off the pot, peer inside, replace the lid, pick up a pastry, take a bite, lick his lips, put it down and pour the tea or coffee while he chewed. Xavier waited, counted the steps and watched the sequence unfold. Phineas dropped a spoonful of cream into his coffee and then looked up only to catch Xavier watching him.

'Anything wrong, Mr Jones?'

'No, sir,' Xavier said. It was a mistake for him to draw attention especially being so fresh from the dungeon.

'It isn't what I'm hearing. If I catch you stepping out of line, I'll be on to you.'

'Yes, sir.'

'Good.' He threw a piece of chalk that stung Xavier's cheek and bounced onto the floor. 'When you find it, go to the blackboard and draw the graph for problem three.'

Xavier got on his hands and knees to fossick for the chalk. One of the boys kicked him in his side as he crawled past, causing him to grunt.

'What now?' Phineas asked as he tapped the switch on his palm.

'Nothing sir, just banged my head on the desk.'

'Do it quietly.'

Xavier turned around to see who had kicked him. Felix grinned at him. When he found the chalk, he thought of hiding it. It would be preferable to stay on the floor for the rest of the class rather than embarrassing himself at the blackboard. He needed to avoid another detention so soon after spending a week in the dungeon. Shuddering, he recalled Ratti's tea and chat. There was no way he wanted to experience one of her detentions again. The last time he had problems in Phineas' class, he had called upon the Celestial Force. He tried the same tactic but heard nothing.

'Ahh, you've found the chalk, I see.' Phineas was standing over him.

'Umm yes, sir.' It was useless trying to deny it.

'Help me, please,' he called again to the voices.

Focus

They were listening. He walked to the front of the classroom with his exercise book, stared blankly at the blackboard for a few seconds, and then drew a horizontal line, the x axis. He then drew a vertical line to represent the y axis. He turned around to find a few boys staring at him. Some nodded encouragingly. Felix however, was grinning stupidly. All he wanted to do was pitch the chalk at him right between his eyes.

Focus on Felix

Xavier obeyed the voices. Matron had said not to trust anyone and that probably included voices in his head, but they didn't bear any resemblance to the voices he had heard below the dungeons, yet he couldn't be sure. He turned his attention to Felix, who was still grinning. Suddenly an image popped into his head. It wobbled and flickered for a moment. Stunned, Xavier placed numbers and a series of crosses on the graph and then linked them with a sinuous curve.

Phineas stepped towards the blackboard and examined each of the crosses he had drawn.

'Show me your book,' he demanded.

Slowly Xavier handed him the exercise book.

'I see you've written down the question, but where's the graph?'

'It's not there, sir.'

Phineas stared at him.

'I j-just worked it out on the blackboard,' he stammered.

Phineas' eyes narrowed. 'Right then. Do problem four.'

Once again Xavier focused on Felix. Like a snapshot, the answer came quickly and easily. He turned back to his book before sketching the graph on the board.

'Enough. Sit down. You appear to have had a mathematical breakthrough, Mr Jones. Mark my words; I'll be following your progress with great interest.'

Xavier slunk back to his seat. He didn't know whether to be elated about escaping detention or worried about Phineas' approval. While using Felix's mathematical ability to help him was dishonest; he didn't care. It was payback for the kick in his side and for the day he was shoved in the mud at football. In any case, he couldn't help what had popped into his head.

Xavier relaxed as the morning settled into a quiet routine with Phineas strutting along the aisles while occasionally flicking hapless students with his switch. It felt normal or as close to as it could be. Just before the class ended, Ratti bustled in with two people in her wake.

'I'll be quick, Mr Phineas. We've two new staff members commencing at St Griswold College today.' She turned and nodded at the first person. 'Nurse Oakshof, will be replacing Matron.'

Xavier's heart thudded so strongly that he worried that everyone in the classroom could hear it.

'She'll be moving into Matron's old room on first floor.' Ratti waved her hand in the direction of the tall man beside her. 'And this is Mr Ligh, who'll be instructing students part-time in metal and woodwork. Not all of you have academic leanings and we thought some of you might be more interested in pursuing a trade. We are all differently-abled. Here at St Griswold we want to help you find your special place in the world,' she gushed.

Artemis bowed stiffly with her introduction. He didn't blink, wink or show any sign of recognition when he looked over his glasses at the boys who were sitting to attention at their desks. What if they had turned him into a shell, Xavier thought for a horrible moment.

'I'm honoured to be joining the staff,' Artemis said. 'If any of you would like to drop by and introduce yourselves, I'll be staying here on Thursday nights for Friday classes in the room on first floor at the end of east wing.'

Ratti bristled. 'Ahhm, while that is a very generous invitation, Mr Ligh, it won't be necessary, as I'm certain you'll get to know the boys quickly in class.'

'I understand, Ms Ratchet.'

Xavier relaxed as Artemis didn't sound like a shell. Shells barely said little more than 'yes' or 'no'. He wished he could just stand up, walk over and talk to Artemis. He especially wanted to know about Gustavius and Merewyn.

* * *

After maths class the boys returned to their rooms to change for sport.

'I can't believe Artemis will be teaching at the school,' Xavier said once the door was safely closed.

'Yes, it's unbelievable,' Gabe said. 'We'll need to be very careful.'

Xavier thought about Matron's warning to Ethan about trusting people. He tried to put the thought out of his head.

'Why do you suppose Artemis is here?' Ethan said.

'Hopefully to help us,' Xavier said.

'My ankle's killing me. I rolled it in my last game of football when you were in the dungeon. I think I might go and see the new nurse.'

Gabe and Xavier glanced at each other.

'What? You're jealous, right?' Ethan said. 'I'm looking forward to a nice restful spell in the library while you sweat and heave with Ugly.'

'Didn't you recognise her?' Xavier asked in disbelief.

'Who?'

'Nurse Oakshof.'

'I heard Ratti introduce the new nurse, but I was so distracted I tuned out. I didn't pay any attention. There was so much going on outside. I saw this black van pull up in the driveway from my seat next to the window. All these strange looking people got out of the back and carried boxes and things up the steps. They were so weird.'

'Nurse Oakshof is Beauty, the same woman who tied you up in Lanoris or have you forgotten?'

Ethan seemed embarrassed. 'Like I said, I was distracted.'

'Be wary what you tell her,' Gabe said.

'On second thoughts, I might stay here,' Ethan said.

'No, you can't do that. You've either got to come with us or go to Beauty, otherwise they'll notice you're missing and you'll end up on detention,' Xavier warned.

Ethan paled.

'It'll be okay,' Xavier said. 'She doesn't remember you or Gabe from Lanoris.'

'Are you sure?'

'Definitely,' Xavier said. 'We convinced her the first time she met you and Gabe was at the assembly in the girls' school.'

'There's something else I was going to tell you,' Ethan said.

They both looked at him expectantly.

'While you were away I had bad back pains. I even had to see Matron.'

'Are you okay?' Xavier said.

He grinned. 'I think I'm one of you now.'

Xavier and Gabe looked at him in astonishment.

'Congratulations, that's wonderful.' Xavier patted him on the back. 'I'm really pleased for you.'

Ethan nodded. 'They've only just started growing, but it won't be long and I'll be able to fly too. Will you teach me?'

'Of course! We can't wait,' Xavier said. 'You'll need to be extra careful with Beauty. Until your wings are mature, you'll need to bind them. He rummaged under the mattress and brought out the band of elastic Gabe had given him a few months ago. 'Only two previous owners,' he said as handed it to Ethan. 'Whatever you do though, don't leave the binder lying around, especially with the new room searches.'

'I'd say you've a couple more months to wait before you can start learning to fly,' Gabe said as he checked the small semi-formed wings on Ethan's back.

'I can't wait,' Ethan said.

'It will be a challenge though,' Gabe said. 'We need a place free of observers.'

'I think I've found the perfect place,' Xavier said thinking about the tunnel to the outside trapdoor and the freedom it might offer.

* * *

The next morning, Xavier was lying face down over the edge of his mattress. It was Saturday and the heavy rain had led to sport being cancelled. 'I'm bored already,' he said and sighed. 'The stuffing's falling out of that mattress.' He rose to his feet and peered at the hole in the mattress of the spare bunk. 'Looks like rats have got to it.'

'Can't blame them,' Ethan said. 'There isn't much else on offer.'

Someone banged on the door. The handle turned and Crowley walked in. 'You boys are getting your new roommate today.'

'Can't,' Ethan said. 'Rats have eaten the mattress.'

'What are you talking about?' Crowley sounded tired and irritable.

Xavier got to his feet and lifted the edge of the mattress so the teacher could inspect it. He was amazed to see how massive the hole was.

'That's disgusting. It's a wonder the whole thing hasn't collapsed.

All right, I'll organise a replacement and I think we might put out a few traps. I'll bring Edward by later so he can settle in, but he might need to sleep in another room until we organise the bedding.'

An hour later, Crowley returned with Edward. After introducing him to the boys, he said, 'Edward just arrived at the school last week and will be taking the same classes as you boys, except for geography, maths and sport. That's correct, isn't it?' he asked Edward, who nodded.

'Would you boys help him with the timetable?'

Xavier smiled at Edward. 'Yes, we'll do that.'

'When you've finished here, Edward, come and see me. I'm going to chase up a new mattress for you as this one's had it,' he said as he kicked it. A handful of stuffing fell from the mattress to the floor. 'See.'

'Thank you, sir'

When Crowley had left, Gabe turned to Edward. 'What's your full name?'

'I'm Edward Eppworthy.'

Edward was tall and agile in appearance with dark skin and hair. However, Xavier noticed he moved with a slight limp. 'Have you hurt your leg?'

'No, actually I have a knee deformity. That's why I won't be doing sport.'

Xavier felt embarrassed he'd commented.

'It's okay. It doesn't worry me. I've had it since birth,' Edward said and smiled.

'So why aren't you doing maths with us?' Ethan asked. 'You didn't use your gammy knee to get out of that too, did you?'

Xavier frowned at Ethan, but Edward burst into laughter.

'Just ignore him,' Xavier said to Edward. 'He can be thick at times.'

'Actually I love maths,' Edward said.

'So why aren't you doing it?' Gabe asked.

'I am—with an older class. Mr Phineas said I'll also be taking some extension classes with Mr Ligh instead of geography on Thursdays.'

'Mr Ligh's only here on Fridays,' Xavier said.

'He's agreed to come in on Thursdays as well,' Edward said.

'How come *you're* in extension classes?' Gabe's tone was slightly shrill.

'After Mr Phineas looked at my school reports and gave me a test, he decided I'd be happier in the other class.'

'I was never given a test,' Gabe said moodily.

'Gabe's amazing at maths too,' Xavier explained. 'You might have a bit in common.'

'I'm sorry. Perhaps you need to ask if you can do the test. We could go to the classes together,' Edward offered. 'To be honest, I thought Phineas was a prat.'

The boys looked at him.

'Sorry, do you like him?' he said with his eyes wide open.

They laughed.

'You're dead right, he's a massive prat,' Ethan said. 'And a bully and a bore. Do you know, he gorges on pastries and coffee in front of us kids and has a slave called Tomkins to deliver it every morning. He's a pig.'

'Really? That's disgusting,' Edward said. 'What about the other teachers?'

'Well, you've met Phineas and Crowley. Crowley takes language and history. He's okay. Have you met Ms Ratchet?' Xavier asked.

Edward shook his head.

'Ratti's the principal. Looks prehistoric and harmless, but she's seriously scary. Actually she's the worst,' Ethan said. 'You're lucky as you won't have to worry about Kennedy, or Ugly as we call him, because he's the sports teacher. He's a thug.'

'What about Mr Ligh?'

'No idea,' Xavier said. 'We haven't had a class with him yet.'

'Oh, okay,' Edward said.

'We've old Pittworthy for science or natural history as they call it here. He's obsessive and ancient but doesn't usually hit you. Hortense is newish. Don't laugh, but he's our etiquette and ethics teacher,' Xavier said.

'Etiquette?' Edward sounded puzzled.

'Yeah, I know it's a joke, isn't it?' Xavier said. 'But you learn to just go with whatever they tell you to do here. It's not worth going against them. There are other teachers, but we don't have them this year,' Xavier explained. 'The gardener's called Grubner. Sometimes you'll get him if you do detentions, which everyone eventually does. Matron left recently and now there's a new first aid person. Her name's Nurse Oakshof or Beauty as we've nicknamed her.'

Edward grinned.

'Obviously she's pretty good looking,' Xavier said.

'So where are you all from?' Edward asked as he sat on the spare bunk.

'Green Isle originally,' Ethan said.

'I've never been there,' Edward said.

'I don't remember much about the islands. I was young when I came here.'

Edward looked at Xavier. 'And you?'

'Ravenwood in the Northern Lands.'

Edward glanced at Gabe, but he had wandered over to the window and stuck his head out as though he was distracted by something in the school grounds.

'Don't worry about him,' Xavier said in a low voice. 'He's just brooding over the maths business.'

'Jealous,' Ethan whispered.

Edward seemed embarrassed.

'Gabe's a local from a farm between here and Clearview,' Xavier said.

'I can still hear you,' Gabe said in a steely tone.

The others grinned at each other.

'So where are you from?' Xavier asked Edward.

'Illwarthe.'

Ethan and Xavier looked at him with surprised expressions.

'You've come a long way,' Xavier said.

'I know. We visited Clanarde last year and my parents loved Ambrosia. They wanted to move there but couldn't get jobs as chemists. But about a week ago they received this letter. They wouldn't tell me what was in it, but they said I had to come here while they settled some business. I've no idea what it was about.' Edward's voice trailed away.

'Don't worry, that's a common story here,' Xavier said.

'You too?'

Xavier nodded. He was beginning to warm to Edward. The boy was open and talkative and his story was so similar to all the other boys. He hoped they would all be good friends.

* * *

Later that night, Xavier couldn't sleep so he sat on the edge of the desk. He sat staring at the night sky as he done many times before and wondered if his parents and Allie were doing the same thing. Were they still on the island of Clanarde? Perhaps they were now just shells in a Darklaw camp; that's if they were still alive.

'Can't sleep?' Gabe whispered from his bed.

'I just want to fly away.'

'Me too,' Ethan said as he rolled over.

'We can't though, can we?'

Gabe sighed.

Xavier turned back to the window. 'We can't because we're bound. Bound to save Griswold's children.'

'And probably bound to save Clanarde and no doubt, Illwarthe,' Gabe said.

'Why stop there? How about Kepler too?'

'You know it's destined now, don't you?' Gabe said.

'Yes, I don't want it to be, but I know it's true. I know what Raphael and the Boundary Keeper said was the truth.'

'At least we have each other.'

'And me too,' Ethan said from under his blanket.

They laughed.

'I hope Edward fits in,' Xavier said. 'Who knows, perhaps we'll have another angel in our ranks.'

'We'll need the support,' Gabe said.

'You know what I was thinking? If we get sent to the dungeons again, we'll need to be ready with torches and supplies. Maybe we could leave a tool or two down there as well. We just need to find trapdoors outside the dungeons.'

'We could explore the tunnels together,' Ethan said excitedly. 'You know—safety in numbers.'

'It might not be so scary being down there together and I'd like to know more about that voice below the tunnels,' Xavier said.

'What's our next step?' Gabe asked and looked at Xavier.

'Why are you asking me?'

Gabe and Ethan laughed.

'What?'

'You're the leader, aren't you?' Gabe said.

'Well …,' Xavier said and broke into a broad grin.

'Yes?' Gabe and Ethan said in unison.

'The three of us should go on a holiday. How does Green Isle sound?'

THE END

I hope you enjoyed book two of the Xavier series, 'Flight to Ambrosia'. If you did, please leave a rating or comment on Amazon.

Book three of the Xavier series is due for release in early 2016. If you would like to join my mailing list for news about the series, please send me an email: e.m.cooper@outlook.com.

E.M. Cooper

37654133R00164

Made in the USA
Middletown, DE
04 December 2016